Three Perfect Gifts by

Chapter One

Golda

Golda's mother named her after Golda Meir. It wasn't because she had firm political views or was interested in Israel. It was just that she liked the name and thought it would make Golda stand out. Golda, however, hated standing out and always had done, even as a young girl, though this trait became more pronounced as she grew older. She much preferred to exist somewhere in the background of life. Her own and other people's. It was, she liked to think, her mission in this world, and she'd done it well.

She had good reason for that.

So, at the age of sixty-two, she was a happily well-off widow with a widow's routine of gardening, reading, attempting the odd crossword if she was in the right mood, and attending her weekly Thursday afternoon Pilates class. She lived in Elstead, a particularly beautiful village in Surrey, which was exactly right for Golda, but in ways other people didn't necessarily understand. It was situated halfway between two main towns, both handy for shopping, and the train journey to London (if Golda ever bothered to go to London) was less than an hour. When the trains were running.

Elstead possessed a village green, a very good doctor's surgery, a hairdresser, a pharmacy, a beauty salon, a marvellously well-stocked village shop, a village hall and youth centre, a primary school, two churches of different denominations, and no less than three cafes and two pubs. There was also a small business estate (where one of the cafes was situated), a football field, a cricket ground, a tennis court and a set of allotments. So, there was really rather a lot going on.

In terms of facilities, the village was in fact a miniature town in all but name, although it still possessed the appearance and characteristics of a village. In addition, there was a great deal of social activities – quiz nights, WI meetings, garden clubs, regular school fetes and so on. Golda never attended any of these events and did not often visit any of the other village amenities either. Even though her neighbours had never really stopped inviting her, she'd always politely declined. She wasn't a fan of people. And this was the reason the village was so very well suited to her: it had enough

2

going on to allow her to fall gently but inexorably between the cracks, and only appear when it pleased her.

In short, her life was exactly as she wanted it and she had no desire for change of any sort. Until one particular Thursday afternoon, that is, when everything changed.

As always, Golda had arrived at the United Reformed Church where the Pilates class took place about ten minutes early. She hated being late. As usual, she parked next to the memorial garden – which was beautiful and very calm even with the main road through the village next to it.

That June afternoon, when Golda turned the ignition off and opened the window to let the breeze flow through, she could hear a blackbird singing in the shrubs and it made her smile. On a whim, she got out of the car, took her handbag and went to have a few minutes' relaxation in the garden. There was a small bench in one corner facing the road and a couple of larger seats on the other side. She chose the bench as it was more secluded, the bushes around it shielding her from both the road and the car park.

When she sat down, Golda saw someone had been busy planting up the bed nearest the entrance. It was filled with marigolds. Not a flower she liked though she had to admit that – as her mother used to say – it was a 'good doer'. But these ones were rather pleasing – large and creamy coloured, rather than bright yellow or that horrid orange shade she hated.

She was settling into a few moments of peace when there was a sudden screech of brakes and a bicycle came flying up the church drive. On it, Golda caught a glimpse of a small blonde woman peddling as if her life depended on it just at the same moment as the cycle hit the corner of the garden wall and the woman somersaulted over the bricks onto the bed of marigolds Golda had only just been admiring.

Golda froze. This wasn't the kind of crisis she was good at. She'd never been good in a crisis. Neither did she want to be. She sat and stared for a long moment at the woman – no more than a girl really – who was lying flat out across the flower bed. Then she grasped the edge of the bench with both hands, the knotted wood digging into her skin, and looked frantically around to see if anyone else had seen the accident who would be better placed to help. Sadly, there was nobody. Nobody at all. She would have to get involved, which was something she absolutely hated doing.

4

So Golda got up from the bench and crept slowly towards the woman who was – as she'd suspected – nothing more than a girl. Maybe no more than early twenties.

"Are you all right?" she whispered, crouching down and trying to see without actually touching her if the girl had any terrible or life-threatening injuries.

For one awful moment Golda thought she might even be dead, but then the girl opened her eyes, which were dark blue, and stared up at her.

"Oh," she said. "Are you an angel?"

Golda smiled at that thought, even in spite of the circumstances. "No. I'm just an ordinary woman. Are you all right? That was quite a fall."

The girl sighed and closed her eyes for a moment. "Yes, it was, wasn't it? I didn't want to be late for Pilates. It's my first time, you see."

With that, she got up, dusted herself down and gave another sigh. "I'm alive then," she added.

There was something about her and about what had just happened that worried Golda, but she couldn't work out what it was.

The girl moved cautiously from one leg to another whilst pushing her hair away from her face. Then she looked down. "Oh."

"What is it?"

"The flowers. I've ruined them." She blinked for a few seconds as if the fate of the marigolds was of more importance than anything else.

"Oh no, you won't have," Golda replied, moving with the girl as she limped across to the bench. "They're crushed now but give them a couple of days and you would never know anything had happened."

"Really?"

"Oh yes," Golda said as the girl sat down. "Marigolds are tough. Tougher than people. Are you *sure* you're not injured anywhere?"

The young girl shook her head. "No, I'm fine, thank you. My name's Miranda, by the way."

"Hello, Miranda," Golda said, thinking how formal this was. "I'm Golda."

Miranda looked up and stretched out her hand solemnly. After a moment's pause, Golda took it and the two women shook hands.

At the same time, a pale yellow four-by-four swung into the car park driveway and came to an abrupt halt.

"Oh! My bike," said Miranda and got up.

"Don't worry," Golda said. "I'll sort it out. You stay there and catch your breath."

By now, the woman in the sunshine-coloured four-by-four had got out of her small tank and was surveying Miranda's bicycle with a frown. Golda recognised her from the class but she didn't know her name. As a rule, she tried not to learn people's names. It was safer that way. The new arrival was wearing the kind of professional Pilates outfit Golda would never dream of owning and had tied her brown hair into a neat bun at the back.

The front wheel of the bicycle was bent over where it lay crumpled against the wall at such an angle that she doubted Miranda would be cycling anywhere in the foreseeable future.

"What's this?" the newly arrived woman said. "Who's left this here? Honestly, people dump rubbish everywhere these days, don't they?"

"It's not that," Golda said, glancing behind to make sure Miranda was still on the bench and couldn't overhear. "There was an accident. A new member of the class came off her bike."

"Oh no," the four-by-four woman said with a gasp. "How awful. I'm so sorry. Is she all right?"

"I'm fine," Miranda's voice came drifting through the shrubs. "What's wrong with my bike?"

The next moment, Miranda was standing next to the unfortunate bicycle, looking pale but well able to walk by herself.

"Oh shit!" she said. "My poor bike!"

"Don't worry," said the four-by-four woman. "I'm sure it can be mended. The good thing is that you're all right."

This statement was hopefully true, but Golda was unconvinced the bicycle would ever be its usual self again. However, she thought saying so wouldn't help matters.

"Let's move it out of the way," Golda suggested. "We don't want cars to hit it and make things worse."

Together the three women picked up the damaged bicycle and carried it to the side of the church where it would be out of sight of the road. Miranda glanced at the bike rack the council had recently provided but didn't bother attempting to lock it up. The four-by-four woman then returned to her enormous car and reversed it with enviable expertise next to Golda's Fiesta, just as the Pilates teacher Carol arrived.

"Afternoon, everyone!" Carol said as she jogged over, carrying a bucket of exercise balls and an armful of Pilates mats and bands. "Everything okay?"

She then caught sight of the broken bicycle. Golda explained what had happened, and Carol gave Miranda a gentle hug as she unlocked the church door. "Poor you! Are you sure you're okay? What an awful thing to happen at your first class, or at any time really. Let me get you a glass of water."

Carol deposited her kit in the corner of the room and headed to the kitchen. By the time she came back with the promised glass of water, the group had been joined by a couple of the other regulars, though there were always one or two who arrived just as the class was starting. Which Golda always thought was very annoying indeed. Why couldn't people simply be on time?

"Are you sure you're okay to do the exercises, Miranda?" Carol said again as she handed the glass over.

"Yes, honestly, I'm fine. Just a bit startled."

"Of course. Anyone would be," said Carol. "Now take it easy and don't push yourself too hard. The routine this afternoon isn't too challenging but if anything feels too much, just don't do it and have a break. I'll keep an eye on you. Will you be okay getting your bike home?"

"Oh!" said Miranda. "I'd not thought of that."

"Don't worry," said the four-by-four woman. "There's plenty of space in my car. I can give you a lift home if you'd like?"

"Thank you," Miranda replied. "That's so cool. I'm only at the other end of the village."

"Thanks, Frankie," said Carol as she switched the music on. "You're a star. Now, come on, everyone. Let's get started."

Frankie, Golda thought, and wondered what it might be short for. It would be Francesca, she imagined. The woman looked like a Francesca. Organised, efficient and capable. Golda couldn't imagine anything had ever gone wrong in her life. This was exactly the sort of woman Golda tended to dislike on principle. She hoped they wouldn't have to have any interaction again.

Carol kept her promise of not having too many challenges in the session. Golda suspected she might have downgraded her usual routine to ensure Miranda wasn't too stretched, but she didn't much mind. She was always happier with the relaxing exercises and less enamoured of the more strenuous ones anyway. Nobody should ever be forced to do the plank, in her view.

As the women were packing up after the class, Miranda came over to where Golda and Frankie were gathering their belongings. She looked a little brighter than earlier on.

"Hello," said Miranda, her eyes darting between the two women. "Are you still happy to take me and my bike home, um, Frankie?"

"No problem at all."

"Oh, thanks so much. In that case, would both of you like to have a coffee or something? My treat. I *definitely* owe you. If you have time?"

"That's very kind," said Frankie. "There's honestly no need as I'm happy to help. But a coffee or a tea somewhere is always welcome."

"Great!" said Miranda. "How about you then, Golda? Would you like a coffee?"

No, Golda absolutely didn't want to. Coffee and chat weren't in her repertoire so it was on the tip of her tongue to refuse. But Miranda looked up at her, her blue eyes wide open.

"Please," she said. "It's the least I can do."

There was something in Miranda's expression that changed Golda's mind. Some need or vulnerability she couldn't interpret. Or perhaps it was the way the afternoon had been pushed out of kilter by the accident, she didn't know. Either way, it made her alter her decision. Just this once.

"All right," Golda replied. "Thank you, though I can't stay long."

They had a brief discussion in the car park as to where they should go as they loaded Miranda's broken bicycle into Frankie's car. Golda couldn't help but be impressed with the pristine state of her four-by-four. If Frankie had any children, she obviously kept them well under control.

"What do you say to the Little Barn Café up the road?" Miranda asked. "Great cakes."

"Perfect!" said Frankie. "Let's see what they've got on offer today. You've got transport, haven't you, Golda? It is Golda, isn't it?"

"Yes," Golda said. "It is. Nice to meet you, Frankie."

Which was an odd thing to say, she knew, as they'd been part of the same class for weeks, but meeting someone outside a class was very different to smiling at them politely inside a class. She supposed it was what made them British.

The Little Barn Café was at the other end of the village from the church and was part of the Royal British Legion buildings. There was also a pub and a small exercise hall there. Golda had never been to either.

Inside the café, Frankie took off her dark glasses and dropped them into her extremely smart handbag. "Oh, this looks different. They've changed the layout. Very nice indeed. Much better to have the counter opposite the door, than near the kitchen where it was before. They can get more tables in now. Makes it look really spacious."

Golda murmured something non-committal. She was already feeling as if she'd made a terrible error in agreeing to come at all.

She wished with all her mind that she'd made up an excuse not to be here, but it would be rude to back out now.

"They still have the best cakes," Miranda said. "Though of course the best coffee is at the cyclists' café. Nice loos there too."

Frankie laughed. "So the ideal afternoon would be cake here and coffee with the cyclists?"

Miranda smiled and nodded. "Sounds like a plan."

Conversation paused as the waitress arrived and took the orders. Latte and lemon sponge for Golda, a good strong tea and a hazelnut cookie for Frankie, and a decaff cappuccino and flapjack for Miranda.

"So," said Frankie. "What are you going to do about your bike, Miranda? Have you got insurance on it? I'm not sure if it can be mended or not. It looks fairly damaged to me."

Miranda shrugged, though she softened the gesture with a smile. "I don't know. Not really. I've got a mate who knows someone good with bikes so I'll ask him. I don't have any insurance. I only ever really go round the village with it."

"I don't think you'll be able to do that for a while," Frankie said. "Have you got any other transport?"

14

"No, I walk if I don't get the cycle out. Or use the bus."

That was impressive. The neighbours, on the rare occasions Golda had to socialise with them, were always saying that the local bus was one of the bugbears of village life. Apart from the sheer numbers of potholes. The Number 46 which serviced the village rarely arrived on time, if at all, and the drivers had a certificate in rudeness. Apparently, it was the main topic of conversation on the village Facebook page, alongside lost dogs and the condition of the local horse population. Golda had never seen the point of any social media so had to take this fact on trust. So if Miranda had used the bus and survived, that was very much a miracle in itself.

Then again, the younger woman walked away from this morning's accident with no after-effects, so perhaps she was used to miracles.

The waitress arrived back with the drinks and Golda took a sip of her latte, as Frankie poured her tea from the small floral teapot provided.

"How's your decaff, Miranda?" Frankie asked.

"Pretty good," Miranda replied. "Though still not as strong as the coffee from the cycle place."

"I'll have to try that one sometime," Frankie replied. "Though I'm a tea drinker at heart. And isn't it mainly for teenagers and young people? At least, that's who I always see in there whenever I drive by. Very terrifying indeed!"

When the cakes arrived, the three women sampled their selections in a satisfied silence. Golda couldn't help but agree that the Little Barn produced a marvellous assortment of cakes. They were the best she'd ever tasted.

"We're not all that bad, the young people," Miranda said, continuing the previous conversation and giving Frankie a cheeky wink. "When we're not falling off our effing bikes."

Frankie blushed. "Sorry. I didn't mean to be rude. It's just not a place I'd ever thought of going, that's all."

Miranda shrugged. "No problem."

There was a short but tense pause, during which Golda glanced out of the window at her car and wished once more she'd never agreed to this.

"So," Frankie said with a hint of desperation in her voice. "Here we are. Anyway, do you both live in the village? We're on the Thursley Road. Well just off it really, on one of the service roads towards the cricket pavilion. You must be fairly local, Miranda, what with the bike?"

Miranda nodded. "Yeah, I live in one of the council flats. I moved in with my ex last year. I'm on my own now, as he buggered off at Easter. Good job really. The council might move me somewhere else at some point, I don't know."

"Oh, I'm sorry," said Frankie. "What a horrible thing to happen."

Miranda shook her head. "It's okay. I'm glad Rob's gone. He was a bit of an arse. It wasn't working out anyway."

"Oh," said Frankie, looking startled, but obviously trying to make the best of the way the conversation was going. "That's good then. If relationships don't work out, best to get rid of them and get something better."

Miranda smiled. There was something about her expression that seemed odd to Golda but, once again, she couldn't work out what it was.

"So what about you, Frankie?" Miranda asked in return. "Are you married or living with someone?"

"Yes indeed. I've been married for about ten years and we've been in the village for eight. Gareth works for an accountant in Guildford. He's very ambitious. I'm an administrator for a training company. Mornings only which suits me. I like having the afternoons free. For Pilates and cake."

"Any children?" asked Miranda.

Frankie coughed as she took a sip of tea and then signalled the waitress over to ask for a glass of water. Which arrived with a jug and two other glasses.

"Goodness," Frankie said when she'd stopped coughing. "That's a question and a half, isn't it?"

"Sorry," Miranda said, though to Golda's mind she didn't look that sorry. She was obviously the kind of young woman who didn't mind asking straight questions. "I just thought that with the big car you'd definitely have a family."

"Good point," Frankie said, though her brief smile wasn't echoed in her eyes. "There's just the two of us. That big car is Gareth's pride and joy, and it gets all his camping equipment in when he goes off for his occasional adventure weekends. It's also good for shopping. Which is where I was planning to go today before tea and cake became an option."

"Camping weekends sound interesting," Golda said, suddenly aware that she wasn't contributing to the conversation and knowing she really ought to make an effort. As she was here.

"Maybe," Frankie said with a smile. "Not my idea of fun though. I went camping once, in France, when I was very young. It was horrible. It was cold and wet all the time and I couldn't understand what anyone was saying. Since then my holiday of choice would definitely involve a hotel with a decent bar. And a good salon too. I do love a facial."

"But all of the fun of it is getting back to nature," Miranda said. "As long as you've got a good tent and sleeping bag, the rain doesn't much matter. I slept out under the stars once on a school trip to Belgium and I loved it."

"Goodness, you're brave," Frankie replied. "I'd be too frightened to sleep outside. Well done, you, for going for it."

Miranda smiled. "It was great. Maybe I'll do it again soon, I'm not sure."

There was a strange expression in her eyes for a moment before she shook her head, and then it was gone.

"Anyway," she said. "What about you, Golda? Are you local?"

Golda felt a part of her shrivel inside as the questions turned inevitably to her. How she hated being the centre of attention. "Yes. Yes, I am. I live on the side of the village near the hairdresser. In one of the cul-de-sacs. Not too far from where you are, Miranda. I've been here for about six years, so not as long as Frankie. I think it's going to be the final home I move to, and I moved a fair number of times after my husband died."

At once, Golda stopped talking. She hadn't intended to say anything remotely personal. It must have been something about the day, or the occasion, or perhaps even the company of the two women. She wasn't sure. Usually she made a point of not talking about her husband.

"Oh, I'm so sorry," said Frankie. "How awful for you. Many commiserations. But good for you on deciding to start afresh after your husband died. That takes real courage."

Golda wasn't sure it had taken any courage at all, but she wasn't going to say so. Not here and not now.

"I'm sorry," said Miranda, quietly. "Was it an illness?"

"Yes. Yes, it was. But it was a long time ago."

"That's truly terrible," Frankie said. "No matter how long ago it was."

Golda didn't reply to that and, thankfully, the conversation moved on.

Half an hour later, the three women had finished their second round of drinks, and the café was getting ready to close, so it was time to go home. For Golda, this was a relief.

"That was nice," Frankie said as Miranda flashed her card at the till. "Unexpected but nice. We should do it again at some point."

"Mm-hmm," Golda replied, hoping that would be enough for Frankie. She had no intention of doing anything like this again, ever, if she could help it.

The women walked out of the café into the late afternoon sunlight, Frankie still making plans for another get-together, to Golda's dismay. "Yes, we'll have to treat ourselves again after next week's class. Those cakes are to die for! Come on, Miranda, let's get you and your bike home. Lovely to have a chat with you both. See you next week, Golda."

Golda nodded as she unlocked her car but kept her silence. Frankie disappeared off with an enthusiastic wave, taking Miranda and the damaged bicycle with her.

Driving home only took a few minutes. The house where Golda lived was in a relatively new area of the village. Shortly after Golda had moved in, she gathered from one of the new neighbours that when the development had been in the planning stage back in the 1960s, a fair number of local people had been unhappy about it, but once it was completed, the fuss had died down. Now the houses on the development – which had once been home to a small garden centre – were rather admired and they all had good-sized but manageable gardens. Which had been a draw for her when she'd been looking.

Golda had been lucky too. Her new home was at the very end of the cul-de-sac so there was no through-traffic. Some of the houses she'd viewed when she started her search had been eminently suitable but too near busy roads. Which meant that in the gardens she seen, all she could hear was the sound of passing cars. In her home now, the only sound in the back garden was the gentle putter of the fountain. For Golda, it was one of the most relaxing sounds in the world.

She was still surprised at what she'd said to Frankie and Miranda earlier on. It puzzled her and she didn't like to be puzzled by things. She liked things to be understandable and under control. It was how she had survived her life.

As she sat down in the living room and gazed out at the garden, this issue was still eating away at her. Golda never talked about her marriage and she certainly didn't talk about her husband. It was hard to explain and so, by default, she often let people assume she was single, and always had been. This was made easier these days as she used "Ms" to describe herself rather than "Mrs'.

But today, she'd made known her widowhood to two women who were strangers. She wasn't sure what she'd been thinking. She was also worried about Frankie's eagerness in immediately suggesting another get-together, as she had a feeling the other woman would be hard to refuse. Not because she was horrible, but simply because she wasn't. Posh, yes, but not horrible.

Golda would therefore have to think of a decent excuse not to go, if asked. She would, she told herself, bow out gracefully in such a way that no-one would get hurt. It was the safest thing to do.

Chapter Two

Frankie

As she left the café car park, Frankie gave Golda a quick wave but was unsure if the older woman saw her. It had been an unexpectedly nice way to spend a post-Pilates afternoon, but she had the impression Golda might have thought otherwise. She'd hardly said a word when they'd been having their coffee and tea, though Frankie had been wondering if she might have found a new friend. She certainly needed one. She wondered if Golda would make an excuse not to join them next time. That would be a shame as there were obviously hidden depths there. If she did cry off, would Frankie be able to cope with Miranda on her own? The younger woman wasn't really her type. All those personal questions!

Next to her in the car, Miranda took out her phone and started jabbing at it. Frankie couldn't help smiling. She couldn't bear being parted from her phone herself, but young people were seriously obsessed with them. The work experience girl at the office seemed to be surgically attached to hers. Whatever had they all done before mobile phones existed?

Talked to each other, probably.

"So what are you going to do about your bike?" she asked as she took the turn onto the main road through the village. "Do you really think it can be mended?"

Miranda looked up and shrugged before placing her phone, screen-side down, on her lap.

"Not sure," she said. "I'll ring my mate about it when I get home."

"Good idea. Because you never know, do you?"

Miranda smiled at this but didn't respond. After a couple of moments, she picked up her phone again, so Frankie concentrated on her driving instead.

As they approached the street where Miranda lived, Frankie noticed, not for the first time, how the houses were built in small terraces and the gardens were open to the road, most without fences. It was funny, she thought, how even a fairly affluent village in a fairly affluent part of the world could have areas of need in it. Then immediately she told herself not to be so stupidly biased. People couldn't help their backgrounds, could they? Just because she and Gareth were well off, it didn't mean everyone else was.

"This is it," said Miranda suddenly, pointing at one of the terraced houses. "That's my flat."

Frankie wasn't sure which one Miranda meant but she drew up at the kerb and parked in the most suitable space. She was the only four-by-four in a line of old estate cars. She hoped her car would be safe.

"Okay," she said. "Let's get your bike inside, shall we?"

Together, she and Miranda removed the bike and began taking it towards the house Miranda had indicated.

"Hang on a minute," Frankie said.

She rested her end of the bike on the pavement and clicked her key fob to lock the car.

"Honestly, it'll be fine," Miranda said. "Just because I live in council housing doesn't mean we're all thieves."

"I know!" Frankie replied quickly and with too much conviction. "I always lock the car. It's a habit."

It was too, but she had to admit that if Miranda had lived anywhere other than here, she wouldn't have bothered to lock up for a short drop-off visit. Once again, her prejudices were all too clear.

And not only to herself. Miranda gave her a brief hard stare but said nothing. She didn't need to. With a sigh, Frankie picked up her end of the bike and the two of them made their way down the path to Miranda's front door. There were two doorbells on the side, numbered – sensibly enough – 1 and 2.

"I'm number 1," Miranda explained. "I'm downstairs so we can just put the bike in the hall and I'll be fine, thanks."

"Are you sure?"

"Yes, honestly."

Miranda was definitely being more distant than she'd been in the café earlier on. And Frankie couldn't blame her for it. She thought that next week at Pilates the three of them would probably just smile politely and leave their separate ways after the class. Maybe that was for the best? She had lots of other friends after all. It was just that she couldn't talk to them right now.

Today, all Frankie could do was leave the bike where Miranda asked her to and go home. She gave the younger woman a quick smile and left. The front door was already closed by the time she reached her car so she didn't bother to wave. Nobody was looking.

And nobody was staring suspiciously at her vehicle either. There were a couple of women walking by with shopping bags and neither of them paid her or her car any attention at all. Miranda had been right.

There was a lesson in there somewhere. As a result, Frankie drove home in a less upbeat mood than she'd been expecting.

At home, everything was quiet. Molly, her cleaner, had already left for the day, and Gareth would be home in just over an hour. He only worked a few minutes' drive away and usually cycled the route in summer unless the weather was really bad. She sat down in the living room and flicked through one of her women's magazines, although her mind was churning over the events of the afternoon. She hoped Miranda's bike would be okay and she wondered again about her own attitude to the less affluent parts of the village. Then she wondered about how things could be improved for the people who lived there. Perhaps she could raise the issue at the next village committee? They usually spent most of their time planning for the summer fete on the green, the quarterly litter picks and then the big Christmas tree decoration celebrations. Last year they'd raised over £900 for local charities at the Christmas tree event on the green, which was the most they'd ever raised. Mind you, it had been a fairly warm night, unexpectedly, and so people had joined in who probably wouldn't have bothered if it had been cold or raining. But maybe, this year, they could focus on local people more? Or would that be just too patronising for words? Perhaps, less well-off people, such as Miranda for instance, didn't need their help. Really, it was a muddle.

With a sigh, Frankie tried not to second-guess herself and turned back to the celebrity gossip she was still flicking through.

It didn't work. She couldn't concentrate on anything right now. No matter how worthwhile. And she knew perfectly well why that was too. All those things she'd done today after work – tidied out Gareth's jumper drawer and added those he was unlikely to wear again into the charity bag; made notes on what books might be suitable to suggest at the next book group meeting; gone to Pilates of course; and then had a get-together with two women she'd really only just met, although of course she'd known Golda by sight for ages at the class. All these things she'd done just to distract herself and to stop her having to be at home quite so much.

She was here now though! So she might as well go upstairs and check that the shock she'd received this morning and which was likely to upend her marriage and her whole life hadn't just been her misreading things, and doing a whole lot of worrying about nothing.

Slamming the magazine down on the coffee table, Frankie leapt up and ran upstairs, her heart pounding. She was being stupid, she knew it, but she couldn't help herself.

She arrived in a matter of mere moments at the main bathroom. She needed more time to think. There was no time. Gareth would be home soon and she absolutely did not want him to find her in the bathroom, doing this.

Frankie opened the door. She went into the bathroom. She reached for the bathroom cabinet. Opened it. She took out the package she'd bought secretly in town (she could never have bought it at the village pharmacy where everyone knew who she was. Never!). She'd placed it in the cabinet this morning and she absolutely needed to find another place to hide it now. She unwrapped it. She looked at the contents. Read the instructions for what must surely be the one hundredth time, and did the test again. She'd thrown the first test away before going to work, and it was currently buried at the bottom of the rubbish bin outside. Gareth would never think of looking in there. Not that he would ever think of looking in the bins anyway. What reason could he have to do that? None.

Then she waited. Not thinking of anything and also thinking of everything, at the same time. She could feel the beginnings of a headache sneaking up on her.

When the time came, she stared at the results. Yes. The same facts which had made her skin grow cold this morning were still there this afternoon. Two lines. Blinking hard, she once more unfolded the instruction paper and checked that the results were what she had interpreted them to be.

Still yes. One missed period (and she never missed a period, ever) and two lines.

She was pregnant. All she could think was it must be because of that stupid vomiting virus she'd had about a month ago. She hadn't been able to take her usual birth control pill then as she couldn't keep anything down. And then she and Gareth had made love when she'd been feeling better and she'd not thought of the possibility of getting pregnant at all. She was thirty-seven years old. There was nothing to worry about. After that night, she'd just started taking the pills again as usual and hadn't even given the matter a single thought. How stupid had she been?

Very, very stupid was the answer to that.

Abruptly, Frankie sat down on the toilet seat and put her head in her hands. Then she cried.

*****

Frankie had never wanted children. It was something she'd grown up knowing, though everyone used to laugh about it. They'd told her that she'd change her mind when she grew up but she never had.

She much preferred reading and learning things. She liked finding out about history in particular, although English literature had also been a favourite. She loved Dickens and Jane Austen and felt as if every moment away from those two great authors was time wasted. Once she opened the pages of a book, she was in another and magical world.

Because she loved reading so much, Frankie worked hard at her studies, did exceptionally well in her A levels and ended up at Newcastle University studying history and English.

It was at university that she'd met Gareth. He was in the same year as she was but studying Maths. They had only met because she'd spilled her tea in the library while she'd been studying late one night, and he'd helped her clear it up and hide the evidence. They really weren't supposed to take drinks apart from water into the library.

After that first meeting, they'd slowly and gradually become a couple. When things had become more serious, towards the end of her university course, Frankie had realised she didn't want the two of them to split up. But, at the same time, she didn't want to change the life plans he might have. Whilst her own relationship with her parents was strangely formal and mainly distant – the result of being away at boarding school for most of her life, she assumed, plus the fact her parents now spent most of their time in Spain – Gareth had a close relationship with both his parents and his younger sister. So she supposed he might assume children would be part of their future. If they stayed together.

She'd waited until after the final exams were over for them both before she'd raised the issue. Anything else would have been cruel. She remembered how she'd invited him round to her bedsit, made him a cup of coffee and an extra strong tea for herself, and then sat down on the bed next to him and told him how she felt.

"I think the world of you, Gareth," she'd said. "In fact, I love you. I know we've not said that before to each other. Not properly. But I want you to know that, first of all. The other thing you need to know is just as important. And I want you to think about what I'm going to say before you respond. And you absolutely must respond in the way that's right for you. Promise me?"

He'd taken her hand and held it in his own. "This sounds serious, Frankie. What's wrong? Are you all right?"

She'd been quick to reassure him everything was fine and then she'd told him.

"If we stay together after university," she'd said, "and believe me, I really do want to. If we stay together then you need to know that I don't want children. I never have and I never will. I can't see that changing. Ever. So if you want a family, you need to think about us and our relationship, and you must do what is most important to you."

There was a short silence and then Gareth let go of her hand and reached to hug her instead.

"Frankie," he said, his voice muffled slightly in her hair. "Frankie, I love you. I'm glad you've told me this, and I think you're so incredibly brave. But you don't need to worry. I don't want children either. I was building up the courage to ask you about it, but you've been braver than me. As usual. So, let's say a big fat no to parenthood and a big fat yes to a life of exotic holidays and fun. What do you say?"

The relief had been overwhelming and Frankie could hardly believe it. From memory they'd spent the whole of that afternoon giggling and making plans for their gloriously child-free future together. It had been the best.

*****

So, right here and right now, and clutching her latest positive pregnancy test in her fingers, Frankie could see no way out of her dilemma.

Chapter Three

Miranda

What a frigging awful day that had been. If Miranda had thought Pilates would make her feel calmer, she had been wrong. So wrong.

Not that it wasn't her fault. Most of it anyway. Because as she'd been cycling to Pilates, she'd thought to herself that, yes, she *could* end it all. She didn't have to wait it out, try to live the life she had as she was supposed to do, as everyone thought she should. She could end it now. Her decision. Her way. Her life, and her death.

The thought had powered through her with almost as much oomph as she was giving her pedals and she'd thought: *what the hell! Why not?*

So she'd pointed her cycle at the wall of the building where the class would be held and gone for it. She'd hit the bricks at speed and plunged over the top onto what she'd hoped would be tarmac on the other side. Where the car park was. But all her sudden and startling plans had gone so wrong as she'd automatically gone into tumble mode, rolling herself into a ball and covering her head as she flew through the air. As if her body wouldn't obey what her mind wanted. Which was just bloody typical, wasn't it?

She'd not even landed on tarmac, but in a little garden she hadn't realised was there in her desperate and overwhelming need to end her life. The flowers had helped cushion her fall and she had lain there for a long moment winded and confused. Wondering if she was glad to be alive and wanting to weep because she still wasn't dead.

Then that lady. The older lady with the grey hair and the closed-in face. What was her name? Golda. That was it. Golda with the grey hair. She'd been helpful and it was absolutely the last thing Miranda had wanted her to be. It was other people being helpful that cracked her resolve.

And then Frankie – *effing* Frankie – had come along as well and Miranda had thought for one horrified moment that she might run over her bike. But she hadn't, even though the bike was the most damaged she'd ever seen it. Far more damaged than Miranda herself.

Not really a scratch on her. She should have clung on to the bike when she drove towards the wall and crushed her head on the bricks instead of somersaulting over them. That would have finished her off for sure.

Wouldn't it?

Yes, it would. In her own time and in her own way.

All through the Pilates class, Miranda had felt sore, though more inside than out. Physically, this once anyway, she'd been lucky. Her instincts as to the best way to fall off a bike had saved her. Stupid, but there it was. And in the end, she'd enjoyed the class. So much so that she'd suggested coffee and cake to the two women who had come to her and the bike's rescue. She supposed it was the least she could do.

To her surprise she'd enjoyed it, even though the women she was with had been weird. Seriously weird! This meant that the class and the cake were the first things she'd enjoyed doing for ages. So it was annoying that when Frankie had given her and her bike a lift home, she could feel the other woman judging where she lived as if Frankie had said the words aloud.

In some ways, Miranda wished she had – then she could have shouted and screamed in the way she'd desperately wanted to. But people here in Surrey didn't do shouting. They were too posh to get really angry. And if you did get angry with them, they didn't get angry back. Which was totally *frigging* annoying.

Because having a good row was one of the things that made Miranda feel most alive. You couldn't have a row with just yourself. You needed someone else there. But she couldn't be bothered to get angry with Frankie. Who probably wouldn't shout back anyway – she was too posh for that, just like every other woman in this effing village.

So, instead, Miranda had kept quiet and ignored Frankie and her *stupid* opinions about her life. Frankie had absolutely no idea about anything. No idea at all. Neither did Golda.

All this thinking made her angry and it also made her sad. She couldn't bear another get-together with the two women now, knowing what Frankie thought of her life. She would bet everything she had that Frankie didn't have any problems at all, or none worth speaking about. She'd probably never been poor or desperate, and she'd certainly never panicked about where the next meal would be coming from.

Frankie had riches written all over her face. Lucky bitch. For a moment, Miranda wished Frankie was still here so she could shout at her anyway, tell her *exactly* in detail what she thought of her. That would show her.

But Frankie wasn't here, and Miranda had missed her chance for honesty. No point crying over it, which was exactly what she wanted to do. She had no time for tears. She had to get on with her life. She had to get her bike mended and get back on it again. Cycling was her favourite thing and she wanted to do as much of it as she could.

So she rang Jake. He lived in Guildford, one of the nearby towns, and she'd known him since school. For a while they'd even got together when they'd been teenagers, but that hadn't lasted. They were better off as mates. They had each other's backs. This was important, now more than ever.

Jake answered on the second ring. It was one of the things Miranda loved about him. Wherever he was and whatever he was doing, he would always answer her calls. And she would answer his. Though most often – typical bloke – he preferred to text.

"Babe," he said with a cough. "What's up? You okay?"

She could tell at once he was smoking. Probably on a break at the depot where he worked.

"I had an accident," she said. "I'm fine, but my bike is buggered."

There was a silence. She didn't fill it.

"What sort of an accident?" he said at last.

"Usual sort," she said. "A stupid car made me swerve in the road and I came off the bike."

It was a lie of course, but if she told him what had really happened, then he would put it all together and know what she'd been trying to do. And she didn't want him to know. It would freak him out and wouldn't be fair on him.

"Is it rideable?" he asked.

"No."

"So where is it now?"

"At home," she said. "A woman from the Pilates class brought me back."

He grunted and she heard him take a draw of his smoke. "It's not the person who knocked you down, is it? If so, sue the bitch. She owes you."

"No! I don't know who was driving the car, but it wasn't her. I didn't get any reg number."

Jake swore. "You don't have much luck, babe, do you? But you're okay, are you? Not injured?"

"No, I was lucky," she replied. Though that was as far from the truth as it possibly could be. "No injuries. I just thought you could look at the bike, see if it's mendable. Please?"

"Course I can. My shift finishes in a couple of hours, and I'll drive over. I can borrow a work van, no problem. So I can be with you at about 8. I'll bring Chinese. That okay?"

"Yeah," she said. "Thanks. See you later."

Chinese was good. Miranda liked Chinese. Even better if she didn't have to pay for it. Then again, she'd probably scrounged off Jake enough in the last couple of weeks. She owed him. So she went into her bedroom and opened the drawers of the cabinet to see what money she could find. She tended to stash money in the nearest drawer if she ever had any spare and then do a round-up before going out for drinks or clubbing. Not that she'd done that for a while, had she? She should probably put the money in the bank or something but she couldn't be arsed. Miranda preferred having cash immediately available for when she needed it.

Sure, most things could be paid for with a card, but cash was better for evenings out.

After putting all the cash together in a heap on her bed, she had precisely £42 and 15 pence. Hopefully that would be enough for paying her share of the Chinese, unless Jake went completely mad with the food order. Which wasn't his style.

She sat down on the bed and looked around. Honestly it was a tip, this place. Since everything had changed for her, she'd let it go to a level of mess and dust she'd not known before. She had always liked to think of herself as neat and clean. Not so now.

She took the money and moved it to the bedside table. She'd put what she had left back in the drawers later once she'd paid Jake. She deliberately didn't look at any of the health flyers piled up on the table. Instead, she pushed those to one side so a few of them fell on the floor and put the money in their place.

Maybe she'd pick up the flyers later. Put them somewhere she didn't have to see them. The last thing she wanted was any effing flyers. What was the point of them? They wouldn't make anything better. She'd only accepted their presence in her bedroom because the nurse who'd come round last week to see her had put them there. And she hadn't had the heart to scream, cry or tear the ruddy health information into a hundred thousand pieces, which was what she'd wanted to do. But the nurse – Diana, she thought her name was – had been so kind that Miranda couldn't bear the thought of upsetting her.

Which was stupid because for the rest of her life, she should be able to do exactly what she wanted to do.

But things didn't work out like that, did they? Not for her.

Suddenly, everything Miranda had been holding on to and keeping shut up deep inside for what seemed like ages came rushing out, and she began to sob. Really sob. Like it was a whole new skill and going out of fashion. She couldn't stop. She had snot coming out of her nose which she had to wipe away on her sleeve as who could find a ruddy tissue when they needed one, and her eyes felt sore and sticky as she tried to rub them.

In the end, she lay down on the bed and kept on sobbing until she fell asleep. And this was how Jake found her when he arrived straight from the Chinese at about 8.15pm. He'd used his key to get in when she hadn't answered the bell. When Miranda woke up and saw him leaning over her, his face was lined with worry and he looked sick.

"Jake!" she said, sitting up in the bed and making herself feel dizzy with the sudden movement. "What are you doing?"

At once the lines in his forehead faded away, and his expression was transformed into a smile.

"You didn't answer the bell, babe," he said. "I thought … I mean …"

He didn't finish his sentence and Miranda didn't want him to. Not now and not ever.

"Sorry," she said, running her hands through her hair and blinking furiously. "Was asleep. Have you got food?"

"Sure. Is your oven on?"

"No," she said. "Must have slept for ages."

She must have done too – which was good news as she wasn't getting much sleep at night. These days, she spent most of her night-time hours worrying. Obviously.

"No problem," Jake said. "I'll put it on. This stuff won't take long to warm up. And I bought wine. Is that okay? Can you …?"

Another of those unanswerable questions he'd started to ask her. She nodded. She had no idea if wine would be a good idea or not – it was probably in one of those leaflets if she had the will or the energy to read them – but she was going to have wine, whether or not it was good for her. And even if it was bad, what did it matter?

"Sure," she said, fingers crossed where Jake couldn't see. "Wine's fine. Is it red?"

"Is there another colour?" he asked, the grin definitely lighting up his whole face now.

"No," she said. "Of course not."

He disappeared, presumably to turn the oven on and find glasses. Hopefully not in that order. Taking the opportunity, Miranda scrambled to her feet and stared at her face in the mirror.

God, she looked like shit. Even more than usual. Her blonde hair was sticking up like she'd had an electric shock or something, and her blue eyes (usually her best feature!) were red with crying. She wondered why Jake hadn't said anything, but maybe he hadn't noticed. Boys, however great they were, were weird.

Or worse. Perhaps he thought she always looked like that. The thought made her half smile and half grimace. With a sudden burst of activity, the like of which she'd not had all day apart from her bike disaster, Miranda grabbed her hairbrush and tried to get her hair sorted. In the end she put it in a ponytail. Which sort of did the trick. Then she wiped her eyes and face carefully, which didn't do much good but at least it got rid of the evidence of her crying.

Finally, because she wasn't a make-up kind of girl and didn't in fact have any in the house, she pinched her cheeks so she looked nearly human and went in search of Jake.

He was in the kitchen, sorting out plates and cutlery. The oven was switched on and the containers of Chinese takeaway were lined up in neat rows on a couple of trays ready for heating up.

The wine was already open and two full glasses poured. Thank God. Miranda grabbed the nearest glass and took a swig. It was rich and smooth and totally what she needed. Health issues or no health issues.

"That's amazing, thanks, Jake."

He turned round and gave her a nod. "Nothing but the best for my babe, don't you know."

And that was what broke her. Just his casual admittance that she was worth something in this horrible world. Just his friendship and the way he treated her. She started to cry once more, this time with less fury but more despair, and once again she couldn't stop. Surely she'd cried enough? But her face didn't seem to realise it.

"Oh, babe," Jake said, stopping what he was doing and folding her into his arms. "I know, I know."

She hugged him right back. It felt comforting, and she wished he'd been here earlier but then again maybe she'd needed to be alone. There were some things that even enduring friendship couldn't solve.

But right now, Jake's warmth and strength eased her tears so that after a few minutes Miranda was feeling better. Thank God.

She gave him a gentle push to let him know the hug was over.

"Get away," she said. "You're keeping me from my wine."

He let her go and gave her another big grin, though she could see the concern in his eyes that wouldn't go away. "Sorry! Refill?"

Miranda nodded and stretched out her glass. She hadn't drunk that much, but she never said no to a refill.

He topped up her drink and then turned his attention back to the oven. She was beyond grateful he didn't question her over the crying, particularly as she wasn't the crying sort. That was the best thing about her best friend – one of the many best things, anyway: he had the kind of tact she'd never experienced elsewhere in her life. He somehow knew when to speak and when not to speak.

It was one of the things she'd miss.

No, she didn't want to think like that. If she thought like that, she'd be lost again. Which was the last thing she needed. She had to live in the moment, didn't she? Not think about any possible future and what it might be like. It was one of the things the nurse had told her. Hell, it was probably the only thing the nurse had said that she'd remembered, so she'd better learn how to do it.

"With any luck, the oven won't take long," she said, putting her new living-in-the-moment resolution into immediate effect and feeling ridiculously proud. "The rest of this flat might be pretty crappy but the oven's fine."

"It's not a bad flat," Jake replied. "At least you get to live in the country, rather than on the dirty side of town like I do."

Miranda laughed. His town flat wasn't that bad, but he did like complaining about it. And she was only in this village because she'd moved here to be with her stupid, cowardly *pig* of a boyfriend who'd been higher up on the council housing list than she was. She'd thought they'd been in love, *really* in love, but she'd been proved wrong.

But she wasn't going to dwell on the past. There was no point. So she concentrated instead on the taste of the wine, waiting for the oven to heat up and then enjoying the Chinese that Jake had brought over. It was a good one too – all their favourites with extra soy sauce. Prawn toasts, duck pancakes, chicken chow mein and fried rice. Lots of it.

As usual, they ate it in the kitchen which was the tidiest room in the flat. Even though Miranda had been letting things slide, she had been keeping the kitchen on the right side of bearable. She didn't want to eat her meals in dirt. That would have been even worse than everything else going on.

Okay, maybe not worse, but it wouldn't have made any damn thing better either. There was only so much of a slob she could become.

"How was Pilates?" Jake said after a good time of munching and comfortable silence. "Did you manage to go to it, what with the accident? Or did that woman just bring you home?"

"Yeah," she said. "I went to the class. Felt a bit stiff after the bike thing, but I still did it. Didn't want to waste my money."

He nodded at that. Jake saved money whenever he could. Like her he'd grown up poor, but unlike her he saw his family. Not all the time as they lived over in Kent, but some of the time anyway. His family were also real family, unlike hers. Miranda had been fostered out to a few families during her years in care but had never grown close to any of them. She was glad to be out of that system now.

"I even went out with two of the women from the class afterwards for cake," she added. "They were the ones who helped me with the bike."

"Good for you," said Jake, speaking around half a mouthful of prawn toast. "You see, it's what I always tell you. People can be pretty nice sometimes."

Miranda shrugged at that. It was her opinion that people could be frigging awful most of the time and generally there hadn't been a lot of evidence in her life to the contrary. It was one of the things – one of the *fundamental* things – she and Jake tended to disagree about. He had a deep-seated belief that people were basically good and, given half a chance, would choose to do nice things rather than horrid ones. She felt exactly the opposite. In her opinion, people needed to be made to do the nice thing rather than the nasty one, which was usually easier. It was, she believed, because people were lazy.

She thought for a moment or two about Golda and Frankie before speaking again.

"Sure," she said. "They were nice, but I paid for coffee and cake to say thank you, so they got paid for being nice. The older woman, Golda, was a bit tight-arsed, didn't say much. And the woman with the car – Frankie – was really snobby about the flat when she dropped me off. That's definitely not nice, is it?"

"What?" Jake said, eyebrows raised and with his forkful of chow mein pausing on its way to his mouth. "What the hell did she say? There's not a bloody thing wrong with where you live, babe."

"It's not what she said," Miranda replied. "You know Surrey women – too posh to say anything. It was her attitude. I just *knew* what she was thinking and not saying and that's the effing thing about living here. People never say what they mean."

Jake put down his fork and started to laugh.

"What?!"

"It's you," he said, still laughing. "I bet you were bursting for a fight and thinking things about this poor woman that she'd not even imagined. I can just see it – you probably went all bitter and twisted on her and she couldn't get away fast enough."

"No, I did not!" Miranda protested, though maybe he was nearer the truth than she liked. "I didn't say anything at all to her."

"No," he replied. "You probably gave her the silent treatment and one of your scary looks. That would have frightened her off. And I should know as I've definitely been on the receiving end of a few of those myself."

This time, Miranda couldn't help it. She started to laugh and gave him a friendly punch on the arm. It was true that at the start of their relationship all those years ago, she'd not been sure about him and had taken a while to warm up to Jake's friendship. But she'd been protecting herself as no other bloody person would. Nothing wrong with that.

"Only because you deserved it," she said.

Jake grinned at her and tried to look innocent, but it wasn't an expression he did well. She snorted at him and focused on her meal instead.

"Are you going to see those two women again?" he asked her after a while.

That was typical Jake. He was constantly on the look-out for more friends that he thought she ought to have. Whereas she was more than happy with having Jake himself as a friend, and the one or two casual girlfriends she occasionally saw. Though she didn't see them so much now, not since her illness started. It was just the way things were.

"Well, are you?" Jake persisted, not content with a silent response.

"I'll see them again at the Pilates class," she said.

"Yes, but after that? You going for a coffee and cake again?"

"Not if I have to pay for it!"

"It'll be their turn though, won't it? Go on, you should. Give this poor woman who was kind enough to bring you and the bike home another chance. And maybe the other one might talk to you a bit more next time. You know you always think everyone is more of a bitch than they really are. There's more to people than you think."

"Yeah, more weirdness and nasty stuff. The world's not all Disney fantasy land, you know."

Jake put his hand up in defeat. "Okay, okay. You win for now. But see how you feel next Thursday after the class. Never say never. Now, let's finish this food and I'll look at your bike. See what I can do."

Which, to Miranda, seemed like a plan. She and Jake finished their meal, washed up the plates in the sink, and poured out the last dregs of the wine. She then showed him the bike.

"Bloody hell!" he said, crouching down and peering at the damage. "That was one hell of an accident."

He glanced up at her where she stood above him and gave her a searching look. She didn't want to respond to that so she just nodded.

"Yeah, it was," she said.

Jake sighed and turned back to the bike. He gave it a quick once-over and sighed again.

"It's not looking good," he said, standing up, "but I'll take it home and see if I can salvage it. I've got a couple of contacts who are genius at this sort of thing. Are you going to be okay without a bike for a while or do you want me to get a replacement for you? I'm sure I can grab a cheap one from somewhere."

"Yes, please," Miranda said. "That would be great if you could."

"Okay, leave it with me. But no more accidents, okay? I mean it, Miranda."

She knew he did.

"All right," she promised him. "No more accidents."

She only hoped she could keep that promise.

Chapter Four

Golda

Golda spent the week after meeting Miranda and Frankie doing the kind of activities carried out by retired women all over the country. She did a spot of gardening, some shopping and a whole lot of reading. She kept up with *Homes under the Hammer* and *Escape to the Country* on the television. Occasionally she even wondered if she should buy and do up another house herself – there was certainly more than enough money for this – but she didn't have the energy or the talent. Though she always admired those who did.

And so the week ambled by. Golda would never stop being grateful that her life wasn't exciting. She didn't want excitement, of any description. She'd had more than enough of it. She could be accused of hunkering down, avoiding the light. But that was exactly what she wanted.

Then it came to Thursday afternoon, Pilates day. Golda had been thinking of the two women every now and again since last week. She'd wondered if Miranda and her bicycle were all right, and whether Frankie would suggest another post-class coffee. The former she hoped for, but she wasn't so keen on the latter. Still, by now, it would all be forgotten, and the other two women would surely be busy with other things. Wouldn't they?

When Golda arrived at the class, Frankie's car was already in the car park, and the woman herself was waiting next to the church door.

She gave Golda a friendly smile. "Hello, Golda. How are you?"

"Very well, thank you. And you?"

Frankie's smile became strained for a moment or two. "Oh yes, fine. Same old, you know. Do you think Miranda will be here after the drama of last week? I was thinking if you're both free, we might go for coffee and cake again. I definitely need the distraction. Though I'm not sure Miranda will want to."

"Oh?" Golda replied, when it looked as if Frankie was expecting a response. "Why is that?"

Frankie sighed and then paused as if making a decision.

"To be honest," she said slowly. "I'm not sure Miranda and I parted on the best of terms. She was fine when I left her but I think she thought I was judging her."

"Oh," Golda said again. "What happened?"

Frankie explained where Miranda lived. "I think it was when I had a good look round and locked my car after we'd got the bicycle out. She thought I was judging her for where she lived, and I wouldn't have bothered locking up if it had been anywhere else."

"And were you judging her?"

Frankie grimaced. "No! Well, not really. I don't think so, not in that way. Oh, well, I suppose that means yes, doesn't it? I really did judge her. If she's here today, I'm going to say sorry. I was going to anyway, but now I'll *really* mean it."

In spite of her reluctance to get involved, Golda had to smile. "Don't be too hard on yourself. We all judge everything all the time. It's what people do. We can't help it."

"I suppose we do," Frankie said.

After Carol and the rest of the Pilates class had arrived and set themselves up, the door burst open and Miranda came rushing in.

She gave a quick glance at Frankie and Golda before apologising to Carol, who waved away her apologies and waited for her to grab a mat and the weights.

There was a space just behind where Frankie was standing, but Miranda hesitated a fraction of a second before heading to the opposite corner. Frankie didn't say anything, but her posture stiffened a little in response.

After the class, Golda took the mat and weights, and deposited them near Carol's bag with a quick smile before slipping her shoes back on and heading to the entrance.

Outside, she almost bumped into Miranda.

"Oh, hello," Golda said. "How are you after last week? And the bicycle?"

Miranda glanced back into the church room where Frankie was still struggling with her shoes before giving Golda a brief smile.

"I'm fine, thanks," she said. "And the bike is okay. Look."

She pointed to where her cycle was hidden by the wall and Golda gasped.

"Heavens! Is that really your bicycle? I thought you'd have to get a new one."

"I know," Miranda replied. "I thought so too, or at least have a replacement for a while. But one of my friends, Jake – he knows someone and got it fixed up really quickly. Though probably more than half of it is changed including the front wheel and handlebars.

Not a bad price either, but Jake got me a good deal. He's great at things like that."

Golda nodded and, at the very moment, Frankie emerged into the outdoors, holding her shoes in one hand and her bag in the other.

"Miranda!" she said. "I'm so glad you're here. I wanted to apologise for being a total idiot last week. I'm so sorry I upset you. Please, can I make it up to you by buying you cake? And a coffee too of course, or whatever you like. You too, Golda, if you'd like to come?"

Miranda took a couple of steps back and looked as if she might turn and run from Frankie's enthusiastic apology. But then she gave a slight smile and nodded.

"Okay," she said. "Thank you for saying something, but it's fine, honestly. And yes, cake would be lovely. You can come too, can't you, Golda? Please?"

Miranda turned and looked at Golda, her blue eyes pleading, and Golda saw that, reluctantly, she had no real option but to agree. She only hoped this outing wouldn't become too much of a tradition.

"I'm a bit busy this afternoon," she lied, "but, yes, I do have some time to spare."

So the three women made their way to the Little Barn Café, Frankie and Golda in their cars, and Miranda on her bike. Naturally enough, Frankie and Golda arrived first and waited outside near the hanging baskets for Miranda.

Frankie gave Golda a wry smile. "Thank goodness Miranda agreed. I was worried she might not even give me the time of day. It's such a relief!"

Golda nodded, but wondered if Frankie had ever known things not go entirely her way. She didn't look like the kind of woman life would dare to challenge. On any level.

A few moments later, Miranda cycled in and sprang off her bike before putting the lock on it. It didn't appear that having an accident last week had affected her speed on the road.

Once seated, the women gave their drink and cake orders, which were quick to arrive.

"So, how's everyone's week been?" Frankie asked. "So glad your bike is sorted out, Miranda. That's good news."

Miranda nodded as she put her fork through the blueberry sponge she'd ordered. "Yeah, I was lucky. As I was telling Golda, my friend Jake knows a lot of people in the area and one of them is a genius with bikes so he came round at the weekend to have a look and it was sorted by Tuesday."

After that, the conversation turned to Frankie's job. She worked as an administrator for a training company but mornings only. Which explained the afternoon Pilates class. Ideally she would have liked to have Fridays off as well to get a long weekend but her boss never worked Fridays so Frankie didn't have that option.

"The trouble is," she said, "that I always get nice and relaxed on Thursday and then have to find my work-head again on Fridays just for one morning. Plus you can guarantee there'll be some terrible crisis on a Friday which I have to try to deal with and then explain to the boss what happened on Monday. I'm sure she must always arrange it that way. If I'm ever the boss anywhere, I'll be sure to take Fridays off and let my staff deal with it. I like to think of it as payback."

Miranda snorted with laughter. "That's mean! Anyway, you must like your job. As, if you don't, you can always decide to start a family, or something. Doesn't that get you a year off?"

When Golda glanced up, eyebrows raised at the assumption Miranda was making, Frankie's face looked as if someone had slapped her. Miranda must have noticed too as she started to apologise.

"Oh shit," she said. "I'm so sorry. I didn't mean to upset you. Sometimes I just open my mouth and crap comes out. I don't have a filter on it – Jake is always telling me off for saying things I shouldn't. I'm *so stupid*!"

Frankie shook her head and took a big gulp of air.

"No, no you're not," she said. "It's just … well … it's just …"

And then she began to cry. Not huge sobs but simply a slow stream of tears which spilled from her eyes.

Golda turned at once, mouthed the words, *water, please*, at the waitress and was pleased to see her nod quickly and head towards the kitchen.

When the water arrived, Frankie downed it in one go and gave the waitress a grateful smile.

"Sorry," Frankie said in the way of all English women everywhere. "Didn't mean to do that."

"It's my fault," Miranda said again. "Me and my effing mouth!"

"No, *really*," said Frankie. "It's fine, honestly. It's just that …"

She paused, took a deep breath, and then appeared to make a decision.

"It's like this," she said, leaning forward and whispering so that nobody else could hear. "I've found out recently that I'm pregnant. And I've never wanted children, and neither has my husband. So I don't know what to do."

"Oh," said Miranda. "Why don't you want children? Oh shit, sorry! Forget I said that. I mean: what a frigging nightmare for you! What do you *want* to do?"

"I'm so sorry," Golda interrupted gently as Miranda was still floundering. "What does your husband think about it?"

"I don't know!" Frankie gulped. "He doesn't know yet. I haven't dared tell him."

With that, Frankie took out a pretty white lace handkerchief and blew her nose before putting the handkerchief back in her bag and wiping her eyes with her hand.

"Ah," Golda said. "I see. And are you sure about it? The pregnancy, I mean?"

Frankie nodded. "Yes. Yes, I'm sure. I must have taken the test about ten times at least. I'm definitely pregnant."

"Then I think you should talk to your husband. Gareth, is it?"

"Yes, it's Gareth. But I don't know what to say, how to explain it. And I don't know what to do. I just can't stop being terrified and wishing the whole thing would just go away. But it won't, will it? It just won't."

"No, it won't," Miranda chipped in. "Some things don't, and you just have to deal with them. Even *I* know that. So Golda's right. You have to talk to your husband. But just because you once decided neither of you want children, it doesn't mean things can't change, does it? After all, you've everything you need. You've got a husband who presumably isn't a prick or you'd have left him by now. You've got a big car you can get several babies in, not just one. And you must be rich enough to have a nanny. So maybe a baby might not be as awful as you think. You might even find you love it. Lots of mothers do, apparently."

After this long speech, Frankie stared at Miranda for a few seconds and then, unexpectedly, started to laugh.

"What?" Miranda said, half frowning and half-laughing herself. "What have I said?"

"Nothing!" said Frankie between snorts of laughter. "Nothing bad anyway. I just hadn't thought about it like that before. That's a very positive view."

Again that secret smile from Miranda.

"Being positive does nobody any harm," she replied. "Or so I'm told."

"No, you're right," said Frankie. "And I'm sorry for springing my news on you like this. Sorry our get-together wasn't as relaxing as I'm sure we'd all hoped. What a week, eh! But thank you so much for hearing me out. You're both right. I need to talk to Gareth. Work out what he thinks and what we're doing to do."

"And work out what *you* want to do as well," Miranda said. "You have feelings that are just as valid as any man's. And it's you that's pregnant. Not him."

Ten minutes or so later, the women were saying their goodbyes and Frankie had paid the bill.

"You can get the bill next week," she said to Golda as they left. "After all, we'll need buckets of coffee and tea so I can let you know how I got on with telling Gareth this news. Wish me luck, as I'll need it."

Once home, Golda had meant to put her handbag in its usual place in the hallway before sitting down in the lounge and reading, or perhaps tackling a crossword. Something normal and sane. Something familiar.

She did none of that. Instead, she started to cry, just as Frankie had at the café, but far more fiercely. It was as if something inside her had been loosened by the other woman's honesty and Golda couldn't help herself. Sinking to her knees next to the front door but in a position where nobody could see her, she began to sob. Not because of any issues Golda had about children, but for another reason entirely.

Golda cried because Frankie was so lucky in her marriage, and *she had no idea.* No matter what problems she was facing, Frankie lived with a man she could think of talking to, which was a gift Golda had never had. Frankie's marriage seemed to be a two-way street, whereas her own marriage had been so very different, hadn't it? Different in a way that she already understood Frankie would never experience and she hoped Miranda would never know.

*****

The street in Golda's marriage had eventually been only one way, and there had proved to be no escape. Not until her husband's death but, for good and for bad, it had made her who she was now.

Not that it had been like that at the beginning. When Golda had first met Alan, she'd been twenty years old and had thought he was wonderful. Kind and very attentive in a way she'd not experienced before. He was the nephew of one of her mother's distant friends and they'd met at a party thrown by his family. It had been for a birthday – not his – but Golda had brought a card and flowers to the occasion. Her mother had been swept off by her group of friends soon after they arrived, and so Golda had been alone in a strange kitchen, putting the flowers in a vase she'd found under the sink.

"Hello," a male voice had said, and when she turned round, she'd come face to face with a tall young man with light blue eyes and floppy fair hair. "What are you doing here?"

In her surprise, she'd almost dropped the vase. He'd sprung forward to save it.

"Gosh!" he said. "I thought that vase was a goner. One of my mother's best ones too."

"So sorry," Golda said. "I was just putting the flowers I brought into water."

"No need!" the man replied. "You're a guest, so I should be doing this sort of thing. My name's Alan, by the way. This is my mother's home. And you are …?"

"Golda. I'm here with my mother, though she's gone off to speak with her friends, so I don't know where she is at the moment."

Alan nodded and stretched out his hand. Golda shook it, rather liking that he was being so formal.

"Don't you worry, Golda with the flowers," he said. "Let's go and find your mother and you can join the party. I'll look after you."

And he did. All through the party, Alan was at Golda's side, making sure she was all right and had enough to eat and drink. When, later on, someone put music on, she withdrew to the edge of the room, expecting not to take part as usual and to watch other people dancing instead.

However, after a couple of minutes, Alan approached her. "Come on, Golda, dance with me. Please?"

"No, thank you," she started to protest as dancing wasn't her thing. "Honestly, I'm quite happy watching other people."

"Go on," he said. "It'll be fun. Really it will."

Alan looked so appealing that Golda couldn't find it in her heart to refuse. The next moment, he was holding her in his arms and swaying around to the music. As she was whirled round by Alan, Golda saw her mother smiling and winking in one corner of the room before she lost sight of her again.

Soon the music changed and a slow number started. It was a tune Golda recognised but she couldn't think of the title.

Alan put his arms right round her, whereas he'd only been holding her lightly at the waist before, and pulled her close as he swayed to the new music. She gave a muffled squeak against his shoulder but he laughed softly and kept on dancing.

"This is nice, isn't it?" he whispered.

And, again to her surprise, Alan was right. Dancing in this way with him was nice. More than nice. She'd never danced like this before. At parties with the few friends she had, Golda would be the one behind the record player or tape-deck, making sure the music was in the right order, and watching from the shadows while other people enjoyed themselves. That is, if she went to parties at all.

She didn't know how long they danced for but eventually the music stopped and people began to disperse. She thanked Alan for the dance. It seemed as if he was about to say something to her, but then a guest asked him a question Golda couldn't hear and he had to turn and respond. It looked like whatever it was would take some time and so she slipped away to find her mother. She didn't want to be a nuisance.

When Golda found her mother, she was smiling as if the smile would never leave her face.

"Well, my dear," she said. "It looks like you've made a conquest. What a charming young man. You can't go too wrong there, I think."

As Golda's mother drove home, she chattered away, telling her daughter what she'd found out about Alan at the party. Remembering how it had felt being in Alan's arms, Golda was desperate for any information she could find. She heard he'd just come back from college and was living at home temporarily as he looked for a job. He was very bright, quite a whizz with finance and had interviews lined up with the bank. He'd had a girlfriend at college, but they'd broken up at the end of their course. So he wasn't

74

with anyone right now. This detail made Golda smile and feel sparkly inside.

At home, Golda and her mother said their goodnights. Her mother was already asleep by the time she got under her own covers – she could hear gentle snores through the wall. But it took Golda a long time to drift off. Her mind was going over and over the evening, and the dances she'd shared with Alan. She kept thinking of his kindness, and how handsome he was too! She wished they'd had time for talking at the end of the party, but Alan had been busy with guests. It was his house after all. Of course he'd be needed elsewhere. She shouldn't be selfish about it.

Although perhaps his kindness was the reason he'd asked her to dance? Perhaps he was simply being polite and making sure guests weren't on their own. Perhaps even now he was laughing and congratulating himself on a lucky escape from her? No! She couldn't bear the thought of that, but how she wished they'd been able to talk more. And how she hoped she might see him again, but she didn't know how. Perhaps she would ask her mother what she should do. Yes, that would be sensible, wouldn't it? Eventually Golda fell asleep dreaming of soft fair hair and those lovely blue eyes.

But she didn't need to ask advice from her mother. Because the afternoon after the party, and for the first time in her life, Golda received a beautiful bouquet of flowers. It was her mother who answered the doorbell and exclaimed with surprise at what she found there. Golda heard the muttered conversation from the living room where she was engrossed in reading her book. Even now, so many years on, she remembered exactly what she'd been reading. It had been *Jane Eyre*, one of her favourite novels and one she'd read and reread countless times.

When Golda's mother shut the door and came marching into the living room, a fresh bouquet of orange roses held in triumph before her, Golda could hardly believe it.

"Look, darling!" trilled her mother. "You have flowers. From that nice young man at the party. Isn't that lovely!"

Golda took them and inhaled their glorious scent. She felt all her worries of last night simply vanish away, and a thrill of expectation flared up inside her.

Under her mother's excited instructions, she took the roses into the kitchen, found a suitable vase, filled it with water and placed the flowers inside it.

"Oh no, darling, not like that! You need to make a proper arrangement of them. Here, let me. And, look, there's a card too. Why don't you open it?"

She hadn't thought of a card, but of course there would be one. Golda tore it open and read the note inside as her mother snipped the ends of the roses at an angle, removed some of the leaves and then rearranged them in the vase.

Thank you for a wonderful evening, Golda, the card said. *It was so lovely to meet you!*

The message made her want to jump up and shout with happiness, but Golda wasn't the jumping type. Instead, while her mother wasn't looking, Golda kissed the note and slipped it into her pocket for poring over later.

"Now, darling," her mother continued once the bouquet had been arranged to her satisfaction, "I'm sure Alan will be calling you soon so please do thank him for his lovely gift."

Yes. Yes, Golda supposed he would. She hoped he would! And she hoped it would be soon.

Thankfully, as she couldn't have coped with waiting for long, Alan rang her that evening. Golda found out later he'd been at work, helping his father in the office, while he waited for a more permanent position. But at the time she hadn't known that and so, every time the phone rang that day, Golda would jump up and wait while her mother answered it. And her mother was a sociable woman, involved in most things that went on in the town they lived in. So she received a lot of calls from friends or neighbours.

By the time it came to 8pm, Golda's expectations had begun to fade. Perhaps Alan wasn't going to call after all? Perhaps the lovely flowers were just him being polite, and she would never see him again. She couldn't bear the thought and she couldn't settle to anything. Not even reading.

However, at just before 8.30pm, the phone rang again and something in the way her mother answered it told her that this time, at last, it was Alan.

She sprang up.

"Darling! Golda!" her mother yelled out from the hallway. "It's for you!"

Golda took a deep breath and ran out of the living room. Her mother was holding the phone out, eyes shining. She grabbed the receiver.

Her mother squeezed Golda's hand as she left.

"Don't forget to thank him for the flowers," she whispered.

Golda put the receiver to her ear. "Hello? Alan?"

"Hello, Golda," Alan replied. "Did you get the flowers?"

"Yes. Thank you. Thank you so much. They're lovely," she replied. "I really love them. The scent is wonderful."

"Oh, I'm so pleased you like them! I had such a lovely time. Listen … Golda …"

"Yes?"

"Would you like to have a drink with me sometime? I'd like to see you again."

Golda closed her eyes for a moment. She couldn't believe this was actually happening and she could hardly get her words out.

"Yes, please, Alan," she said. "That would be lovely. Thank you. Thank you so much!"

They arranged to go for a drink together in a couple of days' time. The date seemed a lifetime away, but at the same time there wasn't enough time to prepare. Golda had never been on a date before, not really, though she had gone around for a while with a group of friends from school. Now she was in her last year at the local college finishing off a business and secretarial course, that friendship group had ebbed away. Neither had she bonded with any other group in the classes where she studied now. She didn't find it easy to make friends.

During the days before the drink with Alan, Golda's mother insisted they go out when she returned from college on her half-day to buy a new dress. As a rule, Golda hated dresses – she was always happier in skirts or even trousers though she disliked jeans with a vengeance. However, her mother knew far more about dating than she did – though this wasn't exactly difficult – and in the end Golda's mother bought her a simple green dress which was almost the same colour as her eyes.

Once the perfect dress was sorted out, the next step was, of course, a new handbag and shoes. It was what all the women's magazines encouraged them to do. This time Golda insisted on paying as she didn't want her mother to spend all her money. Both the handbag and shoes were a darker green than the dress and Golda felt she was now prepared to look good on her date. At least that was one worry dealt with. She just hoped Alan wouldn't be disappointed.

On the day of the date, Golda's tingling sense of anticipation grew as the hours ticked by. When evening came, she was in a state somewhere between incredibly anxious and incredibly excited, and didn't know which was worse. She was starting to get ready and trying to ignore her mother's suggestions when the doorbell rang. Her mother tutted and rushed to open it, but then exclaimed in pleasure.

"Alan! How lovely and unexpected. Please do come in! Golda, come down and see who's here!"

In a flurry of confusion and delight – *had she got the time wrong? Was he coming only to say he'd changed his mind and, if so, however could she bear it?* – Golda ran downstairs to find her mother already installing Alan in the living room and offering him a cup of tea.

When she entered the room, Alan leapt up to greet her. The sight of him made her feel overjoyed and shy at the same time.

"Hello!" he said. "Sorry to turn up suddenly like this. I know it's a bit of a surprise, but I thought you might like a lift to the pub?"

"Oh, how kind of you," Golda's mother replied. "What a thoughtful gesture. My daughter would love a lift, I'm sure."

Golda had been planning to take the bus as it was only a ten-minute journey away, and the buses ran every twenty minutes until 9.30pm so that would have been no problem.

This new offer was a delight and would only mean more time with Alan, which would be wonderful. Hurriedly, Golda accepted the lift and ran to get ready now that the man himself was here. From the bedroom as she changed into her dress and grabbed her shoes, she could hear her mother and Alan laughing as if they'd known each other for a lifetime. It made her feel good.

Twenty minutes later, Alan and Golda were walking out of her house towards his car. He rushed round to the passenger seat to open the door, and she saw her mother give her a thumbs up sign from the house. A minute later and they were on their way, Golda's mother waving frantically as they left.

Golda had, in the middle of all her excitement, been nervous about what to do and say that wouldn't put him off but she hadn't needed to be concerned. All through the date, which consisted of the promised drink and a walk by the river, Alan was happy to talk. And Golda was equally happy to listen, smile, and offer encouraging remarks.

After about an hour or so in the pub, Alan reached across the table and squeezed her hand. She could feel the warmth of it in her bones.

"Let's have a walk around town," he said. "If you'd like that? We can take a stroll along the river. What do you say?"

"That sounds lovely, thank you," said Golda.

He got up, still holding Golda's hand, and pulled her gently to her feet. Outside, the evening wasn't cold and there was more than enough light to see by. It was the height of summer. She could hear laughter coming from the High Street, and the cinema light display was flashing its message at the end of the road.

But they didn't go that way. Instead, they turned to the right and walked towards the river. The path took them alongside the theatre and over the little bridge next to it. A scattering of people in the theatre foyer were slowly making their way back into the auditorium. It must have been the end of the interval.

Alan had kept hold of Golda's hand since they'd left the pub and her fingers felt protected and safe inside his. She assumed he'd carry on talking as he had whilst they'd been drinking – she was sure she could have listened to his voice forever if he'd let her – but he was quiet. However, every so often, she glanced up at him and caught him looking back at her. He was so very handsome, and Golda wondered if he might kiss her. Was it too soon? What did the magazines say? She couldn't remember. Even so she hoped he might, and wondered how his lips might feel on hers.

On the other side of the bridge, the path wound to the left past the lock and through the west side of the town. Golda knew that in about ten minutes, there was another, larger bridge across the river, making it a circular walk back to the theatre. It was often used by summer tourists and the holidaymakers who hired boats out. When she'd been at school, the end-of-year boat trip had been one of the highlights of the term. The class had even taken picnics and eaten them in the clearing by the larger bridge. Looking back, she was surprised none of them had ever ended up in the water but in general they were a fairly well-behaved group.

As they walked along the river tonight, Alan spoke again. "Do you like this town, Golda?"

"Yes, I suppose so," she replied after a moment. "I mean it's my home. I've never known anywhere else. It's fine."

Alan laughed. "Yeah, I get that. But just because something's fine doesn't mean there aren't other things that are better. Don't you want to get out? Find out what it's like in other places?"

"I don't know," Golda said. "I'm happy enough where I am. This is a nice place to live, isn't it?"

"But do you want to be here your whole life? Wouldn't that be dull?"

Golda wasn't sure. She'd never thought of it like that before. After her course finished, she was planning to have the summer off, with the intention of looking for a job locally in the autumn. She hadn't thought much beyond that, and hadn't considered moving elsewhere at all.

"I don't know," she said at last. "I suppose it might be dull. One day. But I like living here for now. Don't you?"

"I do now," he said, with a smile which made her heart beat faster. "But I don't want to stay here for ever. You know what they say – travel broadens the mind."

Yes, it did. Of course. Even though Golda liked the town she lived in, it didn't mean to say she'd never left it. She and her mother had been on regular holidays abroad together in recent years, to

Spain, France and Belgium. They'd always enjoyed it though coming back home was just as wonderful too. But when she said so, Alan laughed and pulled her close.

"I didn't mean holidays," he said. "Though they're great and it sounds like you've had a fantastic time. Good for you! I meant for life."

Then he turned Golda round so she was facing him where they stood on the river path, leant down and kissed her.

It felt wonderful and strange and, for a magical moment, everything around and within Golda went quiet as Alan kissed her for the first time. His lips felt warm and comforting, and he tasted of the beer he'd drunk in the pub, but that didn't matter. She kissed him back and then, to her surprise, felt his tongue easing her lips apart and entering her mouth. She moaned as Alan pressed her even closer to his body. She wished they could have stayed there forever as she reached up and wrapped her hands round his shoulders.

But, all too soon, Alan ended the kiss and took a step back. He was panting hard and so was she.

"You're so beautiful," he whispered. "So very beautiful."

Golda didn't know what to say. She was still catching her breath from the shock and delight of his kiss. Nobody had ever called her beautiful before and, in any case, she didn't think she was beautiful. She was just an ordinary girl.

"Thank you," she replied, when she could speak again and not knowing what else to say.

Alan smiled and took her hand once more.

"You're so very lovely," he said and then they continued their walk.

Soon, they reached the second bridge, crossed it and retraced their steps on the other side of the river, hand in hand. Golda noticed the scented shrubs at the side of the path and the way the rising moon shone on the water. She heard the faint rustle and splash of ducks or geese on the river as they played near the bank. Everything felt so much larger than life, so much more vibrant.

Finally, they reached Alan's car and he let go of Golda's hand to open the car door. She longed with all her heart to feel his touch again.

They drove home in silence though, every now and again, Golda glanced across and saw his sideways glance at her. When he pulled up in front of her home, Alan took her face in his hands and kissed her on the lips again. This time it was a peck only, and Golda couldn't help regretting that he didn't ask for more.

"Thanks for a lovely evening," Alan whispered. "I've enjoyed it so much. Can I pick you up on Saturday? If you like, I'll take you out for a meal this time. Please, Golda, please say yes."

Wordlessly, Golda nodded. Saturday was perfect but it already seemed a lifetime away before she could see him again. How would she bear all that time between now and then?

"Thank you," he whispered. Then he leaned forward and kissed her again. "See you on Saturday, Golda."

By the time Golda reached her front door, her mother was already at the threshold, her face shining with excitement. Once inside, she asked Golda a thousand questions about how the date had gone, why Golda hadn't invited Alan in for coffee, whether they'd stayed at the pub or gone on somewhere else afterwards, and – this one seemed to be the most important question of them all for her – whether they would be seeing each other again.

"Saturday," Golda told her. "He's picking me up on Saturday. For a meal."

Her mother's unbounded joy was almost as powerful as Golda's own.

This time in Golda's life was the happiest she had ever experienced and also sped by too fast. Alan was all the things her mother repeatedly praised him for, and more: charming, handsome, kind and ambitious. She couldn't believe he'd chosen her as his girlfriend. About a month after they started dating, Alan began his job at the bank and was excited and eager to learn.

At about the same time, Golda began her own job in the local library. It was temporary but she hoped it might become permanent. She enjoyed the routine and the sense of quiet contemplation she gained amongst the books. It gave her more time to daydream about Alan and she loved it.

Alan and Golda would see each other once during the week and then once on a Saturday night when they would usually go to the cinema and then on for fish and chips somewhere. Occasionally, if Alan was feeling flush after pay-day, they skipped the film in favour of a meal at the local pizza restaurant. For Golda, it was a magical time and, whenever they parted company, she couldn't wait to see him again.

So, when about ten months after their first date, on a warm May evening, Alan took hold of Golda's hands across the restaurant table on one of their non-cinema Saturdays and told her he loved her and wanted her to be his wife, Golda was absolutely overjoyed and absolutely astonished.

She opened her mouth to say *yes, of course, a thousand times yes*, but Alan had already slipped out of his seat, still gripping her hands, and was going down on one knee beside her. Golda couldn't believe it and could sense the sudden expectant interest from the tables around them: the gasps; the whispers; the waiting.

"Yes, Alan, I love you too," she said, blinking back the tears of joy. "*Yes*, I will be your wife. I will marry you. Of course I will!"

Alan's eyes, in harmony with her own, glistened with tears and he reached up to kiss her. At the same time, the people around them began to cheer and clap, a response which filled Golda with equal measures of delight and horrified shyness.

The waiter brought over a bottle of complimentary champagne which tasted silvery and rich, and the rest of Golda's and Alan's meal was spent gazing at each other, smiling broadly and listening to the congratulations of their fellow-diners. When they left, people were still offering their good wishes and congratulations.

Alan drove through the town, one hand on the steering wheel and one hand holding Golda's on her knee. He kept on glancing across and smiling, his eyes gleaming with pleasure. An echo of Golda's own expression.

However, at the junction where he should turn right in order to take her home, he turned left and began to drive in the opposite direction.

"Where are we going?" she asked him, surprised. "This is the wrong way, isn't it?"

"Yes," he said as his face reddened. "Would you mind? I thought we could go to my home instead tonight. Have a coffee? And I wondered if we might ... be together? I've got protection. You know?"

Golda blinked. It was what she'd been dreaming of but at the same time she was scared. So very scared. She'd never done this before. What if she couldn't do it right? What if he wasn't happy with her? What if she was frigid or something? She'd read about that lately in one of her magazines and had immediately begun to worry about it. She needed to let him know how she felt. It was the perfect time, after all. They were engaged. But she was still afraid.

"That would be lovely," she said quietly, hardly daring to look at him. "But I've not done this before. So you mustn't expect too much. Is that all right?"

Alan laughed gently and gripped her hand more tightly.

"Yes, of course it is," he replied. "It's more than all right."

Even now, so many years on, Golda could remember so very clearly how their first time together had been. It had hurt a little, but not as much as she'd feared and then that wonderful feeling of closeness had driven all other thoughts away. For a long while afterwards, Alan held her in his arms. And, on his bed in his tiny flat, being safe in the warmth of his embrace had somehow been the nicest part of it all.

When she arrived home later, much later than she'd planned to be back, Golda told her mother that she and Alan were engaged, and her mother's happiness thankfully swept away any other questions about the lateness of the hour.

A week later, Alan presented her with a ring that had once belonged to his grandmother. It was a simple gold band with a single diamond set in the middle and Golda loved it.

Four months later, in September, she and Alan were married in her mother's church. Golda wore a slimline white dress her mother had chosen, and which looked perfect on her. She felt for the first and only time in her life, almost like a princess.

She could remember the white roses in the church which her mother had arranged for her; how solemn the minister had sounded as he joined them in holy matrimony; the look of tenderness on Alan's face as Golda promised to love and obey. And she remembered the comfort of the wedding ring against her skin, and how it had felt like a key unlocking a door into a life she'd never imagined she could have. She remembered the smiles and excitement of the few guests; the sparkle and glitter of the wedding breakfast champagne; and the tangy sweetness of the wedding cake.

Their wedding night was spent in Alan's flat. It was everything Golda had imagined it would be, though with a glorious golden sense of freedom now they didn't have to sneak around to be together anymore. She was glad it wasn't her first time and she knew more about what Alan liked and what she wanted too. It made a difference.

For the first year or so of their marriage, Golda couldn't have been happier. Alan continued to do well at work and was keen to advance his career, whilst Golda enjoyed her job at the library. Six months into their marriage, Alan had suggested trying for a family together now they were settled into their new home, and Golda, delighted at the thought, had agreed at once. She stopped taking the pill the doctor had given her, and she and Alan made love as often as they could. She hoped for a boy, someone just like her husband, but so far nothing had happened. They had youth on their side though and there was no need to be concerned just yet. Children would come along in their own good time.

That particular Wednesday afternoon when everything changed so utterly for Golda, she arrived home, more than ready for her half-day off. Usually she would get the housework done so she didn't need to do any cleaning at the weekend, but today she decided to have a quick nap first. The library had been busy this week as there'd been lots of school groups having various tours and she was tired.

The moment Golda lay down on the sofa, she was almost instantly asleep. It was only the sound of the front door opening and closing, and Alan's greeting that roused her.

"Hello, Golda! I'm home!"

Golda was awake at once and struggled to sit upright on the sofa.

"I'm in here," she shouted back, getting to her feet and attempting to smooth down her hair. "I've been asleep. Can you imagine!"

There was a silence and then Alan walked into the living room. Golda went to kiss him, but there was something about his expression which stopped her.

"Is everything all right?" she said. "How was your day?"

He glanced at her but didn't respond. Instead, he gazed around the room which was a little messy as she'd not started tidying up yet.

"Well," he said at last, walking to the coffee table and frowning at the magazines strewn across it. "I've been working hard at the bank all day and I'd hoped to come back to a nice neat home to relax in."

"I'm sorry," Golda started to say. "I would have done the housework, but I was so tired. I'll do it now. You don't have to worry."

She would have said more, but Alan held up his hand in a way he'd never done before and Golda fell silent.

"You're sorry?" he said. "You're *sorry?* You're so tired you fall asleep in the afternoon? What have you got to be tired about? I'm the one who should be tired, not you. I'm the one with a challenging job. I'm the one dealing with finances and difficult people all the time. All you have to do is stamp a few books out every day and then put back another few books onto shelves. How can any of that be tiring? I slog away at my job all the hours I can to give both of us a nice home, and the least I can expect is that my wife cares enough to keep that home clean and tidy. How can I relax in this ... this ... *mess?*"

As he'd been speaking, Alan had become louder and louder so that his last few words were all but shouted. Nobody had ever shouted at Golda and she had no idea what to do. What on earth was going on?

The moment he'd finished, Alan grabbed the magazines from the table and threw them up into the air. Golda yelped in protest and tried to stop him but he pushed her away. Then he stared wildly round before marching to the mantelpiece and grabbing the two cups she'd not yet taken back to the kitchen.

"What are these doing here?" he yelled. "These are from *last night!* Why don't you put them in the kitchen where they belong? Why can't you wash them up like normal women would do? Why are you so bloody lazy all the time? Honestly, if you're like this now, Golda, *what sort of mother are you going to make?"*

With that, Alan began to take everything in the living room that was moveable and hurl it to the floor. The books on the shelves, Golda's beloved set of Dickens and Austen novels. The candle holder her mother had given them as a wedding present. A vase full of early autumn flowers she'd picked from the garden only this morning as a treat. All of them ripped apart or smashed in front of her eyes. Again, Golda tried to get him to stop the madness, but he was too strong. He shoved her away so she slipped and fell, banging her shoulder on the corner of the coffee table.

Alan didn't even pause. He just continued yelling and smashing things. Unable to believe what she was seeing, Golda scrambled to the far corner of the room and watched him. Finally there was nothing left in the living room to destroy and Alan stopped shouting.

Golda was unable to speak, unable even to think. Alan walked over to where she was sitting on the floor.

"What a mess," he said. "Make yourself useful and clear it up, would you? I'm going to have a shower."

And then he left the room.

Golda sat where she was, her heart pounding. The living room felt unnaturally silent. As if it was holding its breath and waiting to see what would happen next.

Then she heard the shower being turned on upstairs. She looked round the living room. Her magazines lay torn across the carpet, and broken china was scattered everywhere. She couldn't grasp what had just taken place here. It felt impossible. What had happened to her husband today? Slowly, she got to her feet. Trying not to think, she stumbled to the kitchen, took out a bin bag from one of the drawers and walked back to the living room.

The sight of it made her eyes fill with tears but she refused to let them fall. That wouldn't help anything, would it? She made her way through the living room, picking up all the scattered items and putting them in the bin. She wrapped the broken crockery in the magazines to avoid cutting herself on the sharp edges. Some of the magazines were fairly intact and she could have put them back on the table to read later, but she didn't want them in the house. Not after this.

Was he right about her? Perhaps she *was* lazy. Perhaps she *would* be a terrible mother once children came along. Perhaps she deserved his anger. She didn't know, but she couldn't think about it now.

By the time Alan returned downstairs, the living room was as tidy as Golda could get it in a short space of time, and she was in the kitchen, busying herself with making dinner. She heard the living room door opening and almost forgot to breathe, hoping he wouldn't get angry again. She couldn't bear it. When he came into the kitchen, Alan rushed towards her and Golda froze, dreading hearing him shout again. But he didn't shout. Instead he wrapped her in his arms and hugged her until she could hardly breathe.

"Oh, my darling," he said. "I'm so sorry. I didn't mean to get so cross. I'm so sorry for shouting – that's the last thing I want to do, believe me! I'm so sorry for the horrible things I said – you're not lazy! Of course you're not And you'll be a *wonderful* mother when we have children. Let's hope it's soon, eh – I can't wait to be a father. I really can't. But I'm so sorry and it'll never happen again. I promise you. *Please* forgive me, Golda, I can't bear it if you don't. I love you so much!"

Of course Golda forgave him. She loved him. It was a one-off and he'd promised it wouldn't happen again. That was what he said and, of course she believed his promises. He was a good husband. She was so lucky to be married to him.

Wasn't she?

Chapter Five

Frankie

Golda was right. Of course she was. Frankie needed to get help and try to make sense of the terrible fact of being pregnant. But, most importantly of all, she needed to tell Gareth. Keeping this shocking news from him was being unfair.

It was equally shocking that she'd told two women she'd only just met about it. She should have told her husband first. Of course she should. But, at the coffee shop when it had all come pouring out of her, Frankie hadn't realised how much she'd needed to talk. She felt a tiny bit lighter now, as if she wasn't entirely on her own any more. It made a difference.

Still, she needed to tell Gareth and she needed to do this soon.

So late Thursday afternoon, when she finally arrived home, she decided to talk with her husband when he got in from work. Not immediately, as she knew how much he needed at least ten minutes down-time to relax from being at his job. The world of accountancy could be very intense sometimes and was probably more people-orientated than Gareth was necessarily happy with. But he liked the set-up and his colleagues, and the pay was good. Very good. So much so that his salary was the main reason she was able to work on a part-time basis only, and she was grateful for it.

Frankie thought briefly about leaving her news to the weekend, but she knew that if she put it off any longer, she would never do it. It had to be tonight.

So Frankie switched the kettle on at about 5.30pm in preparation for her husband's return. Her shoulders felt tense and she could feel the start of a headache which she hoped with all her heart wouldn't develop any further. To give herself something to do, she retrieved the teapot from the cupboard near the back door as Gareth always swore tea tasted better from the pot. She herself could never tell the difference and secretly preferred the simplicity of a teabag popped straight into the mug, but she was determined to make the effort.

She heard his car drawing up in the driveway and walked to the door to greet him. When he saw her, he smiled and hugged her. "Good day?"

Frankie nodded, not sure how best to answer that one. "You?"

"Yes, not bad," he replied. "Glad to be home though."

She had to say something. Now. Before the evening got caught up in the usual routine of their marriage and she lost her opportunity to be honest.

"I've boiled the kettle," she said. "I'd thought about a cup of tea together in about ten minutes before I put the dinner on. There's something I need to tell you. Something we need to discuss."

There! She'd said it. She'd started the process and she couldn't change her mind now.

Gareth frowned. "Okay, tea sounds nice. Thank you. But is anything wrong though? Are you all right?"

"I'm fine," Frankie replied, a response which was as far from the truth as she could imagine. "Well. Anyway. Tea. Ten minutes. Is that okay?"

"Sure," he said, still frowning.

Frankie turned and walked back into the kitchen. She heard him go upstairs to get changed. He would then, again as usual, switch on the computer in his study and catch up with the news. Her husband was a bit of a news junkie.

Exactly ten minutes later, she reboiled the kettle and made the tea.

"Gareth, tea's ready now!" she called up the stairs. Her voice sounded high and strained but she couldn't help that.

When he came into the kitchen, she handed him his mug before walking into the living room and sitting down. Gareth followed, joining her on their leather two-seater sofa.

"Look," she said. "I need to tell you something. Something I don't like, and which I know you won't like either."

Gareth put down his mug on the coffee table, shuffled up to get closer and hugged her.

"Whatever it is, I love you," he said. "Tell me. What's wrong?"

She gave him a quick squeeze and moved out of his arms. "I don't know any good way to tell you this, but I'm pregnant."

Her announcement was met by silence.

Utter silence. It seemed to Frankie that Gareth wasn't even breathing, let alone moving. It was as if her words had turned him to stone and she wished with all her strength that she could unsay them, but she couldn't. And it seemed also as if the terrible silence lasted a lifetime but it couldn't have been any more than a few moments.

"What?" he said quietly, staring at her as if he couldn't look away.

Frankie gulped. "I'm pregnant. I took a test, then I took several more tests just to make sure. They were all positive. All of them."

He blinked at her. "But how could that happen? You're on the pill. Did you forget to take it or something?"

She shook her head. "I don't know for sure. I think it was last month when I was sick with that virus. I didn't forget to take anything. But I was throwing up a lot for a couple of days, and it must have been then."

Gareth sprang up and began pacing across the carpet. "But are you sure? Have you been to the doctor? Got it confirmed?"

She shook her head. "No. Not yet. I didn't want to think about it, but the tests were all the same. Like I said. What else would the doctor be able to do?"

Her husband stopped pacing – which was a relief as watching him was making her feel dizzy – and his frown deepened. "I don't know, Frankie! These tests. They're not always right all the time, are they? You could be wrong. You should get it confirmed for definite. What's the point of worrying about things before we know for sure? I'm surprised you didn't at the very least get it checked out before springing it on me like this!"

"I don't know," Frankie wailed, feeling the tears pricking the back of her eyes. "I just thought you ought to know! Golda and Miranda at Pilates said ..."

"What?" he said, stepping back and staring at her accusingly. "Golda and Miranda said ... *what exactly?* You've been discussing this at your Pilates class before telling me?"

"Not the whole class!" she protested. "Just the two women I've seen for drinks afterwards a couple of times and I didn't mean ..."

"These are women you don't even know that well?" Gareth interrupted her before she could explain properly, his voice rising almost to a shout. "You told them before you could even be bothered to tell *me*? Your *husband?*"

"I didn't mean to tell them first!" she yelled. "I was just so worried and it all came out before I could even think about it. And they were helpful, you know! *Really* helpful. A whole lot more helpful than *you* are being right now. Because I don't know what to do!"

Gareth stared at her. He opened his mouth. Shut it. Then opened it again.

"Well, in that case," he said, coldly. "If these women are so very helpful, why don't you go and ask *them* what you should do then? Unless, of course, you already have!"

With that, her husband swung round and stormed out of the living room, slamming the door behind him. She heard his footsteps pounding up the stairs, then his study door being opened and banged shut. Then, silence.

Frankie groaned and sat back on the sofa. That hadn't gone how she'd hoped. Not at all. And she definitely had that headache now.

She sat there, alone, for half an hour but Gareth didn't come back downstairs. He must be on his computer. She wasn't going to get any help from him. Not this evening anyway. His reaction had shocked her – of all the ways Frankie had thought her husband would react to her news, this hadn't been one of them. Not that she'd made things easier herself, but it wasn't her fault, was it? She hadn't deliberately got pregnant. It took two to bloody tango, didn't it?

With a sigh and blinking back tears, Frankie retrieved her laptop, opened it and began searching for what to do if you had an unwanted pregnancy and where to get help. There certainly seemed to be a lot of opinions on the issue and she spent a fair amount of time trying to unravel them. That evening, dinner remained uncooked and uneaten, and there was no more conversation of any type. At about 8pm, Frankie heard Gareth go into the kitchen and she wondered if he might be making a meal of some sort, but ten minutes later, she heard him going upstairs again.

When, exhausted by her research and with far too much information now filling her head, she went into the kitchen, she saw Gareth had made cheese on toast and left the grill pan near the sink. Not feeling remotely hungry, Frankie took a hunk of cheese, grabbed some biscuits from the larder, and returned to her research.

This time, she made notes in one of her notebooks. It was the one that Gareth had bought her a couple of Christmases ago with *Run the World!* on the front. She didn't much feel like running the world, but it was the nearest one to hand.

Frankie always found that making notes on paper crystallised her thoughts and plans far more clearly than making notes on her phone or online. There was something special about the physical act of writing that was brilliant for clarification.

She turned to a blank sheet of paper, added the headline *Pregnancy: Possible Options* at the top and then began to revisit the websites she'd visited earlier and write down key points she wanted to remember.

When she'd noted down everything she could think of, she typed it all up on the laptop, taking a bite from her cheese & biscuit supply every now and then.

She ended up with three main possibilities with variants of each.

The first was abortion. She didn't like the thought of that but she and Gareth didn't want a baby so it was the most practical option. Apparently, this could be done surgically or with a pill, depending on how far along she was. As Frankie thought she was only probably about a month or so along, a pill would be her preference.

The second was adoption. She could have the baby and then give it away. It felt like the morally more acceptable option, but then everyone would know, wouldn't they? All her friends in the village, all the people she knew at work or on the various committees Frankie was part of would know she'd had a baby and then given it away. Yes, she knew other people's opinions shouldn't matter but they did, and she could help that. Plus there was always the possibility that one day the baby might want to come and find her, and she didn't want to live under that shadow. She also had no idea how she'd feel if that happened, though she could put an embargo on ever being contacted at all. And what kind of woman would that make her? She didn't like to consider that.

The third and final option was basically having the baby. A baby she didn't want and which her husband didn't want either. That wasn't an option in reality, was it? It would never work in a thousand years and she couldn't even begin to imagine it. The thought was exhausting. She liked her life too much as it was. Yes, it was selfish to think like that, but surely at heart every decision was selfish? Whether it was to have a baby or not to have a baby, or any other decision in the world, there was a selfish impulse behind them all.

By now, Frankie's brain – not to mention her heart – was feeling fuzzy and she didn't think she could take any more information. Neither could she decide between the first two options and, in any case, she couldn't think about it now. No matter how much she liked making decisions and moving on with her life, this pregnancy crisis didn't just involve her. There was Gareth too, whether or not he was speaking to her.

The weekend after her pregnancy confession was the worst Frankie had spent for a long time. She couldn't sleep much, as her mind kept going over the possibilities and thinking about what she should do and whether she could live with any decision she made. The realisation that she couldn't spend much time on it but needed to make a life-changing decision *now*, before the decision was made for her, didn't make things any easier. Neither was it helped by the silence between herself and Gareth. They'd not had this kind of falling-out for a long time and the silences between them had never lasted this long either. One or the other of them would make tea, apologise and make up. So much so that more often than not the tea would be stone-cold by the time they got to it. Frankie didn't think that would work now, and she couldn't think what to say to Gareth anyway. She wasn't the one who had started the argument! Bloody, bloody men.

On Saturday evening, Frankie attended the quarterly committee of the village hall committee, which seemed to go on for longer than usual. Though she was in no real hurry to get back home. It felt as if she were watching proceedings from a distance, floating somewhere above her own head. She watched herself in astonishment as she chatted to the committee members, voted for decisions and agreed to organise the autumn litter pick weekend. It was amazing how normally she was behaving even when everything was so out of control. She managed to fool everyone there too, as nobody asked her how she was or how things were going. Thank goodness they didn't! They definitely wouldn't have been expecting her response, though of course she would have said everything was fine, wouldn't she? That's just what people did.

By the time Frankie arrived home after the obligatory post-meeting chat, Gareth was already in bed. She didn't think he was asleep as his breathing wasn't steady enough, and she thought about trying to thrash everything out now, but she didn't have the heart for it. She was too shattered. So she undressed in the dark and got quietly under the covers, trying to calm her breath and empty her mind. If only that had ever worked. After a couple of minutes, Gareth turned and rolled away from her, leaving her alone in her empty space of bed. Frankie felt like crying and wondered if she'd ever get to sleep now, but she must have done because when she woke up on Sunday morning, it was already light outside and the bed beside her was empty.

She was wondering how on earth to cope with the day ahead when the bedroom door opened and her husband walked in. He was holding a tray with two mugs of tea and a plate of biscuits. Chocolate digestives, by the look of it. Her favourite.

"I'm sorry," Gareth said, as he put the tray down on the dressing table. "I'm an idiot, and I'm sorry I shouted. I just didn't know how to respond to what you said. About being pregnant. I didn't know what to say or what to think. I still don't, but I know it's not your fault."

With that, he took the mugs and carried them over to Frankie's bedside table before sitting down on the bed next to her. She leaned toward him and the next moment they were hugging. She could feel the pounding of his heart through his dressing gown, as she struggled to wipe away her tears.

"I don't have a clue what to do either," she said once the hug had ended as all hugs had to end at some point or other. "I've been looking at what the options are on the web and all of them are dreadful."

"Oh," Gareth said, taking a sip of his tea and frowning. "What do you mean?"

Frankie explained as succinctly as she could and then started her tea as well. She definitely needed it. Gareth put his tea down and stared at her.

"But you're going to get rid of it, aren't you?" he asked her. "I mean the last thing we want is a baby, isn't it? We don't like children. We never have. And you don't want to be pregnant, do you? So the adoption choice isn't ideal, is it?"

"No," Frankie said. "No, it's not. I couldn't bear it. It will have to be abortion, won't it? Even though I don't like the thought."

"But it's the sensible choice."

Frankie swallowed. She knew it was. Of course she did. But even so, it was a big decision to make. Though it looked as if her husband had made that choice easily enough. Still, he wasn't the one having the baby, was he?

"Yes, I know," she replied at last. "But I think you're right about needing to get it confirmed first. I'll make an appointment next week with our doctor and then we can go ahead."

"With the abortion?"

Frankie nodded. "Yes, with the abortion. You're right. It's really the only decision to make."

And it was. She knew it. So why did she not feel as sure as she wanted to about it?

In the following days, and in the way of all marriages facing big decisions but not now and not yet, she and Gareth carried on with their lives. Work continued for them both in the way it always did. Of course, nobody at either of their workplaces knew about Frankie's condition. It was the last thing she wanted to talk about to her work colleagues, and she knew Gareth would be the same.

Frankie managed to get a doctor's appointment on Tuesday afternoon. She'd tried for Monday but that was impossible. She was lucky to get a Tuesday, but she'd said it was urgent and she managed to get a slot at the end of the day. Not her usual doctor, but Frankie thought that was all for the best. She liked her usual doctor and didn't want to have to discuss something as personal as this with her. She was stupid to feel that way, probably, but that was how it was.

Frankie arrived at the surgery about ten minutes earlier than she needed to and signed in. She glanced around the waiting room but didn't recognise anyone there, thank goodness. She wasn't up to having any kind of conversation right now. And the less people knew of her medical appointments, the better. It was a shame there weren't any spare magazines on the table any more but they'd been taken away when Covid had started and had never returned. Sensible enough, Frankie supposed, but she could have done with the distraction. She thought about taking her mobile out and checking for any What's App messages, but there were at least two posters pinned up warning her not to do precisely that so she didn't dare.

The overpowering sensation of being out of place here wouldn't leave her, however, and she tried to work out why that was. The surgery wasn't somewhere she visited very often but it certainly wasn't unfamiliar. Heavens, she knew a couple of people from the village who were on the Patient Participation Group and she'd regularly dropped off her women's magazines here herself back in the day. She shouldn't be feeling so edgy.

Then again, people usually visited the doctor because they were ill or were attending a check-up for some reason. They didn't usually visit because they were pregnant and wanted a termination, did they? Most pregnant women, Frankie imagined, were supremely happy to be in that condition. It was just she herself who was out of place, not the surgery. At once she felt as if everyone in the waiting room knew why she was there, though of course that was impossible! The elderly woman in the corner was reading a book and paying her no attention at all, and the woman and her young son on the other side were chatting together quietly. They weren't paying Frankie any heed either. It was all in her own head.

The sound of her name being called by the doctor on duty made her jump and she had to scrabble around for her jacket and handbag before she could follow him back into his appointment room. He was one of the new doctors who'd joined last year. She'd never visited him before and she would definitely have preferred to see a woman, but she didn't have the choice as the slot she'd chosen was the only one available.

"So," the doctor began as she sat down on the chair he indicated. "What can I do for you? I gather it was urgent?"

For a very long moment, Frankie considered lying about something random, like leg pain or a headache that wouldn't go away, but doing so wouldn't help anyone, least of all herself. Besides, she couldn't bear the thought of having to make another appointment and going through all this again, so she opened her mouth and blurted it all out at once.

"I'm pregnant," she said. "At least, that's what the tests all said and I did a lot of them. Just to make sure. But my husband thought I should come here to get checked and I had to agree."

"Okay," the doctor said. "That's very sensible. We can easily do that. A urine test is much the best – it's similar to what you've already done, but more accurate. Here, take this, pop to the loo and then come back and we can find out properly for you."

With that, the doctor opened his desk drawer, took out a sample tube and handed it to her. Frankie took it numbly. "Should I bring it back to you now?" she asked.

"Yes, please do. You've got a ten-minute slot and the test is quick, so that's no problem."

She nodded, stood up, leaving her handbag and jacket on the seat, and went to the loo, as asked. She wondered briefly if she'd be able to use the tube as she was still so tense, but she managed it after all. After washing her hands and staring at her own face in the mirror, she returned to the appointment room.

"Here it is," she said, handing the sample to the doctor. She was feeling rather light-headed as if all this was taking place behind a curtain she was unable to open.

118

The doctor smiled, took the tube and tested it for her. Then, before she'd fully prepared herself for the full weight of medical confirmation, he gave her a great big smile.

"Congratulations!" he said, beaming. "You're definitely pregnant."

Frankie gasped and stared at him in horror. Even though all the tests she'd done herself at home had already told her the truth, it was still a completely different thing to hear it from someone else. Someone with professional knowledge.

The doctor was now saying something else, which sounded full of information and also very positive, but Frankie couldn't concentrate on that. The last thing she wanted was information or to be remotely positive, in any way.

"Look, you don't understand," she interrupted him, as clearly as she could bearing in mind her throat was somehow unable to work. "I don't want the baby. Neither of us want it. Getting pregnant has been a terrible mistake. Please, you have to tell me how to get rid of it. *Because we just don't want a child.*"

And that was the truth of it.

Two days later, it was the first post-Pilates get-together after Frankie's melt-down. And it was Golda who raised the subject of the unwanted pregnancy.

"I'm probably being too forward," Golda said quietly as the three of them sipped their drinks at the café and waited for the cakes to arrive. "But I didn't want you to think we weren't interested. And you can tell me to mind my own business, but I *have* to ask if you've talked to your husband since last week about what we discussed."

In spite of everything, Frankie couldn't help but smile, a response which instantly produced an expression of relief on both Golda's and Miranda's faces. Maybe she wasn't the only one who'd been worrying, even though these women didn't know her that well, and this fact touched her more deeply than she'd imagined.

"Yes," she said. "Thank you for asking and, yes, I did take my courage into both hands and I told my husband what I told you."

"Good for you!" Miranda said. "How did it go?"

"Pretty badly at first," admitted Frankie, though the ins and outs of her relationship with Gareth wasn't her usual topic of conversation with her other friends. "I think it was the shock, but we were talking again by Sunday, thank heavens, and I had a doctor's appointment on Tuesday to confirm it."

She was about to explain more about the discussion she'd had with the doctor after her revelation, and also the decision she and Gareth had made, but Miranda interrupted her flow.

"Result!" the younger woman said. "High five!"

With that Miranda raised her hand in the air and waved it at them both. Smiling, Frankie copied the gesture and high-fived her in response. Golda looked utterly bemused but followed suit in a more restrained fashion, just as the cakes arrived.

"Is this something you young people do?" Golda asked.

"Thank you for counting me in that category," Frankie said. "But yes, the high-five is a young people's thing."

"Marvellous," said Golda. "And well done on booking that appointment and getting everything confirmed. That's a real plus point."

"So," Miranda said. "Now you've had time to get used to the idea, are you going to have the baby? When it's due anyway?"

Frankie shook her head. "No. Gareth and I have talked about it –
at the weekend and then again after I saw the doctor – and we've
agreed. I'm not going to have the baby."

Miranda put down the forkful of cake she'd just picked up and
stared at her. "What do you mean? You're going to have it
adopted?"

"No," Frankie replied. "I don't even want to be pregnant. I'm
going to have an abortion. It's much easier now, apparently, and I've
already rung the number the doctor gave me and they're sending me
a pill I can take. I'll be so relieved when it's all over."

Golda nodded and laid a hand on Frankie's arm, but Miranda's
eyes widened.

"What? You're going to get an abortion?" she said, her voice
rising. "You're going to *kill your baby?*"

"Hush," Frankie said, glancing around to make sure nobody had
overheard, but the tables next to them were empty while the family
in the corner were laughing together about something and paying no
attention to anything else. "I don't want everyone to know. But I'm
not killing anything, Miranda. It's not even a baby yet. Just a
collection of cells that aren't a person. Nobody's getting hurt."

Miranda, however, didn't look like she could agree. She pushed her plate to one side and leaned across the table towards Frankie.

"Yes, it is," she hissed. "*It is a baby*, no matter what everyone might say. It's a person, no matter how small it is, and you're going to kill it!"

"Miranda, my dear ..." Golda started to say, but the younger woman wasn't having any of it. She just carried on regardless.

"You have no idea how lucky you are!" she continued, her eyes swimming with tears. "You're going to have a baby and, even though you don't want it for some reason I can't frigging work out, it's life, isn't it? It's *life*. And I would do anything to be able to have a baby one day. But I can't, I effing can't. And do you know why I can't? I can't have a baby because ... because I'm *dying*. And it's all so frigging *unfair!*"

Then she jumped to her feet and ran out of the café without looking back.

Chapter Six

Miranda

Miranda stared at herself in the tiny mirror in her equally tiny bathroom. Her blonde hair was sticking out and her blue eyes were wide. As if someone had given her a terrible shock, the sort of shock you couldn't see coming and could never be prepared for.

Which was true, wasn't it? Because she'd done it today. Just now. She'd actually told someone the truth about herself. Two someones. Two someones who weren't Jake, who of course knew everything already. And telling him had only felt like telling herself. Which was the way she'd thought she'd wanted it. It was the only way she could cope with it.

Or so she thought.

But this afternoon, the fact of hearing what Frankie intended to do to her baby – and how could she even *think* about doing such a terrible thing when there was nothing physically wrong with her? *What the frigging hell was wrong with people?* – well, that had changed something inside Miranda and she'd opened her mouth and said the words *in absolute fury* before she even knew that was what she was going to do.

She should have kept her effing mouth shut, no matter what her personal feelings were about Frankie's decision, and then everything could have carried on as it had been doing: Miranda getting on with her life and trying not to think about the very scary things that lay ahead; seeing Jake and not talking about it after that first time she'd told him everything; ignoring the calls from that nurse she didn't want to see and who Jake thought she should see; and more than anything thinking about death and wishing she didn't know about that. About any of it.

And now other people knew her terrible secret. Two other people. Did that make it better, or worse? She didn't know.

She continued to stare at her reflection and felt all those pressing things she was spending so much time holding down inside where they couldn't hurt her come streaming upwards into her heart.

Turning, she dropped to her knees, flung open the loo seat lid and was sick into the bowl. Her heart was thudding and her head slammed with pain. She'd not been this sick for a long time and she rested her head on the cool porcelain of the loo and tried to take deep steady breaths.

Flashes from the moment she'd stupidly told Golda and Frankie flitted through her brain; Frankie's shocked face and Golda's expression of concern; the way she'd instantly regretted her confession and stood up; how she'd run to the door and outside where the air was warm on her face; the way she'd flung herself onto her bike and cycled home without looking back, all the while tears stinging her eyes so she could hardly see and it must have been lucky, so lucky, she'd not had another accident. Not that it mattered if she had or not. Not really. She wasn't supposed to think like that, but she did, and what did that matter either?

The moment she was at home, her heart still pounding and the keys slipping in her grasp until at last the door was open, Miranda had rung Jake, left a voicemail for him that made no sense but she couldn't find the words. He'd be on his shift, wouldn't be able to answer, but maybe he'd get the message later when he got a chance, understand it was from her (because who else could it be?) and ring her back. She needed to hear his voice more than anything, didn't know how she could wait for him to respond but she just had to.

126

And then she'd come into the bathroom, stomach churning, and now here she was, sprawled across her loo with sick clinging to her lips. She wished she was dead already, honestly she did.

She began to sob, this time for real, and it was then that her frigging doorbell rang.

For a moment of pure relief, she thought it might be Jake. But no, it couldn't be, could it? He would still be at work until at least 6pm. If it wasn't him, then she didn't want to see anyone else. Not now and not ever, for as long as that was for her. Maybe whoever it was would go away, because she didn't want to see anyone but Jake, especially not with sick on her shirt and the taste of it in her mouth.

The bell rang again.

"Go away," Miranda muttered, "please, *for fuck's sake*."

Her plea didn't work. The bell rang again, this time for longer. It sounded desperate, if bells could do that.

"For God's *sake*," she muttered again and added a few choice curse words for good measure.

Then she launched herself off her knees, flung open the bathroom door and staggered to the front door. When she flung that one open as well, she blinked as she tried to take in what she saw.

"No, *no*," she moaned. "I don't want to talk to *you*."

She tried to close the door and block out the whole of the outside and all its bloody stupid challenges but she didn't have the strength against the two women who stood on her doorstep.

"Let us in, Miranda," came Frankie's voice. "I'm so sorry I upset you. But, please, you can't just say what you said and then run away."

"Yes, I can!" Miranda protested but in vain as both Frankie and Golda pushed the door open more firmly and stepped inside. "I can do anything I want."

"Yes, of course you can," said Golda calmly as she closed the door behind her. "But, on this occasion, I think you can do that while we're here with you just as easily as if we weren't. Do you have tea?"

For all the world, the older woman sounded like she'd arrived at a party and was just making conversation. Miranda almost laughed but couldn't quite find it in herself to do so. Instead, she nodded and pointed in the direction of the kitchen behind her.

"Good," said Golda. "I'll go and make some then. You can never have too much tea in my opinion. Besides, you and Frankie might need to clear the air."

With that she bustled away, and Miranda was left in the hallway with Frankie. She didn't know what to say, and the two women stared at each other for a couple of moments.

Then Frankie coughed.

"I didn't lock my car," she said.

Miranda shrugged. "Maybe you should. It's a bit rough round here, after all."

"I'll take my chances. Is there anywhere we can sit?"

"Suppose the dining room will have to do. It's tiny though."

Miranda turned and stumbled through to the dining room though in reality it was more of an addition to the kitchen and she hardly ever used it. The landlord had never put a table in there, mainly because there wasn't room for one. It just held one struggling pot plant she didn't know what to do with though she wished it had a flower or two at least. She liked flowers and they always brightened the place up. Whenever she was feeling flush, she bought a bunch or two, but she'd not felt flush for a while. She wished she had some now. There was also a stool and a two-seater sofa that had definitely seen better days. You had to climb over one arm to get to it, but it was better than nothing.

Miranda took the stool. It gave her a height advantage over the rest of the room and she needed that.

There was a slight hesitation and then Frankie squeezed herself over the arm of the sofa and sat down. There was a moment when Miranda wondered if she'd give it a quick dust with her hand first but she didn't. Then Miranda waited. She was too tired and still too angry to be polite and make conversation, though she'd never been one for that kind of thing anyway.

A long and tense pause followed while Frankie gazed aimlessly round the room. Miranda wondered what she was looking for and thought that, whatever it was, she was unlikely to find it here. In her posh-cow house with her posh-cow ways, Frankie had probably never realised that shit flats like this existed. She'd probably never had to rent anywhere. She would have plenty of room for a child, if she didn't get rid of the one she had now. Frankie didn't know how lucky she was.

"That's a nice fern," Frankie said, making Miranda jump.

"What?"

"Your plant. It's nice. I like ferns."

"Oh," replied Miranda. "You're bothered about the fern but you're not worried about an actual baby? *One you're carrying right now?*"

"My decision not to have a family is nothing to do with you," Frankie responded, and her lips were so pursed that Miranda was amazed she could talk at all. "And, besides, your parting shot at the café trumped all of that, didn't it? If it's even true? Or did you just say it to shock me?"

Miranda felt a wave of fury power up inside her and opened her mouth to tell Frankie what an *absolute bitch* she was, but just then Golda pushed open the door from the kitchen and came in, carrying a tray with three steaming mugs, a carton of milk and a plate of biscuits.

Miranda hadn't realised she had a tray and, even if she had known, would never have thought of using it. Never mind the biscuits – where the hell had they come from?

"Tea's up," Golda said.

With that, she looked at them both, frowned and then handed the two silent women a mug of tea before offering the biscuits.

Nobody took one. After a couple of moments, Golda made her way over the obstacle of the sofa and sat down on the one remaining seat next to Frankie.

"So," the older woman said, quietly, "have you two sorted yourselves out?"

"Well," said Frankie. "I think we know where we stand and what we feel about babies a little more than we did, but whether that means we've sorted ourselves out is another question."

"I didn't think you were someone who could throw a baby away like that," protested Miranda.

"And I didn't think you were someone who would pretend you were dying just to make me feel bad," was Frankie's response.

"I'm not pretending! Don't you dare accuse me of things you know nothing about."

"Then don't judge me for things you don't know anything about either."

"I'm not the one who started with the whole judging thing!" was Miranda's furious comeback, her fingers clutched so tightly around her mug of tea that it was amazing it didn't break.

"Wait, please," said Golda, interrupting their growing rage with each other. "This isn't what I meant when I said I hoped you'd clear the air. I understand everyone has a strong view about having children and abortion, but we should be able to live with our differences, shouldn't we? We can't all think exactly the same. We all know that, but let's at least act like adults. All right?"

She paused and eyed first Frankie and then Miranda. Frankie sighed and nodded, and Miranda shrugged.

"Okay," she mumbled, as her face grew red. "Okay, sorry for what I said, Frankie. About the baby. I might not like it but it's up to you what you do. I do see that."

"Thank you," said Frankie. "And I'm sorry too. I didn't mean to upset you."

"Good," said Golda. "That's a relief. I do so hate arguments."

She stopped speaking abruptly and shook her head as if trying to dispel bad memories before continuing. "So, do you want to tell us what you meant at the café, Miranda?"

No. Miranda did not want to talk about it. The only way she was keeping it all under control in the first place was ignoring what she knew to be true. But she'd said something – stupid, so stupid! – at the café and now these two women wouldn't let it go. They wouldn't leave until she'd given some kind of explanation. Older women were always like that. It had been true of her eldest foster mother and it was true of these two as well. They would never leave her alone until she'd talked.

For a heartbeat, she thought about lying and telling them she'd only been joking, just to get rid of them. But one look at Golda told her beyond any doubt that it wouldn't be possible. She had to tell them something and it would have to be true. Maybe then they would leave.

"It's true what I said," she whispered. "I'm dying. I don't know how long I've got. It's a brain tumour. So fucking stupid. I've had so many tests but they can't help me. That's all. Sorry."

She had no idea why she was sorry. There was no need to be sorry, was there? Or maybe she was sorry she'd said anything in the first place, sorry she'd let the two women in and sorry she'd told them her *stupid* health problem. She really wished Jake was here.

"Oh," said Frankie. "I don't know what to say. Except that I'm sorry and it's totally crap. Which is an understatement, I know. I'm so very sorry."

"Don't be. It's not your fault, is it?"

"Yes, I see that. I'm …"

"… sorry, yes, I know," Miranda completed the sentence before Frankie could finish it. She couldn't bear to hear the word again.

Then one look at Frankie's stricken face made her regret her shortness.

"Oh shit," said Miranda. "I don't mean to be rude but I knew this would happen if I told anyone. Apart from my friend Jake, I mean. He knows. I knew everyone would be sorry and then not know what to say or do."

"Well, you were bloody right, weren't you," Frankie replied, totally unexpectedly, "It puts all my stuff about the baby into perspective, doesn't it? Oh, see, I still don't know what to bloody say, do I!"

Golda gasped and looked as if she honestly couldn't take any more, but the next moment Miranda and Frankie were laughing. The kind of laughter with more than a hint of hysteria in it.

"I don't think anyone knows what to say in these circumstances," Golda said thoughtfully, when the other two were quieter. "I don't think there's a rule book. However, I do wish there was. It might have been helpful when my husband had his terminal diagnosis."

Miranda blinked. "Oh, yes, you said your husband was ill. Was it cancer too? Like me?"

Golda nodded and held her mug in both hands as if trying to warm herself. "He was ill with cancer, yes, and there wasn't a cure. He didn't have what you have though. It was another kind of illness. Leukaemia. Cancer of the blood. All cancers are different, you know."

Miranda knew what leukaemia was. One of the pupils in the class above her at secondary school had died of it. Though she'd not known the girl, she'd thought how cruel it had been to die so young. She'd never thought that person might one day be her.

"How long did he take to die?" she asked.

Golda hesitated before answering.

"About a year or so," she said.

"I'm so sorry," said Frankie, softly and then blushed furiously and looked away from them both. "*That word.* I can't stop using it now."

"Don't worry about it," Golda said. "The English language doesn't have enough vocabulary to deal with terminal illness. I've always thought that. It doesn't have the vocabulary to deal with any kind of pain."

There was no answer to that, Miranda thought. And maybe she was right. It was Frankie who spoke next.

"How did you find out?" she asked Miranda. "If that's all right to ask? Just ignore me if you don't want to answer."

Miranda shook her head. "It's fine."

And, oddly, it was.

It had been like this. Just over six months ago, her life had been pretty good. She'd been living with her lovely boyfriend (well, she thought he was lovely back then but now of course she knew what a total effing *bastard* he was), and with a temporary job in one of the local shops. It wasn't ideal but it had been enough for her, and she'd even got to the point where there was a tiny bit of money left at the end of the month, which was brilliant.

Then, in December, the headaches she'd been having for a while, when she thought about it, kept on coming back more and more often. And they got tougher and tougher too, sometimes lasting for two or three days, no matter how many pills she took to try to stop them. They were so bad she was even off sick for a couple of days every now and then, lying on her bed and unable to eat because of the pain.

Jake had moaned at her and told her she should see a doctor, but she'd ignored him. Headaches – no matter how awful – weren't something doctors would be interested in.

Then came the shop's Christmas party. The week before December. Miranda had been looking forward to it and had brought a new pair of trousers for the occasion, at a cost she wouldn't normally have gone for but she deserved a treat after all the bloody headaches. She'd made a special effort too, even buying mascara for once and then – finally! – nailing the smoky-eyed look she'd practised for days.

The party, which was held at a local night club the company had booked for the evening, had started out brilliantly and she'd had several dances with her boyfriend before he'd disappeared to the bar for a couple of beers. She hoped he'd be back soon as she remembered how thirsty she'd been.

It was then that it happened. She'd been standing at the edge of the dance floor, chatting and smiling with two of her colleagues. And then everything around her started to move, even though she herself wasn't moving. She wasn't drunk, not this early in the party. A moment later the whole room turned black and she wondered where the hell the lights had gone and if there'd been an electricity cut. And then the room came back into view again, but it was all foggy, with people moving in odd ways and blending into each other. Her head began to throb and she staggered, trying to find something to lean against. But there was nothing and she heard nervous laughter – though whether that was her own or one of the girls she was with, she never knew – and then everything went black again and she fainted.

Miranda didn't remember anything else until she woke up in a hospital bed with Jake sitting next to her and holding her hand. Her mouth felt dry – so dry! – and her head was sore. When she tried to speak, to ask what the hell had happened, she couldn't. But the movement produced a wave of nausea she couldn't fight and she turned as best she could and vomited over the bed she was lying in. The wrench on her gut made her feel dizzy and even more sick. She heard Jake shouting for help and felt the warmth of his hand smoothing back the hair from her face.

Then there was a nurse – maybe two nurses, but again she couldn't remember – who came in and took charge, clearing up the mess she'd made while she groaned and tried to stay as still as possible. So as not to be sick again.

When the nurses disappeared and she had a new sheet over the bed, Miranda tried to move her other hand – the one Jake wasn't holding – but found she was wired up to some machine which was dripping something into her arm.

"What's that?" she mumbled. "What's happening? Why am I here?"

Jake's grip of her free hand strengthened.

"I don't know what the drip is," he said. "But you've had it since you've been here. You fainted at your shop's party and they couldn't make you wake up so someone called an ambulance. And here you are."

"Oh," Miranda muttered. "Sorry to be a nuisance. How stupid. So I've been here overnight then."

A silence before Jake responded.

"Actually, you've been here a couple of days," he said. "You did wake up a couple of times, but you probably don't remember that."

"A couple of days?" Miranda tried to sit up but the machinery she was attached to wouldn't let her and, besides, Jake at once put his hands on her shoulders – gently – so she couldn't move at all. "What? *Why?*"

"I don't know much," he said. "They won't tell me anything as I'm not family. Not even when I told them nobody is and I was the next best thing. Probably should have said I was your brother or something from the start, but I was too worried to think straight."

Miranda asked about her boyfriend, and Jake said he'd been in a couple of times but wasn't good at hospital visits and had now gone to his family for Christmas anyway. Apparently he hoped to see her in the new year.

"*Fucker*," she whispered.

Jake grinned. "Yeah. My thoughts exactly. No idea why you're with him. Fucker!"

"When's Christmas then?" she asked, trying not to think about her frigging tosser of a boyfriend. "When can I go home?"

"I don't know. They're doing loads of tests. You keep being wheeled away for ages and then wheeled back again. Still at least I managed to grab a packet of cigarettes from the shop to pass the time when you're away. I'm shocked they had them really, in a hospital and everything."

"Yeah," she said, then, "Thanks. Thanks for being here, Jake."

He shrugged. "No problem. We're mates. And Christmas is in a couple of days, if you're interested. It's Christmas Eve tomorrow."

"Oh," she said.

She'd probably be here for Christmas then. Once hospitals got their hands on you, they didn't like to let go, unless you escaped without their knowledge or something. And she felt far too weak to do anything so dramatic. Those machines were probably making her worse rather than better. People went into hospital with one illness and came out with five more. She'd be lucky to get out of here alive. She gave Jake a searching glance and he smiled back. No, she thought, if she asked him for help in getting away from here, he definitely wouldn't help her. He was far too honest for any of that. Effing shame.

After that, Miranda thought she might have slept again but she couldn't remember rightly. It was probably all the drugs they were giving her. The next thing she really remembered in full as if it was seared on her brain forever was her discussion with the consultant and the nurse who came to see her.

Jake was there too. He held her hand as the experts said words and words and yet more words she didn't understand and couldn't believe related to her and her life. They kept on asking if she understood what they were saying and she kept on nodding, but she didn't really. Not at all. And they showed her diagrams of the inside of her head and those didn't make any sense either. Then the consultant left and she wondered if it was over but the nurse stayed and held her other hand for a while.

Jake was crying and didn't seem able to stop. She didn't understand why. She stared at him curiously. She didn't know what to say. She felt numb and sick, and the words that had been pushed into her mind filled it so she could think of nothing else.

She must have fallen asleep again, because when she woke, it was dark outside the window and she was alone. She wondered if she might have dreamt everything and she would wake up properly in a minute or so and it would be Christmas and she'd be at home, doing the stuff she usually did at Christmas. Which was ignore the whole frigging thing and get pissed, basically. That had always worked for her.

But no matter how much she squeezed her eyes and tried to wake herself up to the real world she'd known before, she couldn't do it.

So Miranda spent Christmas in hospital. Jake came to visit her and brought presents and she opened them and tried to be normal, but it didn't seem possible. The nurse who'd held her hand came back too and talked to her some more about what would happen now. But Miranda didn't want to hear anything about this and closed her eyes, turning away on the bed and trying to drown out the woman's words by humming to herself.

After a while, the nurse went away, but she'd left a stack of leaflets on the bedside table that Jake was looking through.

"Don't read those!" she whispered, a wave of anger that he should be interested in them sweeping through her. "You don't need to! I don't know why she left them here, that woman. Stupid cow!"

"Miranda! She's not stupid. Honestly, she's just trying to help. These leaflets are going to be useful. She's a cancer nurse. A specialist one. You need to listen to her."

"No!" Her eyes filled up when the last thing she wanted to do was cry. Because if she cried, then everything she'd been told would turn out to be true and she couldn't deal with that. Couldn't ever deal with it. "It's stupid. *She's* stupid. I don't want the leaflets."

"Okay, okay," Jake said. "I'm sorry. If you don't want them, you don't have to look at them right now. Let's forget them. It doesn't matter."

He dropped the one he'd been holding on the floor and took her hand instead. Then his expression crumpled in a way she'd never seen before and he leant forward and buried his face in her shoulder. She could feel the slight shudder of his crying as he held on to her as if he'd never let go.

In a weird way, Jake's collapse helped her. It didn't help her deal with what she'd been told – no, she was unable to do that, but it helped to comfort her friend as he cried. It gave her something else to do other than trying not to think and worrying. And trying not to think and worrying at the same time was a deadly combination. How well she knew that.

After this, there were more tests and more conversations with people who kept telling her the same thing over and over again. The nurse who had tried to help her the first time kept coming back, though it was Jake who ended up trying to put in place what the nurse had advised. There was a lot of drugs too, and she had to take them though she didn't know how they all worked together or what they were for. It was just easier to submit to anything she was told to do as saying no caused more difficulties than she could handle.

Then she was at home again, in the new year. With the first set of those dreadful leaflets Jake had taken for her and which she didn't want. She stuffed them in her bedside drawer so she couldn't see them. See them and remember that this year – *this year* – was going to be the last she'd ever see.

There was a crazy number of appointments to go to as everyone in the whole of the medical profession seemed to want to watch closely to see how she died. Frigging vultures, she thought. Why couldn't they leave her alone? If there was nothing they could do for her, why the hell bother?

It didn't seem to stop them. And if she dared miss any of her appointments, they were just meaner to her the next time she came, she was sure of it. The only thing that kept her going was Jake. He came with her whenever he could and she was sure he'd skived off work for her first few appointments, though he never told her for definite. Even when she asked him.

She was more than grateful for that though, especially since her effing boyfriend had dumped her and moved out. It was too much for him. She felt nothing when he left. Nothing at all. She didn't have any feelings to spare.

When Jake found out, he'd been as angry as she'd ever known him. In a way, she was glad as she didn't have the strength for it. She'd not gone back to work either – it was yet another thing she couldn't face, but her job had been temporary anyway, so it didn't much matter. She was living entirely on benefits, which the nurse and Jake had helped her with.

She thought about getting another job but the appointments she had to go to made it difficult. Anyway, nobody wanted to employ someone who might die at any time, did they? If she tried to get work, she'd have to tell the agency or employer, and that was a conversation she couldn't face.

When Miranda had finished telling her story to Golda and Frankie, she sat back, leaning against the wall behind her as she perched on her stool. It felt as if a weight she hadn't known she'd been carrying had been ever so slightly lifted.

It was Frankie who spoke first, though Miranda had assumed it would be Golda who seemed to be the strongest of them all.

"When you had that accident," Frankie said quietly, "just before the Pilates class. Was it really an accident?"

Miranda felt as if someone had punched her in the stomach, and she took a moment just to breathe again.

"I don't know," she said. "That afternoon, it hadn't been a good day. The thing in my head – the thing that will kill me – had got a bit larger that week and my headaches were worse. I didn't know how to react so I carried on as normal but then, when I was cycling along, and saw the wall in front of me, something just flipped and I thought: why not?"

"Why not kill yourself, you mean?" This time it was Golda who asked the question.

"Yes, I think so," she replied after a long silence that nobody else could fill. "But I don't think I'll try it again. It hurt too much and halfway over the wall I changed my mind. But it was too late to do anything else by then."

She looked up and met the eyes of the two women. She had nothing else to say. Nothing else to offer. Then, to her surprise, Frankie gave her half a smile.

"Well, that's good then," she said. "I'm glad you changed your mind, Miranda. Even halfway across a wall. Because it's the thought that counts, isn't it?"

Another moment's silence and then, again much to her surprise, Miranda started to laugh. A heartbeat later, Frankie joined in followed, more hesitantly, by Golda. It was as if the laughter eased something that had been building up in the room and made the intensity of the conversation more bearable.

"True," Golda said when the laughter had come to a natural close. "It's the thought that counts. But may I ask another question?"

"As long as it's not serious," said Miranda. "I've had enough of being serious. It's overrated anyway."

"I don't know if my question is serious or not," Golda said. "I was simply wondering if there's anything we can help you with. To make your life better."

Frankie nodded her agreement, and Miranda thought about their offer. It was probably out of the question to say a baby of her very own would be nice as all that was impossible for her. And Frankie would go mad anyway! She looked round the room and her gaze settled on the fern, struggling for life in its tiny pot. Then something popped into her head that was the most astonishing thing she'd ever imagined but it felt right. So she said it.

"I know it sounds weird, but I'd like to have a garden," she said. "I've always liked flowers. They make me happy. But I don't know anything about them. Please, will you help me?"

Chapter Seven

Golda

Yesterday's confession from Miranda had shocked Golda. Of all the things she'd ever thought might be possible for anyone that young to go through – and she had plenty of experience herself to choose from, didn't she? – she had never imagined that knowing you were going to die would be one of them.

She had no idea how Miranda was coping with it. In all her life, Golda had always made herself look forward, to a time when things might be better. She'd learnt not to look back and she'd learnt not to think too deeply about what was happening in the present either. But to know that, whatever this life was, there would not be much of it left to enjoy or endure – well, this was beyond her imagination.

When Miranda had thrown her bombshell into the sudden argument in the coffee shop yesterday and then run out before they could react, neither Frankie nor she had had any idea what to do. They'd stared at each other in disbelief and then Frankie had leapt up from the table.

"Come on," she'd said. "We've got to follow her."

Golda wasn't sure this was a good idea but was swept along by the other woman's decision. So they paid the bill as quickly as they could and went outside.

Miranda was nowhere to be seen.

"She'll have gone home," Frankie said. "Give her a few minutes and then let's follow her."

"Don't you think it's best to let her be, to clear the air a little?"

Frankie shook her head. "No! It doesn't matter if she doesn't like that I've chosen to have an abortion. We have to find out if she's okay. It's the right thing to do."

Golda had her own views about that, but they waited a couple of minutes, which seemed like an age, and then Frankie blew out a quick breath.

"That's it," she said. "I can't wait any longer. Who know what Miranda is thinking? Though I suppose we don't even know if it's true, do we? I'll go first. I know where she lives. You follow me."

And that's what they did. Once at Miranda's flat, Frankie pressed the bell. There was no answer. Golda was minded once more to leave it, but Frankie kept on ringing.

Finally, the door was opened, and Miranda let them in. She looked sick, angry and scared, all at once. Golda had no idea what to do or say, so she offered to make tea. It was stupid but it was all she could think of to do.

After that, Frankie and Miranda nearly came to blows again, but Golda had calmed them down, somehow. Which was something of a miracle as calming people down had never up to now been her strong point. And then Miranda had told them everything.

The younger woman had talked about the numbness she'd felt when she was told she was going to die, and how she didn't want to accept it. Didn't want people to know. And, yes, Golda more than most people understood how someone could feel like that – because of what had happened with Alan – but it wasn't the same at all and so she thought Miranda was being incredibly brave.

Then Golda had asked her what they could do to help her, if anything. The answer had surprised her, though she didn't know what she'd been expecting Miranda to say. A garden. Miranda wanted a garden.

Yesterday, Golda had asked her to show them what kind of garden the flat she was living in actually had – and the question had made Miranda snort with laughter. She'd got up and led them to the back door of her flat. Outside, there was nothing more than a tiny fenced-in area of paving stones with a few pots filled with geraniums. These were probably the only plants that could cope with the shade.

"Ah, I see," Golda had said.

And that was where they had left it. Now, today, Golda was still wondering how she could respond to Miranda's wish and also how involved she herself was willing to become, but she hadn't come up with many good ideas. The tail end of June and the start of July wasn't the ideal time to start a garden. Frankie had already checked to see if the village local allotment association had any spare plots, but they were full for the year and the waiting list was long enough too. Besides of which, the rules on the allotment website insisted that at least some vegetables had to be grown. It couldn't be all flowers. Golda also suspected allotments would be hard work and she didn't know how much energy Miranda would have for it.

Closing her eyes for a good minute didn't help Golda much either as nothing else came to mind. So she got up, opened the patio doors and stepped out into the sunshine. Taking a walk around her own garden always made things better. She admired the hardy geraniums, the clematis and the roses near the fence. Then she turned her back on them and gazed at the side of the house. Next to the garage and just beyond her washing line was an area of soil – not too large and not too small – where Golda tended to put garden experiments or plants she was growing on before planting out properly. The area also contained two raised beds. At the moment, the beds were home to a row of rocket salad and the strawberry plants, which had just finished cropping. There were no garden experiments this year as she simply hadn't got round to it.

Wouldn't this be perfect for Miranda's garden? The thought came out of nowhere and Golda drew in a sudden breath. It was certainly an idea but not one that made her feel comfortable. This garden was *her* garden. Her own private space where she could relax, and heal from the memories that still haunted her after all these years. It was the one place she could feel most truly herself.

Did she want to offer that to anyone else? No matter what terrible circumstances they were facing? After all, Golda had had to face her own terrible circumstances entirely by herself and she'd managed to come through, hadn't she? After a fashion. Perhaps Miranda would find another garden elsewhere?

But, then again, perhaps she didn't have enough time for searching? And if Golda had a piece of land she could offer the young woman on what would after all be a temporary basis, perhaps she was morally obliged to offer it. Once, a long time ago, a woman who'd been a stranger had helped Golda when she didn't have to, when she could easily have walked away, and Golda would be forever grateful for that. Perhaps it was time to pay that gift forward, which was a phrase she'd heard recently on television and hadn't really understood then, but now she saw it more clearly.

Golda closed her eyes, and pondered the issue for another long moment. Then she made a decision.

Inside, she took out her mobile phone and slowly but surely texted Miranda and Frankie to see if they might both be free tomorrow afternoon. It was a Saturday and the weather looked set to continue fine – though in this country, you could never be entirely sure – so it would be the perfect opportunity to let Miranda see the space for herself.

Twenty minutes later, it was all arranged. 3pm for refreshments in the garden. Golda had forgotten how fast things happened in the modern world. When she'd been growing up, invitations had been issued at least a week in advance and had sometimes even been arranged by letter. How times had changed.

The next day started off cloudy but the skies soon cleared and, by the time Frankie arrived, five minutes early, there were no clouds to be seen.

"Gorgeous afternoon!" Frankie said cheerfully as she parked her enormous car on Golda's driveway. "And what a lovely house."

"Thank you," Golda said, stepping back to let her in. "I've been lucky, in recent years."

Frankie followed her through the house and into the garden where Golda had set up the sunshade over the patio table and chairs.

"Wow!" Frankie said. "Your view is amazing. You can see right over those fields, and look at your trees!"

Golda couldn't help but laugh. "Yes, the view is what persuaded me to put an offer on the house. I thought it would be lovely living next to a field and woods and, in some ways, it is of course. I just wish I'd known about the fact I'd be fighting the ground elder and the bindweed for the rest of my life. I might not have been quite so keen."

"Hmm, Yes, I see, but we do always have to take the rough with the smooth."

That much was certainly true. She left Frankie admiring the garden while she fetched fruit juice, a jug of water and the plate of cakes she'd prepared. She'd offer her visitors hot drinks later if need be. When she glanced out of the kitchen window, Golda saw Miranda on the driveway just dismounting from her bike.

Temporarily abandoning the juice carton on the worktop, she made her way to the front door and let her in.

"Miranda. It's good to see you. Please, come through. Do you want to put your bike round the back?"

Miranda gave Golda a quiet smile as she shook her head. "No need. I've put the padlock on it and just rested it against the hedge. Is that okay?"

"Of course."

Golda led the way to the garden through the house and was at the far side of the living room when she realised Miranda was no longer immediately behind her.

"Miranda?"

Her visitor was standing in the doorway to the living room and staring round it, eyes wide.

"Amazing," she said.

Golda hadn't paid much attention to her living room for quite a long time. She supposed that was true of everyone – once you had your house how you wanted it, you didn't pay it much heed. But it was her favourite room: double-aspect windows and a long sliding door onto the garden which took in the view over the fields. She didn't have a lot of furniture – just a cream sofa and a couple of soft chairs and a pine bookcase opposite the fireplace. Not a real fire – Golda didn't like the smell or the effort of those, and weren't they supposed to be bad for the environment? She simply filled the gap with dried flowers in winter or fresh flowers from the garden in summer. Currently she had some early dahlias from the front garden in there, and a couple of roses from the back.

"Those flowers are beautiful," Miranda said as she went over to the hearth and crouched down for another look. "And the scent – it's amazing."

"That's the roses," Golda said. "I always choose ones with a scent – I don't see the point of unscented roses."

"But what are these other ones?"

"Dahlias," she replied. "That's a type called *Café au Lait*. They tend to be a bit droopy so I take the tallest ones for the display."

"They're so … large. I didn't even know you could get flowers that big," Miranda said, getting up and fixing her direct gaze right upon Golda. "If I get a garden, however small, that's what I'll have in there."

"Good," Golda replied, taking her courage into both hands and putting her qualms firmly to bed. "Because ideas about your garden are exactly what we'll be thinking about today. Now, come and join Frankie outside, I'll get the drinks and then we can talk."

Once the juice or water was poured and the cakes chosen, Golda got down to business.

"All right," she said. "Thank you so much for coming. Because there's something important I wanted to discuss with you. I've been thinking about your garden, Miranda. I thought about pots you could have at home that might suit the conditions there more, but I didn't think that was really what you wanted, was it? Then Frankie suggested the local allotments, but their plots are full and there's a waiting list. So, in the end, I wondered if a section of the garden I have here might be suitable."

With that, Golda got up and beckoned for the other two to follow her. She walked to the side of the house and gestured at her two raised beds and the rest of the side garden.

"This is what I mean," she said. "The strawberries are over and can be removed for whatever you might want to put in. And the salad you can see can easily go into pots elsewhere. That's not a problem. Now, I know it's not ideal as if you decide to make a garden for yourself here, you'll have to cycle round whenever you want to visit. And we'll have to work out how you can get in if I'm not here. Though, to be honest, I'm here most days so it's not a real issue. I know this is a big decision for you, in ways I can't even begin to understand, but the offer is there. If you need it. Not only that but you won't have to make a garden on your own – Frankie and I can help with anything you might like. How does that sound?"

Miranda was standing a little ahead of Golda when she finished her not-very-prepared speech. She turned round and smiled, her eyes bright.

"Thank you so much, Golda," she said. "That's really kind of you. I never thought anyone would do anything like this. It's the kindest thing anyone's ever done for me. Apart from Jake. Thank you. But this is *your* home, *your* garden. It's your private space. Are you sure about this?"

Golda nodded. "Yes, I've thought about it and I'm sure."

"What about payment?" Miranda said. "I can't afford much but I'll pay what I can, I promise you."

"Oh my dear," Golda replied. "I'm not expecting any money, of course not. It's not why I wanted to offer it to you."

"Then, why?" Miranda asked simply.

Golda hesitated for a moment. There were things she wanted to say, but she needed to consider them first, and she'd not had time to do so. The other two women had been open about their lives – so very open – but Golda couldn't be like that. Not without thought. But Miranda was still waiting for an answer.

"Because something happened a long time ago," Golda said quietly, at last. "And a woman I didn't know helped me, when she could easily have walked away. I never had the chance to thank her, not properly, and so it seems right for me to try to help you now."

162

Miranda and Frankie gazed at her in silence. Golda knew they were waiting for more, but she couldn't do that. Not now. Not yet.

"So," she said clapping her hands together in a way she never ever did. "That's my idea. Shall we sit down and you can think about the offer?"

"Golda, are you really sure about this?" Miranda asked again, eyes still fixed on her face.

"Yes," Golda said. "Very sure indeed."

"And would you and Frankie help me?"

"Of course we will," Frankie replied with a smile. "It sounds like a lot of fun to me. I wouldn't miss it for the world. Not that I have any gardening knowledge, but I'm good at following instructions which I'm sure will be helpful."

"Then thank you again," Miranda said, as the three women returned to their seats. "It's amazing. And I don't need to think about your offer. I'm happy to say yes."

And that was that. They spent the next half hour or so considering what Miranda would like to grow. She was keenest on the dahlias she'd seen in Golda's living room, as well as roses, both of which were perfect for the time of year.

While Golda suggested other suitable flowers, Frankie got her mobile phone out and started searching for late summer plants. Between the two of them, they came up with crocosmias, rudbeckias, echinaceas, asters, heleniums and anemones.

It wasn't long before Miranda started to laugh.

"What?" Frankie and Golda said in unison.

"You two!" Miranda said, still snorting with laughter. "You should see yourselves. I have no idea what you're saying! Are you talking in a foreign language? I've never heard of any of these flowers. You might be making the names up for all I know."

"No! We're not," Golda said. "But you're right. We're getting too carried away. The important aspect of all this is you. What sort of flowers do *you* want? Or, if you're not sure of the names, what colours would you like?"

"Oh, that's easy," Miranda replied. "Yellows and golds and creams. Those are my favourite colours. They're bright and happy and calming, and make me feel better."

"Sounds perfect," Frankie chipped in. "Then those are the colours we will go for."

"All right," Golda said. "In that case, let's make a plan for the garden. It always helps to focus our ideas."

She went back into the house and found a pad of paper and a few pens and pencils. Then Golda put these supplies down on the table outside and shuffled her chair sideways so she could see what Miranda was doing. Frankie followed suit.

"All right," Golda continued. "Why don't you draw the two raised beds and the soil areas in the side garden, Miranda. Then you can add in the flowers you might like in the colours you want and we'll take it from there. Look, I have coloured pencils for your choices."

Miranda snorted with laughter. "Why do you have coloured pencils?"

Golda smiled. "I had a brief foray into dot-to-dot drawings a couple of years ago and one of the biggest books had all the little series of numbers in different colours so I had to get the pencils to suit. I didn't do it for long – the ones for adults are just so small I had to use a magnifying glass so I thought it was probably not a great idea for my eyesight."

When she finished her explanation, Frankie and Miranda were staring at her in disbelief.

"What?" she said. "What did I say?"

"Dot-to-dots?" Frankie enquired. *"Seriously?"*

"I don't even know what they are," said Miranda.

Golda described them as best she could but, in the face of the younger woman's utterly confused expression, she fetched one from the coffee table drawer. Where she kept them just in case she felt the urge to attempt one again.

By the time she got back, Frankie was helpless with laughter and so Golda's appearance holding her once-precious book of worldwide city dot-to-dot drawings didn't make things any better.

"Oh Lord," Frankie said. "You really do have them!"

"What are they?" said Miranda. "Let me look."

Miranda took the book Golda offered her and leafed through. Her frown deepened and she leafed through again, but in the other direction. Then she looked up.

"Isn't this something for children?" she said.

"Well, yes," Golda had to admit, sitting down at the table. "But, as I say, they make them for adults, and it's surprisingly relaxing. Or rather it would be if the numbers were larger. Perhaps I should try some children's versions? They would certainly be a lot clearer."

"Or maybe you could get a proper hobby," Miranda replied and then started to giggle. This made Frankie laugh even harder, and Golda couldn't help but join in.

"All right, all right," Golda said in the end when her two visitors had calmed down. "I admit to not being the trendiest person in the county but, at the very least, I do have coloured pencils."

Frankie and Miranda had to admit that was true and, yes, the coloured pencils would definitely come in handy. So, with only a slight additional snort of laughter, Miranda put the dot-to-dot book to one side, took the pad of paper and the pens and drew the two raised beds and the remainder of the side garden, as Golda had suggested.

Then she paused. "What if I don't know what I'd like?"

"That's all right," Golda said. "Don't worry about flower names. Just put down colours and whether you want them short, medium or tall. Frankie and I can make suggestions from there."

Miranda nodded. "Okay."

With that, she started to scribble on the page with an expression of pure concentration on her face and using both the everyday and the coloured pencils Golda had provided.

"What are those flowers called again?" she asked suddenly. "The ones you have?"

"You mean the dahlias?"

"Yes, those are the ones. How do you spell *dahlia*?"

Golda told her, and Miranda bent to focus on the paper again. "Thank you."

Another couple of minutes went by with Frankie and Golda idly chatting about the weather and if it might last all weekend. Then Miranda was ready.

"Here," she said. "I think this would be lovely."

They looked at her plan. Miranda had made the whole of the first bed – the one nearest the back gate – and the corresponding half of the soil area nearest to it into a plethora of roses, all bright yellow and gold, mixed in with other flowers in the same colour scheme. For the second bed and remaining soil, she had simply written the world *dahlias* and coloured everything in cream and pale yellow.

"What do you think?" she asked. "Do you think I – we – can do that?"

"We can do whatever you would like," Golda reassured her solemnly. "And if you decide you'd like something else when we're doing it, you can have that too. One thing you should think about, however, is if you'd like to take any flowers home with you or if you prefer them all to remain here. Or half and half if that's what you like best."

Miranda frowned. "Won't cutting them mean they'll stop growing? I really want to see something grow. That's more important than anything. Because … because …"

She couldn't complete the sentence but she didn't need to. Instead, she stopped talking. Frankie half-rose and gave her a quick hug, and Golda refilled her drink.

"Sorry," Miranda said when she could speak again. "I just …"

"I know," murmured Frankie. "You don't have to explain."

"No, you absolutely don't have to," Golda agreed. "But, in terms of your garden, if you want to, you can have cut flowers *and* watch them grow at the same time. Cutting blooms makes the plants grow more flowers, in most cases. Though, with roses, it depends what type you have."

"Really?" Miranda said, wide-eyed. "That's like magic!"

Golda smiled. "Yes, I suppose it is. But that's nature for you. Magical. I never really thought about it before, but it is."

It was too. Golda had never paid much attention to the magic of the seasons when she was younger, but now she found herself appreciating the natural world more and more. Being in the garden was, for her, the most relaxing thing ever. Then again, in lots of ways she'd earned a place where she could really relax. She only hoped this new venture of Miranda's garden wouldn't be too disruptive, but this was a mean thought and, besides, she couldn't go back on her promise now.

The women firmed up plans for a post-Pilates class garden centre visit on a Thursday afternoon in a couple of weeks' time. Miranda was a little concerned there wouldn't be cake, but Frankie and Golda were quick to reassure her that every garden centre in the western world was home to a coffee shop as well as a vast range of plants and flowers, so all would be well.

By 5pm, Golda's visitors had gone home and she was finishing the tidying up. They'd offered to help before leaving but Golda enjoyed pottering about after having company of any sort. Much as she had enjoyed the conversation, she liked being alone most of all, and she also liked putting her home back in the way she preferred it. It made her feel settled. It made her feel safe. It had always been that way.

Once, a long time ago, Golda had needed to find safety but all that was behind her now, wasn't it? With her husband dead and gone, she was truly safe. Safe from everything he'd done to her life. Right now, Golda had something to look forward to in a fortnight's time, which was a blessing. She hoped the planned trip to the garden centre would be a positive one. In spite of the shocking reasons for this garden, plants always made everything special and she found she couldn't wait to begin.

Chapter Eight

Frankie

The package to enable Frankie to stop being pregnant once and for all arrived two days after she'd rung up and asked for it. She hadn't expected this process to be quite as simple as it had proved to be so far. She'd thought there would be more questions from the medical profession and she'd assumed that, at the very least, she and probably Gareth would have to attend a counselling session or two.

None of that was true. She'd chatted further with the doctor she'd seen and she'd shaken her head when the counselling suggestion had arisen, reiterating that she and her husband absolutely didn't want a baby and she didn't want to be pregnant at all. The doctor had nodded and hadn't asked her anything else. Perhaps it was because Frankie wasn't a young girl anymore and she was old enough to know her own mind, or perhaps it was because of the determination in her words. She couldn't be sure, but she was glad beyond reason that she hadn't had to argue her case any further.

She returned from the doctor with the number to call for the medication she would need but, to her surprise, it had taken several days for her to key the numbers into her mobile.

Though that wasn't entirely true, was it? She'd actually keyed the numbers into her mobile several times. It was waiting long enough for the call to connect that took her the extra time.

Frankie wasn't sure why.

She'd been surprised by Miranda's fierceness about the whole issue, she supposed. Taken aback by the younger woman's reaction to her news. Shocked by it too, so she'd been angry but hadn't known how to respond. And then of course all that had been entirely swept away by Miranda's revelation about her illness. Which had been truly, utterly awful.

Frankie couldn't ever imagine knowing you were going to die. Of course, *everyone* would die, that was a fact of life. But the knowledge that it would be soon was unthinkable. She thought Miranda was the bravest person she'd ever met. She herself would never be that brave. If she were told she was going to die from a terminal illness, Frankie thought she would start to cry and never stop crying. There were so many things she wanted to do in her life:

go to New England in autumn; visit Berlin; learn to play piano with more than one finger; brush up her schoolgirl French. To name but a few.

If she was dead, she couldn't do any of these things. It was true what people said. You only had one life and Frankie wanted to live it the best way she could. Miranda would never have that chance. It was unbearable.

And being pregnant was absolutely and definitely not in Frankie's life dreams. Which made ending her pregnancy the only decision she could make.

When she finally made that call, Frankie was relieved it was once more an easy process. The nurse she spoke to from the Advisory Service was both efficient and kind. Frankie answered the same kinds of questions she'd answered at her own surgery and gave the woman her doctor's details as well. Somehow, she felt listened to, without any kind of judgement. It made her feel better about herself.

At the end of the conversation – though perhaps consultation was a better description – the nurse advised her that the abortion package would be sent out as soon as possible and she should read

174

all the information carefully when it was received, usually in two or three days, and ring back or contact her own doctor if she had any concerns. She also briefly explained the process to Frankie so she had an idea of what to expect. Frankie thanked the woman for her time and ended the call.

She felt a strange mixture of relief and terror that at last she'd taken the next step and soon she would no longer be pregnant. When the nurse had been explaining what Frankie would need to do when the package arrived, she'd found it hard to take the details in and it had indeed sounded a lot more complicated than she'd hoped, but she assumed the instructions would help. And, as the nurse had said, if she was really confused, she could ring again or even check on the Internet. Sometimes that could be helpful. The Advisory Service had its own website which Frankie had saved into her favourites list. There was plenty of help out there, and her problem would soon be solved. There was no need to worry.

None of which explained the huge jolt to Frankie's stomach when the package was there on the welcome mat to greet her when she arrived home from work. As she'd been told, it was unmarked in any way – which was definitely a huge relief – and she hadn't had to sign for it. She knew exactly what it was when it saw it, and she took it through into the living room and sat down to look through the contents.

They were laid out in exactly the way she'd viewed at least a hundred times on the service's website: there was a Medabon pack with the numbers *1* and *2* emblazoned on it; two further plastic-wrapped pills with the number *3* on it; a packet of contraceptive pills (a bit late for that now, Frankie thought!); a packet of Codeine pain relief pills; and finally a pregnancy termination test kit.

Plus of course a very detailed instruction booklet for it all.

Frankie didn't think she could read it through now. She needed to give herself time to prepare, and she also didn't want to start any kind of treatment when she was on her own. She would do it at the weekend. It wasn't as if there was a huge deadline on when she should start the abortion as she wasn't very far along in the pregnancy anyway.

So she closed the package carefully, and went upstairs to store it in the bathroom cabinet. She'd tell Gareth tonight that it had arrived, and what her plans were to start the treatment. That was the best way forward.

176

For some reason Frankie couldn't entirely pinpoint, it was only when they were making their after-dinner coffee and tea that she found the words to tell him. Which was silly, really, as it certainly wasn't hard.

"I meant to tell you," she began casually enough as she filled the kettle. "The pills arrived today. In the post. The ones for the abortion. I checked it over and everything is there."

Gareth came over at once and hugged her. "That's good, isn't it?"

"Yes, of course," she nodded. "The instructions say I can begin as soon as I like, but I thought I'd leave it until the weekend. I can start Friday night. I don't want to do anything on my own."

"That's fine," he replied. "We're in this together, you know."

And that was all Frankie needed to hear. At the weekend then, Friday night, she'd take the first pill and then, on Sunday, she'd use the remaining pills for stage two of the process. It was simple and she hoped that everything would be as smooth as possible. And then next week she would no longer be pregnant, and a weight would be lifted from her shoulders.

It was odd then how the few days between the arrival of the abortion pack and the planned start of her treatment should be so terribly full of babies.

Honestly, Frankie kept seeing them everywhere: in prams at the side of the road, with their mother or father of course; at the village shop in the arms of the woman in front of her in the queue for stamps; even at the garage where she was buying petrol. They all seemed to be staring at her accusingly, which was a ridiculous notion to have. She knew that perfectly well, but she still couldn't help herself. Maybe babies would stop popping up at every available opportunity once she'd taken those pills at the weekend. She hoped so. She also understood very well that these babies or ones very like them had probably been around her in such quantities all along. After all, the world needed to be filled, didn't it? It was just that she'd not been interested in them before. Though, of course, *interested* wasn't the word she was looking for. *Aware* would be more suitable for her state of mind.

It was therefore with some relief that Frankie arrived at work on Friday morning, ready for a day of course administration and answering the phone to delegates and enquirers. It would definitely be a break from the current baby influx. She was safe from them at work.

Or so she assumed. But in fact this particular Friday morning was the morning allocated for one of her colleagues, Jackie, who was currently on maternity leave, to pop in with the new addition to her family. Frankie had completely forgotten all about this, even though she herself had been the one in the office who'd sent flowers and baby gifts on behalf of the team just after the birth, and she was the one who'd agreed the visit date with Jackie.

It all came flooding back the moment the office door opened and Jackie pushed the pram inside, whilst smiling and waving at everyone. The other women (and one man) in the office at once leapt up to greet her and started admiring the new baby and chatting about how the birth had gone and whether Jackie was getting any sleep at all. Frankie felt her shoulders grow stiff and her neck suddenly seemed extraordinarily heavy.

From within the clustered group, Jackie looked up and waved over at Frankie before bending down and lifting her baby out of the pram.

"He's awake now," she said, "so it's obviously cuddle time!"

The baby – whose name was Tom – was apparently more than happy to be cuddled by anyone, not necessarily his mother, and so Jackie handed him over to the first eager pair of hands. Frankie could hear gurgling and a heck of a lot of cooing. She felt herself grow hot and cold all at the same time and wondered if she could somehow escape without causing any upset, but there was only one door to their office and Jackie and her pram were right in front of it.

She couldn't just sit here – it was rude, and Frankie hated being rude. So, even though her legs felt weak and she could hear the thud of her own heart, she got up and approached the cluster of baby admirers. They parted as if they'd only been waiting for her and let her into the circle. Frankie's immediate boss was just handing the baby back to Jackie, but Jackie shook her head, laughing.

"No, let Frankie have a look first! Oh, and thank you for the flowers, by the way. I'm sure it was you who sent them."

Frankie smiled and was about to reply when her boss turned and thrust the still gurgling Tom into her arms. Automatically, she put out her arms to take his surprisingly heavy form and then panicked.

"Oh God! I don't know how to hold a baby. I don't want to drop him."

180

She tried to return Tom to his mother's arms, but Jackie just laughed. "You won't drop him! Anyway, even if you do, babies are tough. He'll probably just bounce. Here, this is how you hold him. It's easy."

With that, Jackie laid Tom's head against Frankie's chest, put one of her hands up to support his neck and the other under his bottom.

"There," she said. "Job done!"

For one terrible moment, Frankie stared at Jackie in shock, desperately wanting above all things to be a long way away from this awful scenario. Awful in ways Jackie couldn't possibly imagine. Then, in Frankie's arms, Tom stretched and gave another gurgle before opening his eyes to look straight up at her. He felt incredibly warm and so very *alive* in a way she hadn't ever anticipated. Which was once again weird, she knew, but it was the first thought that came to her.

"Gosh," she said with what was nothing more than a squeak. "He's got such grey eyes."

"Oh yes," Jackie laughed. "My other two were born with grey eyes, but they always turn brown, like mine, before the year is out. So if you like grey eyes, you'd better make the most of it."

Frankie nodded, as if she knew what Jackie was talking about, and felt her shoulders relax just a bit as she held her colleague's new son. Her eyes filled with tears and she had to concentrate hard in order to blink them away. After a couple of minutes, someone else demanded a turn, and Frankie handed over her temporary charge with some relief.

Smiling at Jackie, she retreated to the edge of the circle and tried to concentrate on the conversation. But she wasn't able to listen. Not really. And she couldn't help but be glad when Jackie decided it was time to get on with her day, whilst promising to keep them all updated on the baby's progress. Because Frankie could still feel the weight of Tom's small body in her arms even though he was no longer there.

And she could still sense the way he'd made her feel when he'd opened his eyes and looked up at her.

And now she absolutely, entirely, didn't know what to think at all.

182

Friday night came and she was still thinking. The package in the bathroom cabinet had suddenly taken on a life of its own and she felt threatened by it in a way she hadn't before. Each time she called to mind her plan to start the abortion process tonight so it would all be sorted for her and Gareth by next week and they could get on with their lives, she remembered Tom's grey eyes and his incredible warmth in her embrace.

It wasn't fair! She shouldn't be feeling this way. If only Jackie hadn't come in today, if only Frankie hadn't gone into work, everything would be okay. It was probably her hormones, wasn't it? She should ignore them and get on with what she should do, once Gareth was home. She shouldn't be swayed by one small, impossibly tiny child.

Round and round swirled her thoughts and if she made one decision in the time between arriving home that day and Gareth's return, she made hundreds. If not thousands. Telling herself not to be so ridiculous, Frankie marched upstairs when she'd had just about more than she could stand, pulled open the bathroom cabinet and retrieved the abortion package.

Once downstairs, she opened it and stared at the contents again. No, they'd not changed. They were just exactly how she'd left them. A few tiny pills to get her life back on track. Nothing to worry about. It was stupid that something this small should suddenly feel so frightening. She really needed to get a grip.

Frankie checked her watch. Gareth was due back in about five minutes. Where had that time gone? She couldn't imagine. Anyway, she should probably take the first pill as soon as he was here and just get on with the whole wretched process. Once that was done, then the die was cast and the only direction of travel was forward. Into the utterly baby-free life she'd always expected to have. Life would go on as it was meant to. That was the important thing.

Ignoring the pounding of her heart which was telling her all sorts of crazy things about a life that might be so very different, Frankie took the first packet of pills and opened them. She laid the tablet on a side plate and fetched a glass of water. Then, refusing to look at either of them, she sat in the kitchen and waited for her husband.

It seemed like an eternity before Frankie heard the front door being opened and her husband calling out to her, though it could only in fact have been a matter of minutes. For the first time in her life, she didn't get up to greet him. She simply sat and waited for him to come to her.

When Gareth came into the kitchen to find her, he took in the scene at one glance and hurried over. He bent down to kiss her and reached for her hand.

"All ready then," he said quietly. "I'm so glad you waited for me. Shall we do this?"

Frankie swallowed and looked up at him.

"I'm so very sorry," she said. "Sorrier than I can say. I love you, Gareth, and I love our lives together, but I'm afraid I've changed my mind. I can't do this."

And she knew from her husband's expression that nothing would ever be the same again.

Chapter Nine

Miranda

It was weirdly good how she could surprise herself, even now, Miranda thought as she was doing the warm-up exercises in that week's Pilates session. They were off to the garden centre after the class. Wanting a garden had come as a complete shock. She loved flowers, yes, but she'd not known she was going to say anything like that when Golda had originally asked her.

After all, there were a million other things a woman should be wishing for, weren't there? Long life for one. Ha! She shouldn't think about that and she wasn't going to. Lots of money. Yes, that was a better option – if only! Or a boyfriend who bought her expensive things. And babies. Yes, unlike Frankie, she liked babies. She couldn't understand why someone who was pregnant wouldn't see it as anything other than totally frigging amazing. It was a shame that …

No! Don't go there! She told herself not to think and just concentrate on the Pilates. It was best that way.

A garden though. One of her foster families had owned a brilliant garden and she'd loved playing there. Shame that particular family hadn't lasted very long. They never had – she'd been a difficult child to love, hadn't she? Or so her social worker had kept on telling her. But never mind that now – it was the past and Miranda wasn't interested in it. She should concentrate on gardens and flowers. She wasn't that keen on other plants. Look at how badly she looked after the fern in the flat. But flowers were beautiful. It would be good to see if she could grow one. One flower would do! Please let her have enough time to grow at least one. Even though Miranda didn't believe in prayer or any kind of religion (they were all stupid, weren't they?) how she hoped the universe was listening. It effing well ought to be. The universe was giving her enough crap right now, so it definitely owed her.

Just one flower she could call her own. That was all she was asking.

"Find your core, girls!" Carol's voice broke into Miranda's thoughts and she shook her head, trying to concentrate on the balance work the Pilates teacher was getting them to do.

Golda wasn't great at balance work, Miranda noticed. She was directly behind both Golda and Frankie, and she could see the older woman struggling with having to stand on one leg. It made Miranda feel better about not being great at Pilates herself.

Mind you, she didn't need to bother much about her core, did she? It wasn't as if she was going to need it for very long, according to all those doctors and nurses ... *No! Don't go there*, she told herself once more. Just concentrate on the exercises and don't think!

This she tried to do for the rest of the class. It was weird how quickly the session was over and the cool-down exercises began. Not that Miranda could cool down much today – she was looking forward to the visit to the garden centre too much to be relaxed. She'd even made sure there was enough money in her purse for her purchases. More than enough. She'd not spent anything much over the last fortnight and would have to go easy on her spending for the next month but she was sure it would be worth it. Plus Jake had insisted on contributing to help her out. Of course she'd objected to this at first, but he'd persuaded her in the end, which was brilliant. When she'd told Jake about the garden plans, he'd laughed at first but had then changed his mind when he'd seen how enthused she was about the whole thing.

"Okay, babe," he'd said once she'd explained it to him. "It's weird but whatever makes you happy is fine. That's nice of that woman – Golda, is it? – to let you have her garden. Totally awesome."

She could only agree. "Yeah, they're both great. Well, Frankie's a bit odd and I don't agree with her about the baby thing, *not one bit*, but I'm still glad I know them."

Miranda had told Jake in confidence about Frankie's unthinkable decision, and he'd just nodded and told her everyone was different and you had to let people do what they needed to do. She supposed that was true. Anyway, she was still glad she'd met the two older women.

After Pilates, they made their way to Golda's home first. There, Golda left her car on the driveway, and Miranda locked up her bike near the hedge. Then they all drove in Frankie's car to the garden centre. Frankie had insisted as she said it made the most sense, as there was plenty of room in the back for purchases. Miranda did wonder, not for the first time, why her car was so big when she didn't want a family. Still, as Jake had told her, it was none of her business, was it?

In the car, Frankie was the first to speak.

"I've made a big decision," she said quietly. "I've decided against having an abortion."

"What? Wow!" Miranda couldn't help but respond to this amazing news. "Congratulations. That's frigging wonderful!"

"Goodness, that *is* news," Golda said, reaching across from the passenger seat and gripping Frankie's arm for a moment. "It's certainly a big decision. Are you happy with it?"

Frankie took a deep breath before answering. "Yes, I think so. I ordered the medical abortion pack and everything. The doctor gave me all the details. But when it came to it, I just couldn't go through with it. Mind you, Gareth's not happy about it. Not at all, so I still don't know what we're going to do about the baby."

"But you're going to have it?" Miranda asked. "Aren't you?"

"Yes. I'm going to have it. But I don't know if we'll keep it. We never wanted to be parents, Gareth and me. We knew that from the very beginning. We even discussed it when we were getting serious about each other, so we both knew where we stood. Until now."

"It's difficult," said Golda quietly. "I can imagine. You could go down the adoption route if you wanted to?"

"Yeah, sure," Miranda chipped in. "You could. But it's better to be with your own parents, isn't it? I can't tell you anything about being adopted as nobody ever bothered to try to adopt me, but I *can* tell you that being fostered isn't an effing lot of laughs. Not at all."

Silence followed her words and she shook her head. "Sorry. Didn't meant to come out with all that. Honestly, Jake would be horrified if he could hear me. You have to do what's best for you, Frankie. That's what Jake says. So, if adoption is what you want, then you should go for it. Whatever you do, I'll be pleased for you. Honest!"

Golda murmured her agreement to this, while Frankie turned and gave her a slight smile. And then the conversation moved on, thank fuck, and they heard all about how Golda had prepared her garden area for their new project.

"The strawberries are gone," she said. "I've put them in pots. They're easier to manage that way. And the rest of the plants are now elsewhere too. I've added in a whole lot of compost I've had for ages. So your garden is ready for planting up with whatever you like, Miranda. I can't wait to see how it's going to look."

"Me too," Miranda said, feeling an unexpected sparkle of excitement in her stomach. "Thank you so much."

"Absolutely no problem," Golda replied. "It's good for the ground to have something different going on. You have to ring the changes once in a while."

Once at the garden centre and with Miranda's budget approved, the three women made their way to the entrance. They paused only for Frankie to grab the largest trolley she could find. Golda frowned at it.

"I don't know," she said. "We might need two of those. But we can always pick up another inside."

"We might even need three," Miranda said and the other two laughed.

"We well might," said Golda. "But let's see how it goes first."

They wandered in, Miranda and Golda first, with Frankie behind, pushing the trolley.

Miranda had expected to see plants and flowers. It was a garden centre, wasn't it? There had been a selection of small bright flowers at the entrance to the store, but she'd not paid them much attention as they'd been tiny and totally the wrong colours.

She'd assumed the flowers outside would give way to vast displays of more suitable flowers inside, but in fact there were no plants at all. On her left were tall shelves of packets containing things that looked as if they might be alive – or with the potential of being alive – but which were definitely not actual plants. A closer look told her they were bulbs and seeds. No good for her then. And on the right were more shelves – though not as tall – of plates, mugs and gift sets, most of which were white.

She stopped abruptly, a decision which almost made Frankie run into her, but she swerved her trolley at the last second.

"Oh," Miranda said.

"What is it?" Frankie asked her, just as Golda turned back to join them.

"What are these?" Miranda asked, waving her hand around to indicate the various, very disappointing shelves. "Where are all the flowers?"

Both women started to laugh.

"Welcome to the wonderful world of the garden centre," Frankie said. "They're always like this."

"Yes," agreed Golda. "Lots of homewares and cards. They've become like supermarkets in recent years. You could probably get everything you could possibly want in here, but the prices for the non-garden goods can be pretty high. The plants are further inside. Come on."

Golda turned and headed off down the aisle before taking a sharp right past the customer service desk and into an area filled with bath products and candles.

Frigging hell, Miranda thought, Golda was right. Definitely more of a supermarket feel. The scents filling the air were a peculiar mix of lavender and rose, lemon and what might have been ginger, or something a bit spicier at least. Jake would hate it. He couldn't stand any kind of perfume, especially not all mixed up randomly like this. The thought of the horror on her friend's face made her smile. Maybe she'd buy him something just to see his reaction. No time to stop or browse though as Golda turned again and led them both through an area of books and cards, which looked to be mainly for children, before – at last! – they came to a real-life plant area.

Here the space was full of all kinds of plants in all sorts of shades of green you could think of. She saw tall plants with huge green leaves that would definitely fill up most of her kitchen, and there were tiny containers of plants no bigger than her thumbnail as well.

"These are amazing," Miranda said, gazing round and trying to take it in. "But where's the colour?"

"There's lots of colour over there," Frankie said, pointing to the other side of the space, where Miranda could see a flurry of pinks and reds she'd not noticed yet. "This is the house-plant area. We need to go a bit further on for the outdoor plants."

"These are *house plants?*"

Miranda couldn't believe it. House plants to her were small, dried-up and not very attractive. At least, that was true of all the house plants she'd ever had to endure. But here in this magical place, everything was bursting with lushness, and there were so many shapes and varieties. It was like a whole new world.

Golda must have realised nobody was following her anymore as she reappeared from wherever she'd vanished to. "Is everything okay?"

"Oh yes," Frankie replied. "Miranda's just taking in the house plant section."

"You can say that again," Miranda said. "I've never seen anything like this. It's frigging amazing!"

She must have spoken louder than she'd planned as a couple of old ladies walking past gave her a shocked glance before hurrying on. Golda and Frankie laughed.

"Yes, I suppose it is," Golda said. "We can come back and have a proper look later, if you'd like to, but let's shop for your new outdoor garden first. Priorities, you know."

With that, Golda continued on the way she'd been going. Miranda followed her, with Frankie and her trolley close behind. This shop was a lot larger than she'd thought it would be. If she'd known garden centres were like this, she'd have visited one before, even if it meant shopping with the oldies. Because everyone here was old, weren't they? Were flowers and plants not for the young or something? Then again, she couldn't think of a single person her own age who had any interest in anything to do with gardens or gardening. They were all too busy clubbing or on Insta or Twitter, which she could never get used to calling X. Stupid name anyway.

Miranda was still considering the mystery of garden centres when, following Golda, she stepped out into a vast outdoor space which stretched as far as her eye could see.

In front of her were huge tables filled with a total riot of colours and shapes. There were baskets and pots and trays everywhere, with large signs with different letters of the alphabet trailing off into the distance. People were wandering past, their trolleys filled to the brim with nameless plants and flowers, some of them chattering excitedly to each other and others focused entirely on their purchases.

A little way away, Miranda spotted Golda striding along so she did the only thing she could think of to do in this astonishing new world. She followed her.

Golda walked a lot quicker than Miranda was expecting and she was already at the sign saying 'C' when she caught up. Miranda yelled out her name when she got close enough, and the older woman turned and gave her a wave.

"Have you seen something you like?" she asked. "I thought we could start at the dahlias which are over there, but if you see something else, we can get that instead."

As Golda spoke, she pointed further down the lines of tables where Miranda could see the 'D' sign. Ah, they weren't just random letters with random plants then. 'D' was for dahlias, which were one of the flowers she wanted to have. Suddenly, the strangeness of the garden centre started to make a bit more sense. Not much though. Just a bit.

"No, I've not seen anything particular," Miranda replied. "Not here in the outdoor part. Not yet. But it's just so … so … *big*. How am I going to choose what to buy?"

Golda smiled. "Easy! We have a plan and we'll do our best to stick to it. Come on, you two, let's get started."

So that was what they did. Miranda had thought this would be easy. She knew her colour scheme and she knew she wanted dahlias – now she knew what they were. So it was, in her imagination, purely a matter of getting yellow, cream or gold ones. She'd even had a vague idea that there would be one of each, so choosing would be simple.

Oh how stupid she'd been! To her inexperienced eye, there seemed to be hundreds of dahlias in all the shades of yellow, gold or cream that anyone could possibly think up. And once she'd got over that shock, there was the question of types of flower, shapes of petal and height. Golda started off explaining what each one of the desired colour was called, the variety it was, and how high it was likely to grow.

After a few minutes of this, Frankie stepped in from her position as trolley keeper and tapped Golda on the shoulder.

"Sorry, Golda," she said with a slight smile. "But I think you might have lost your audience. You've certainly lost me. Is there a simpler way to help here?"

Golda's eyebrows went up and she looked from Frankie to Miranda and back again. A second later she started to laugh.

"Apologies," she said. "I know I get carried away with it all. I just love gardening."

That much was true, Miranda thought. She didn't know Golda that well, but she'd never seen her so animated. She hadn't even known the older woman knew what *animated* was.

"Look," Golda continued. "Never mind all the details. It doesn't matter. Miranda, why don't you have a browse around these dahlia tables on your own for a few minutes, take what you like the look of and put it in the trolley. Then we can have a think about what you've chosen."

That seemed like a brilliant idea, so Miranda walked round the dahlias – which definitely took longer than anyone would have thought as there were so many of them – and made decisions about what she most wanted.

Big, she thought. The bigger the better. Now was not a time for being shy or for hiding. Now was the time to be as big and bold as she could. If this was the only time in her whole effing life that she could grow a garden, it was going to be the biggest and most beautiful one she could imagine. So, that decision made, she picked up the plants with the largest flowers in the right colours and started loading them into Frankie's trolley. After she'd chosen about ten or twelve plants, she ran out of large ones to choose so nodded to the two women.

"I think those to start with," she said.

Golda ran a careful eye over her collection.

"I love these choices," she said at last. "They're real statement flowers."

Miranda smiled back though she wasn't sure what a 'statement flower' could possibly be. She'd only ever heard fashion described as 'statement' pieces. She hadn't realised it could apply to flowers.

"Shall we have a look at the rose section now?" Golda asked. "You can pick what you'd like to have there, and after that we can have a look round at everything else and get plants to fill the gaps. How does that sound?"

It sounded pretty perfect to her, though she'd thought that all these dahlias, with a whole lot of roses added to them, would be enough for the space. But if Golda thought she'd need more, she was happy to go along with it. The older woman was, after all, the gardening expert in the team.

"Let's do it," Miranda said. "Will we need another trolley?"

"Yes," Golda said after a moment or two. "We probably will, but there are always plenty around so let's see how we get on once you've chosen the roses."

Golda set off towards where the roses must be kept, and Miranda and Frankie followed on behind. Just as she turned round, a great shaft of dizziness swept through Miranda's head and she had to clutch the side of the trolley to avoid stumbling.

"Miranda?" she heard Frankie say. "Are you okay?"

At first, she couldn't think how to answer, but then the dizziness vanished almost as quickly as it had arrived, and she smiled at Frankie.

"Yeah, sure. I'm fine. Just lost my balance a bit, that's all."

That wasn't entirely true. Miranda had experienced these dizzy spells before. Of course she had. There'd never be any warning and sometimes she fainted with the pain, though that wasn't something she'd told anyone about. Not even Jake. Well, that wasn't true either. She'd told the nurse who kept on visiting her and she'd eventually got some extra pills to take to help her. Had she taken them today? Right now she couldn't remember. It was hard to keep track of what she was supposed to do these days.

"Are you sure?" Frankie said with a frown. "We can sit down if you want to? Or I can get some water?"

"No, it's fine," Miranda protested. The last thing she wanted was to cause a scene. Especially not here when she was determined to have a fun afternoon out choosing flowers. She wasn't going to be ill here if she could possibly help it. "I'm fine. Honest I am. Come on, we'd better keep up with Golda before she thinks she's lost us."

With that, Miranda gave Frankie the brightest of bright smiles and walked away in the direction Golda had disappeared into. For a terrible moment, her vision wavered again and she blinked wildly to try to get it back, and then everything was okay. She felt a bit weak but she'd be fine. She was sure of it.

Minutes later, they caught up with Golda who was at the rose section as promised and was busy looking at the labels there. By now, Miranda felt a bit stronger and, fingers crossed, she wasn't going to do anything stupid like faint or anything.

She smiled with a confidence she wasn't sure she believed in. "Okay. Shall I do like I did for the dahlias? Just go along and choose ones I like?"

"Yes, I think so," said Golda. "But here it's best to read the labels as well or actually smell the flowers if they're open instead of just going for the colours you want. As not all roses are scented, and you want the scented ones, or at least mainly scented."

"Okay," said Miranda. "That sounds like fun. And this time you can both help me, if that's okay? We can all play this game. You know my colours: yellow, cream and gold. Let's get sniffing!"

There were a hell of a lot of roses in the world, weren't there? Surely more than anyone would ever need in a garden. It was easy enough to pinpoint the colours she wanted as, though some of them had buds rather than open flowers, she only had to look at the picture on the label to check. But when she moved onto actually reading the labels, Miranda found there was too much information for her to take in. The one common fact was they all needed sun to grow, but that wouldn't be a problem as Golda's garden was bathed in sunlight. She couldn't remember seeing any shadows at all.

"Bloody hell," she wailed. "I'm never going to remember all this stuff!"

"Don't worry," Golda reassured her. "Just choose the ones you like the look of, add them to the trolley and then we can check them for you."

Miranda nodded and started to pick up the ones she liked.

"Try to go for the ones that look healthiest if you can," Golda added. "You want to give them the best possible chance. That one you just picked up – there's one further back that might be the same variety which looks healthier to me? Take that one instead, if it is."

"Okay, thanks," Miranda said. "Will do."

Just at that moment, Golda looked up, clutching one rose container and smiling broadly.

"I found one!" she said.

"One what?" asked Miranda.

"A Golden Celebration rose. I was hoping there'd be some here. Such a beautiful colour and scent."

Miranda leaned forward for a closer look. It was certainly a gorgeous rose and so cheerfully yellow. The scent was pretty amazing too, and it made her think of summer evenings and days by the beach. She couldn't think why as she'd not spend an awful lot of time by the seaside, but that was the image that came to mind.

"Wow!" she said. "That's my central rose in the garden, isn't it?"

Golda nodded, her expression quietly triumphant. "Yes, I think it is."

After that, the three of them chose several more roses for the trolley and then Golda had a good look through them.

"Yes, they all look lovely," she said. "But you've just opted for one of each variety. You should have at least two or three as that makes for more of a display. I'll go and get that other trolley now before anything gets too squashed – I can see there's an abandoned one over there."

Once the roses were distributed between the trolleys, Golda spoke again. "Right, that's good. We're doing well. Now we should choose some decent ground cover if we can. Nobody likes bare soil in a garden."

"Ground cover?" Miranda asked, not having the first clue what the hell that might be. "What do you mean?"

"Low-lying plants that fill up bare ground quickly but don't get tall enough to hide your main plants. They give everything a nice setting, plus they mean you don't have to do much weeding, as the plants block out the weeds."

"Okay," Miranda said, thinking not having to do much weeding would be great. She'd not considered that side of things. "Where do we get those?"

"Well," Golda said slowly. "There are several you could choose, but I always think the hardy geranium can't be beaten. It's perfect for this kind of project. We need to try to find one with a white flower, as that will be better for your colour scheme, though a lot of them are pink. Let's have a look."

Once again, Golda headed off but this time in the opposite direction and, obediently, Miranda and Frankie followed her.

A moment later, Golda stopped in front of the table with the 'G' sign and began looking along it.

"Come on," she said. "Here are the geraniums. Lots of them too, which is good. Let's see if we can get a white one."

Most of the geraniums on offer were various shades of pink or purple, which was disappointing. But it was Frankie who spotted the prize first.

"Look!" she said, holding up a tray of small white flowers. "This one's white. Kashmir White, it's called. Oh, and there's another one. It's called Album. We have choices."

Miranda liked the look of them both and they were certainly better than any of the purple or pink varieties. One of them was ever so slightly streaked with pink, but that didn't matter, according to Golda, as once in place it would be the white that stood out and set off the rest of the colours. The other geranium was pure white – probably the Album one, Miranda thought, but she'd have to check later. Decisions made, the three women grabbed as many of the two types of geranium as they could get in the second trolley, with Miranda making sure to get the healthiest looking plants first.

"Hardy geraniums are so useful," said Golda. "They're almost indestructible and will grow anywhere, no matter what. When it comes to pruning, you can even stamp up and down on them and tear them up back to the roots, and they survive perfectly well."

Miranda and Frankie stared at Golda. Miranda couldn't imagine the older woman doing anything so mad as stamping up and down on her plants, and she assumed Frankie was thinking the same. Though, then again, she was convinced there were hidden depths to Golda which they hadn't discovered yet.

Golda herself must have picked up on their thoughts, as her face turned red and she rushed to explain.

"Oh, I'm not going peculiar or anything," she reassured them. "It's simply that if I can get away with some aggressive pruning, it saves my knees."

Miranda laughed out loud and Frankie too was smiling, though trying to hide it. Golda sighed and rolled her eyes before encouraging them both to get back to the plant shopping.

They'd soon gathered more geraniums than Miranda was convinced they would ever need, and it was only then that Golda cast her expert eye over their purchases and nodded with satisfaction.

"Yes," she said. "That's enough to be getting on with. At least for now. If we discover we need more, then we can always come back. What do you think about it, Miranda? Are you happy with what you've chosen?"

To Miranda, the trolleys piled up with plants looked like a small jungle, but a very pretty one.

"It looks amazing," she said. "Thank you. Thank you to both of you. Is it okay to have another look at the house plant section before we go? I couldn't believe what was in there."

"Of course!" Golda said. "We have to leave that way in any case, in order to get to the till. We can easily pick a plant for your flat. Perhaps you'd like something to keep that fern of yours company?"

"I was thinking of something for the bedroom," Miranda said. "So when I wake up, it's the first thing I see."

"Something gold or cream or yellow then?" Frankie asked.

Miranda nodded. "That sounds perfect."

Back in the house plant section, Miranda started to have a look round, trying to ignore the throbbing in her head and the faint feeling of nausea in her stomach. Maybe she needed to pay for her purchases, get home as soon as she could and have a lie down. Take that bloody pill she might have forgotten to take this morning. That would do the trick. She was probably tired as well – that did sometimes make things kick off for her, which was something the doctors and nurses had warned her about.

Golda was pointing out some plants to her which she said might be suitable, but Miranda's attention was drawn to something else entirely. This plant was sitting proud on the edge of a nearby display. It had thick dark green leaves, and tiny white flowers. Something about it made her smile.

"What's this one?" she asked, trying to find the label but the words seemed to fade in and out so she couldn't focus on them.

"Oh, that's a begonia," said Golda after a moment and with a slight edge to her voice that Miranda hadn't heard before. "It will need a fair amount of light. Does your bedroom get the sun?"

Miranda nodded. "Yes, in the morning."

"That should be fine then," Golda replied but for some reason her voice seemed to be coming from a great distance away, even though she was standing right next to her. "How many would you like? Just the one?"

"Yes … thank you …" Miranda started to say and it was then that the world around her began to go very hazy and strange.

"Miranda …?" she heard Frankie's voice. *"Miranda?"*

Miranda tried to answer but everything went black and then she could no longer hear anything at all.

Chapter Ten

Golda

One moment Miranda had been talking normally about house plants, and the next she was lying on the garden centre floor. Golda thought Frankie might have yelled a warning but she couldn't remember later if it had been before Miranda fainted or afterwards.

Golda shouted for help and knelt to check how Miranda was. On the other side of her, she could see Frankie dialling 999. For one terrible moment, she couldn't tell if Miranda was breathing at all, and then she caught the slight movement of her chest.

People began to crowd around to offer support or watch and a couple of staff members pushed their way through.

"I'm first-aid trained," one of them – a woman – said as she knelt next to Golda. "What happened? What's her name?"

Golda told the woman what she wanted to know and the staff member began talking to Miranda softly before turning her sideways so she was no longer lying on her back.

She could hear Frankie speaking to the emergency operator and wondered at how calm she sounded. Someone fetched a blanket, heaven knew from where, and someone else brought a glass of water.

Golda didn't know how long Frankie and she sat with Miranda as she lay on the floor before an ambulance arrived. Miranda's breathing sounded so shallow and light. The two ambulance staff assessed her while Frankie explained as quietly as she could the issues behind Miranda's health. The older ambulance man nodded as if this was part of his everyday life and within a few minutes, Miranda was on a stretcher and being carried to the ambulance.

Frankie and Golda hurried along behind in silence. Miranda looked as if she was hardly taking up any weight on the stretcher. It was Frankie who had the presence of mind to ask where the ambulance would take her and if they could follow, or even come in the ambulance with her.

"Are you family?" the younger man asked.

"No," said Frankie. "We're her friends."

"Okay. We can only take one of you in the front, or you can simply follow us in your car if you have one. It will be the local hospital. The cancer services there are first-rate, so please try not to worry. I'm sure your friend will be okay."

"Thank you," said Frankie. "We'll come in the car. But we don't know who to let know what's happened."

"Don't worry," the man said. "If Miranda is under the care of the specialists, they'll have that information already."

With that, they were in the ambulance and away, the light flashing but the sirens silent. Golda wasn't sure whether that was reassuring or not. Either way, she felt too dazed by what had just happened to know what to do for the best.

"Okay," said Frankie, taking a deep breath. "Okay. We need to get to the hospital, but first we should pay for Miranda's plants, and store them somewhere. She's in the best care right now so there's nothing useful we can do. She'll need to know her flowers are all okay when she wakes up."

Somehow, Golda found Frankie's logic steadying.

"Yes," Golda replied. "Yes. We'll do that. I'll pay. It's no problem."

They returned to where they'd left the trolleys and, astonishingly, they were still there. Then they made their way to the tills, though not without having to respond to the concern of people milling around and processing what had just happened.

At the tills, Golda was expecting to queue, but one of the staff members who'd tried to help Miranda was there, with an older woman, who might have been the manager. The two women were waved through to a free till that was just being set up.

"How is the poor lady?" the staff member asked.

"I don't know," Golda said. "I hope she'll be all right. We're going to the hospital as soon as we can. We were shopping together for the plants she wanted to buy. She wants to create a garden."

Then, suddenly, Golda's eyes filled with tears she hadn't expected at all. How very ridiculous of her. And how she hated crying in public. Thankfully, the manager led her to one side for some privacy and fetched a glass of water. It tasted cool and refreshing and made Golda feel a little better.

Frankie sorted out the trolley goods but when it came to payment, Golda did what she'd promised and used her card. Two staff members helped load up Frankie's car. Even with all the space inside, the plants filled it quickly and Golda ended up on the passenger seat holding the begonia Miranda had chosen before she fainted. She couldn't remember putting it in the trolley but she must have done. Or Frankie had. *How she hated begonias.*

Once they'd thanked the staff and were in the car, Frankie spoke.

"This is the plan," she said. "We're going to go to the hospital and check on Miranda's progress. Depending on how things go at that point, I suggest we then drop off the plants at your house, give them a water, and have a cup of tea ourselves. How does that sound?"

Golda nodded dumbly. At the hospital, Frankie turned into the entrance area, and came to a halt outside the main hospital door.

"If you get out here," she said, "you can find out what's happening to Miranda while I go and park. Have you got your mobile?"

"Yes," said Golda.

"Good," Frankie continued. "If I can't find you, I'll text. Okay?"

Golda took hold of her handbag and got out of the car. The moment she was on the pavement, Frankie drove off. She was alone. Checking her mobile phone was actually on, she hurried inside, pausing only to use the hand sanitiser at the entrance.

At the reception, there was a queue of two people but they weren't moving quickly enough. It felt like every second spent waiting was a second wasted, but there wasn't anything Golda could do about it.

Finally, it was her turn. She gave Miranda's name to the tired-eyed receptionist, and a brief recap of what had happened. The receptionist nodded and turned to her computer with a flurry of typing.

Another few seconds ticked by.

"Yes," the receptionist said. "I have a note of your friend. She's in the ICU now, though it looks like she might soon be transferred to the cancer ward. You may not be able to see her at the moment, but you'll need to go to the ICU to check that."

She went on to describe the way to the ICU and Golda thanked her. As she turned to go, Frankie tapped her on the shoulder.

"It's me," she said. "What's happening?"

Golda repeated what the receptionist had said as she started to walk in the direction she'd been given.

"Did they say anything about how she is?" Frankie asked.

"No," Golda replied. "I don't think they're allowed to. We can find out more at the ICU."

"Okay."

The hospital – like all hospitals everywhere – was a universe of winding corridors, hurrying people and the scent of stale antiseptic. Golda hated it. She'd already forgotten the detailed instructions the receptionist had given, but the signage was surprisingly clear.

It seemed to take ages to get there but it was probably no more than five minutes. At the ICU entrance, Frankie and Golda made use of the hand sanitiser once more and then they each took a disposable mask from the box that had been left there. Somehow, that just made everything feel worse.

Once inside, the unit receptionist – again a woman but much younger than the main receptionist – looked up and smiled.

"Hello," she said. "How can I help you?"

This time, it was Frankie who explained why they were there, which was a relief as Golda didn't think she could go through it again.

It was odd how much all this was bringing back bad memories. Ones Golda hadn't thought of for a while. The circumstances were very different, of course. Her husband was dead and could never hurt her again. Miranda, however, was her new friend and Golda wanted her to live for as long as she could. She had to remember Alan was the past, and Miranda was the present. It wasn't the same.

Meanwhile, the receptionist was checking her computer.

"They're assessing your friend now," she said calmly. "So I'm afraid you can't see her until that's done. I can tell you that the emergency number we have for Miranda has been contacted, and that person is on their way in."

"Oh God," said Frankie. "Is it really bad then?"

"I'm sorry, but I can't tell you specifics. But what I can say is that it's standard procedure to contact the emergency number when anyone is admitted to ICU."

"What can we do?" Golda asked. "Can we wait here?"

"Yes, of course," the receptionist said. "I can ask one of the duty nurses to pop out and see you when they get a chance, though I don't know how long that will be. Would you like me to do that?"

"Yes, please," Golda replied. "Thank you."

The receptionist pointed out the water machine and the signing-in sheet. Once they'd added their names to the list, the two women sat down and waited.

"Are you okay?" Frankie asked. "You look pale."

"Yes, I'm fine, thank you. We've both had a shock. Are you all right?"

"I think so," she replied. "I just wish there was something definite they could tell us."

"I know," Golda said. "They never do though, not unless you're family or that emergency contact number. It was the same with my husband."

"Oh, of course," Frankie said, reaching over and taking Golda's hand. "I'd forgotten you know about this kind of thing. I'm so sorry."

Golda squeezed Frankie's hand briefly before letting go. "Thank you, but there's no need. That's all in the past. We have to focus on Miranda now and hope she's all right."

"Yes. Yes, indeed."

After that, there wasn't much more to say but it was only a few minutes later that a nurse appeared with a bright smile and sat down next to them.

"Hello," she said, giving off an aura of calm efficiency which was more reassuring than any words. "I'm Alice. Thank you so much for coming in. Please could you just confirm the name of the patient you're here to see today?"

Frankie answered the question and asked if they could know how Miranda was doing.

"I can only give you general information on Miranda," Alice said, repeating basically what the receptionist had already told them. "But I can say she's improved from the position when she arrived with us and it may be that tomorrow she'll be transferred out to another unit. We'd like at the very least to keep her here overnight and see how she progresses."

"Thank you," Golda said. "That's very helpful. Are we allowed to see her or is that not possible?"

"We only allow one person at a time in ICU," Alice explained.

She might have gone on but, at that moment, Golda heard running feet outside the waiting room, and the next second the door was flung open and a young man burst in. He was in his twenties, with close-cropped black hair and a stocky physique. He wore a short-sleeved blue top which looked as if it might be a uniform and his arms were covered in tattoos.

"Hello, I'm Jake," he said in an accent that sounded softly Scottish. "I got a message about Miranda? How is she? Is she okay? What happened?"

Nurse Alice took charge at once.

"Thank you so much for coming in, Jake," she said. "Yes, Miranda is stable at the moment, and I'm happy for you as the emergency contact to have ten minutes with her. If you could just sign in at reception first?"

Jake nodded, his face pale and his lips drawn tight. As he strode to the reception desk to sign in, Alice continued her brief explanation.

"These two ladies were responsible for calling the ambulance for Miranda," she said, as she followed in Jake's footsteps. "I believe they are friends of hers."

Jake looked up from where he was signing the book on the receptionist desk and stared at them vaguely. "Sorry?"

"Jake," Golda said, standing up. "Hello. My name is Golda and this is Frankie. We know Miranda from Pilates."

His frown cleared. "Oh, yeah. Miranda's talked about the two of you. Thank you for helping."

222

"It was the least we could do," Golda said. "But please never mind any of this. Go and see Miranda. If it's all right, we'll wait here and perhaps you can let us know how she is when you come back out?"

"Sure, yeah," he said.

There was no time for more talk, as Nurse Alice smiled and took Jake away through the door she'd first come through and into the heart of the ICU. There was nothing to do but wait and see what Jake found out. It was strange how he wasn't anything like Golda had imagined him to be when Miranda had talked about him. He looked a lot rougher for a start. But, as Golda knew only too well, appearances were meaningless. What mattered was how someone treated others, not what they looked like.

Frankie sighed and rolled her shoulders. "So, that's Jake. Nice to meet him, though maybe not under these circumstances."

"No, that's true," Golda agreed. "I hope he'll have more news when he returns."

"Yes, me too."

While they waited, nobody else came into the unit and there wasn't much to say, so Golda gazed round at the posters on the walls instead. The messages were all very positive, but they'd have to be. This wasn't a place where people expected to read anything bad. If they were here, then things were already bad enough.

After about five minutes, Frankie got up and poured herself a beaker of water.

"Golda? Do you want one?"

She shook her head. "No thank you."

She wasn't sure water would help right now. Above all, she hoped Miranda would improve soon. Golda didn't want this to be it for her. She wanted her young friend to have her garden.

"Hey, try not to worry," Frankie whispered. "We don't know anything until Jake comes back."

"Yes, you're right," Golda said. "It's hard *not* to worry though."

"That's understandable," said Frankie. "As you said, it's been a shock for us both."

That was certainly true. Golda hoped Jake would remember them and come back this way – she didn't know if there might be another entrance to the ICU ward and, of course, they wouldn't be the first thing on his mind.

When Jake finally returned, his expression was serious as he listened to the end of whatever Nurse Alice had been telling him.

"Yeah, sure," he was saying as the two of them came back through the ward door. "I understand. Thanks for all you're doing."

Alice smiled and nodded, before giving Jake a gentle pat on the arm.

"You can call us any time," she said to him. "If she's not on the ICU by then, we'll update you on which ward Miranda is in, of course. But we'll let you know that anyway as soon as we can if she's moved."

"Thanks," he said again, but it looked as if he might be close to tears and was trying to keep everything bottled up.

With that, Alice bustled off back into the unit to do whatever needed to be done. Saving lives, Golda hoped.

Jake stretched and then ran his hands through his dark hair. Frankie got up, poured some more water and handed it to him.

"Jake," she said. "Would you like this?"

He looked at her as if he didn't have the first idea who Frankie was or what she might be doing here, and then his expression cleared as it all – obviously – came flooding back to him.

"Sure, thanks," he said, before taking the cup and drinking it down in one go.

With a heartfelt sigh, he grabbed a chair and drew it up to sit beside them while Frankie took her seat again.

"How is she?" Golda asked. "Did you speak with her?"

He shook his head. "No. She's not awake yet, though the nurse said she'll wake up when she's ready. It's not that she's in a coma or anything. They're still doing tests, which is mainly why they want to keep her in here overnight. I just sat with her and held her hand for as long as they let me. I told her about my day, because I remember from the last time she was in hospital that they said people can sometimes hear you, even when you think they can't. Weird that. Not that there was anything much to say. I really wanted to tell her not to be stupid and overdo things, but ..."

Jake's voice broke and he wiped at his eyes. Golda took a tissue from the nearest box and handed it to him, but he shook his head.

"No, I'm fine, thanks."

Golda didn't think he was fine, at any level. None of them were. But saying so wasn't going to help.

When Jake could speak again, he told them what the hospital thought had happened. Miranda's tumour would – in his words – go crazy every now and again and this had been one of those times. Apparently, she didn't always take the pills she was supposed to take to ease the pain, but he had no idea if she'd had any of the drugs today or not. When they'd brought her in, they'd put her on a drip to give her a boost of whatever it was they needed to calm things down, and that was the position she was in now.

"How long do they think she'll be in hospital?" Frankie asked.

"They said they'd probably move her over to the cancer ward tomorrow if all goes as they hope it will," Jake replied. "But I don't know when she'll come out of hospital. If she accepts the home help they're offering her and *does what they say for bloody once*, it would be better for her all round and then maybe this would never have happened. But that's Miranda all over – she makes her own bloody decisions and she won't ever take the sensible route. Sorry about the swearing …"

Golda shook her head. "Don't even think about apologising. Thank you for letting us know more, Jake."

He gave her a slight smile, which lit up his face. "Thanks for being Miranda's friends. She's been keeping herself to herself for too long since she was diagnosed. It's nice for her to know other people apart from me. And thanks for giving her the garden idea – she's really happy about it. The nurse said something about a garden centre? Was that where you were when it happened?"

"Yes, we were," Frankie replied. "And we have all the plants she wanted in the back of my car. So when Miranda wakes up, that's one of the things you or we should tell her. Because when she gets out of hospital, she can start making her garden."

There was something about Frankie's determined positivity that eased the mood in the room, and both Jake and Golda smiled.

"Yeah," said Jake. "That's a good idea. She'll be pleased – she hates unfinished business."

After that, there wasn't much else anyone could do. They offered to buy Jake a coffee at the hospital café, but he shook his head, saying he had to get back to work. The three of them made their way in silence to the main hospital foyer, and Jake shook hands with them before he left. Which surprised Golda. He left on a rather intimidating-looking motorbike, which didn't surprise her at all.

"Okay," said Frankie. "Okay. I'll take you home, Golda."

"Thank you," she said. "We do need to give those flowers a drink. I think it's all we can do for now."

By the time they'd got home and taken Miranda's flowers through to the garden and given them all a watering, Golda felt shattered. After they'd briefly discussed Miranda's bike and decided to leave it here for now, she asked Frankie if she wanted to stay for a tea or coffee, but her friend shook her head.

"No thanks, though it's kind of you to offer. I need to get home."

Golda understood how she felt and was at heart glad she'd refused the invitation. After the afternoon they'd experienced, she suspected they both wanted to be alone.

It was odd then that waving Frankie goodbye as she drove off brought a wave of loneliness crashing over Golda. This was ridiculous. She'd not felt quite so cut off since her marriage. Taking a deep breath, she walked into the kitchen, thinking about making a cup of tea.

But no, she didn't want to sit down and she didn't want to think about poor Miranda and how she was doing now. If Golda had thought it through, she'd have given her phone number to Jake. Then again, Frankie and he had exchanged mobile numbers before leaving the hospital so if there was any news, she was sure Frankie would let her know. Golda would just have to be patient and hope for the best.

In order to give herself something to do, she decided to sort through Miranda's purchases. In the back garden, the sight of the plants made her blink for a few minutes until she told herself to stop focusing on the many terrible things that *might* happen and try instead to focus on this one good thing. This approach had helped Golda in the past and she hoped it would help her now.

In normal circumstances, there was nothing Golda enjoyed more than planting a garden. Somebody far wiser than she had once said that planting a garden meant trusting in the future – or something like that. And whoever it was, and what exactly they'd said, they were definitely right. It was the miracle of nature.

As best she could, Golda positioned the various flowers near to the areas she thought Miranda wanted them to be, though she didn't have a copy of the plan Miranda had made. She had to rely on memory. The roses looked incredible and she hoped the dreaded blackspot would stay away from them this year.

The dahlias, however, were looking a little sorry for themselves and Golda wondered if she should pot them on, but thought she'd better wait and see what happened after giving them another good watering. Of course, she could rely on the geraniums to be none the worse for anything you could think of doing to them. It was hard to know where they'd be needed as they were being used as a filler plant, so she put a few of them next to each flower group. That way, they'd be easily to hand once the planting began.

When at last, all the pots were better organised, Golda stepped back and cast her critical eye over them. She'd made sure they had enough but, even now, she wasn't convinced they wouldn't need more at some point. It was one of the rules of gardening: however many plants you bought, there would always be gaps you needed to fill. Still, they'd done their best, and what they had now would be enough to be getting along with.

Glancing at her watch, Golda realised it was time to start making something for supper. It would have to be simple as she didn't have the heart for anything complex. Not tonight. As she turned to go, a flash of white caught her eye and she realised she'd forgotten about Miranda's one house plant: the begonia she'd chosen. Somehow, it had become entangled with a couple of dahlias and she'd not noticed it, so Golda spent a few moments rescuing it to take it inside. This one definitely wasn't an outdoor plant.

As she walked round the side of the house towards the back door, holding the begonia, Golda's heart was pounding. It was only when she closed the patio door behind her that the memories she'd been trying so hard to ignore came flooding back.

There had been begonias in Norfolk, where Alan and Golda had gone for their last and most terrible holiday together.

*****

It was odd, looking back, how it all seemed to have happened so quickly. Golda's marriage years. While she was going through the horrors of her marriage, time seemed to last forever, but now Alan was dead and gone, increasingly Golda remembered it as a long-ago nightmare which was now over. Thank goodness. These days, women had more power and were more easily able to leave abusive men, but it hadn't been the same back then. Not that it was that long ago, but everything had been different when Golda had been

232

younger. In fact it was only now that she realised what her marriage had been. An abusive one with a difficult and manipulative man.

Not that every day had been like that. The beginning of their marriage had been wonderful. Until it wasn't Then there had been weeks – months, even – when Alan had been the man Golda had first met: attentive, passionate and caring. And then something would happen – usually something at work or he would get angry about the fact she wasn't getting pregnant, or it was something he thought she'd done or not done – and everything would change. She was stupidly proud that on a couple of occasions, she'd even fought back, kicking and slapping where she'd been able to, but it had never done any good and it always made things worse in the end. It was better by far to hunker down and wait for Alan's fury to come to an end. Afterwards, he was always apologetic, desperate for her forgiveness and promising he'd make it up to her, telling her everything would be wonderful again if they only managed to have a baby, which they never did, though neither of them ever knew why. Alan, of course, refused to seek any medical opinion about the issue, and Golda didn't have the will to find out for herself. What good would knowing anything for certain do? During her marriage, Golda had in fact moved slowly from a position of wanting a child in order to have something innocent to love and care for, through a growing sense of disappointment and bitterness that it had never happened, and finally to the realisation that their lack of children was probably a blessing as things would surely have been so much worse if children had come along, wouldn't they?

Each time Alan fought her, he would always promise never to hurt her again, but that never happened. Golda quickly gave up believing in his promises though – to her bewilderment – a part of her never stopped loving him. For the man he once was, for the man she had thought he was. And so, she spent her married life with her focus entirely on her husband – trying to assess what mood he was in, what would make him happy or at least keep him calm, how to deal with him when he was angry. It had been her whole existence.

It was *that* holiday in Norfolk that had brought everything to a crisis point and, even now, Golda wasn't entirely sure why.

The week before their holiday, Alan had been very stressed at work. He'd been overlooked for a promotion and not for the first time. On top of that, he'd asked for a meeting with his boss at the bank about it and that hadn't gone well either. That week, Golda made a special effort to cook his favourite foods, keep the house as tidy and sparkling-clean as she could make it, and to avoid him as much as possible. In spite of all that, in the last two days before the holiday (which Golda was now dreading), there were a few times when he slapped her for what he said was her bad attitude. She had no idea what that meant but she simply endured it and hoped – against everything she knew and understood – that things would improve. They did not. The day before they left, he made her pack and re-pack his case for him three times. By the end of this, she was exhausted, every sense on high alert for danger.

They were travelling up to the holiday cottage on Saturday morning. The night before, they had sex and Alan fell asleep immediately afterwards. Golda, however, lay awake for most of the night, wondering what the week would hold. Not that holiday time was always awful or frightening. They'd had some wonderful trips together in the past, when things had been good, and they'd travelled to more places than Golda had ever imagined she would go: Egypt, Turkey, and once a magical week in New York that she would always remember. She didn't think the week ahead would be anything like these.

Early on Saturday morning, she rose quietly so as not to disturb Alan and padded downstairs to make her husband's morning tea. Sometimes this was the best part of her day, watching the sunlight on her beloved garden and hearing the birdsong. It gave her a peace she knew wouldn't last but which was all the more powerful for being temporary.

Upstairs, she put the mug of tea on Alan's bedside table and then returned to the kitchen to wait for him to get up. She'd already made sure the cases were in the hall, alongside their coats and her handbag, so they were all ready to go. While Golda waited for her husband to wake up, she laid out the usual breakfast of scrambled eggs, toast and coffee for preparing later.

After about half an hour, Golda heard the shower being turned on upstairs. Alan always started his day with a shower then, while he was shaving and getting dressed, she would have time for her bath. When she heard the shower being turned off, Golda went upstairs and knocked softly on the bathroom door. Alan opened it, gave her a peck on the cheek and a swift good morning and she ran her bath.

All continued well until she got downstairs where she found Alan peering into the egg pan.

"Are these eggs off?" he asked, without turning round.

Instantly, Golda felt her shoulders stiffen.

"I don't know," she said carefully. "I thought they were fine, but I can check if you like."

"Please do."

Alan turned round and gestured at the pan which Golda had set on the hob earlier. She took a breath and walked to the eggs. She already knew they were fine. She'd worked it out that today they'd eat the last of the box she'd bought and then they'd buy fresh ones when they returned from Norfolk. There wasn't any problem, or at least not with the eggs. Still, she knew she had to do what Alan said. When Golda reached the stove, she glanced into the pan and gave it a quick sniff. It seemed fine to her but, when she looked up at her husband, she knew that whatever she said now would be wrong. Her heart was thudding and she couldn't seem to get her words in order.

"I-I'm sorry," she stuttered. "I don't know. They look good to me. Do you want me to cook them and see how they taste?"

There was a moment, right there and then, Golda swore it, when everything could somehow still have been fine. The birds were continuing to sing, the sun to rise and the day could have been bearable. Alan could have stepped back from whatever decision he was heading towards, he could have been kind, but he wasn't.

"Well, they don't look good to me," he said, his voice low and mean, and his eyes fixed upon her face so she couldn't look away. "They look *disgusting. You're* disgusting. Anyone would think you were trying to poison me or something."

Golda began to protest that she wasn't trying to harm anyone, but it would have been better – far better – if she'd just kept quiet.

Alan exploded with fury. He grabbed the pan of eggs and threw it at the window. Luckily it missed the glass, bounced off the window frame and landed on the floor with a terrible crash. The eggs went one way and the pan another. Alan aimed a punch at Golda's arm whilst shouting something she couldn't make out but she jumped away and his fist landed on the oven. He screamed in pain.

Golda tried to run though she had no idea where she could go, but he grabbed her and pushed her to the floor. Acting from instinct and experience, she huddled down, trying to make herself as small as possible and protecting her head as he started to kick her. Now was not a time for fighting back. Thankfully, he didn't stay focused on her for long, but instead began to march round the kitchen, pulling items out of cupboards and throwing them onto the floor, where some smashed and some rolled away. Cups, plates, saucers, tins of food, all of them were taken and flung around the room. She felt shaky and sick, and hoped the neighbours couldn't hear anything. More than anything, she prayed for Alan to stop.

After a while, he ran out of things to throw and came back to give Golda a final kick or two.

"For God's sake, woman," he growled. "You're so *stupid*. I don't know why I put up with you. Clean up this kitchen and we'll have breakfast on the way."

With that he left, and Golda heard the back door slam as he went out into the garden. Her body ached from where Alan had kicked her but it wasn't as painful as the fear that held her tightly in its grasp. She couldn't catch her breath properly and she was suddenly desperate to escape but there was nowhere to go. Her mother had died only last year but, if she'd still been alive, Golda knew she couldn't have gone home. Her mother would never have believed her but, even if she had, the shame would have been unbearable, both for her mother and for herself.

As quickly as she could, Golda picked up all the crockery and tins, throwing away the ones that were broken and placing the unharmed ones back where they'd come from. Then she filled a bucket of water, added floor wash, and cleaned up the mess of eggs. She didn't know if she should do the whole floor or not, but decided it would be best, just in case that was what Alan wanted. The last thing she needed was to make the wrong decision and then everything would be so much worse.

Golda was finishing off her task when Alan came back into the kitchen. She hadn't heard the outside door opening so was unprepared for his reappearance. She stopped what she was doing at once and watched him out of the corner of her eye. In the past, when this had happened, she'd tried to carry on cleaning, but that had only made him more annoyed. He wanted her to pay attention to him.

There was a moment when she thought he would apologise for his behaviour as usual but, to her surprise, he didn't. His mouth twisted as if there were words inside him he wanted to say but couldn't, and then he simply nodded.

"We need to go now," he said. "Are you ready?"

Golda wasn't, but she got up, hurrying to put away the bucket and hang the cloth over the kitchen tap.

Alan picked up the cases in the hallway and opened the front door. Golda grabbed the remaining bags and her handbag, and hoped against hope that she'd remembered everything. She usually liked to have a final check of things before leaving on holiday, but this wasn't going to be possible today. She quickly set the alarm and locked up, and then ran after Alan who was already in the car and revving the engine.

The moment she was in the passenger seat, he set off. Golda risked a glance at him to see if she could pick up any clues, but his expression was unreadable. The whole scenario felt odd. Different from the usual. More dangerous. She had no idea what to do about it.

So she settled down for a long and silent journey to the holiday cottage. Her legs and side felt bruised from where Alan had kicked her, but at least he'd not touched her back this time, which meant sitting down wasn't too painful.

They drove until they reached the main road and the first service station, where Alan indicated to turn in. By then Golda was desperately hungry and feeling faint. She'd forgotten to put a bottle of water in her bag, so her mouth was feeling dry. She was more than glad to be stopping for breakfast. Perhaps there'd be time for her to buy a water bottle as well. Perhaps Alan would even start talking to her again. That would be a relief.

They parked as near to the café as they could and Alan turned the ignition off. Golda reached round to undo her seatbelt but he grabbed her hand and shook his head.

"No," he said firmly. "*You* don't get out, Golda. You don't deserve to get out. I'm going inside to have my breakfast and I don't want to have to be with you when I'm eating. I don't want to even look at you."

"What on earth do you mean?" Golda said in disbelief, frantically glancing at him and then out at the café. "What have I done? I'm sorry about breakfast at home. Truly I am. I tidied up. As you said. Please, Alan, I'm so hungry."

He signed deeply, as if what she'd said was unreasonable and stupid, and he was trying to keep his temper.

"Oh, Golda," he said. "You have no idea how stupid you are, do you? And how much I have to put up with. I swear I've tried my best with you, but you don't make it easy for me. If you think about it properly, you'll see you don't deserve breakfast so you're not going to have any. If you behave properly, then you get to eat. But today you haven't behaved properly so you don't get to eat. After all, it's mainly *my* money that's paying for everything so I can do whatever I think is right. So what's going to happen is this: I'm going to get breakfast and you're going to stay in the car and think about your behaviour and how you can improve in the future."

Golda must have whimpered or made some kind of noise as he shook her hand roughly before ensuring her seatbelt was still fixed into its slot.

"And don't think about trying to get out of the car," he warned. "I'll be sitting at one of those window seats in the café and I'll be able to see *exactly* how well-behaved you are."

"Please, Alan," she begged him, unable to credit what she was hearing. "I need to go to the ladies at the very least. *Please.*"

"You should have thought about that before you left the house," he said. "Besides, I don't believe you. You're just pretending so you can get out of the car. Well, you don't fool me. You don't need to go to the bathroom. You've not eaten or drunk anything, so there'll be no need, will there? No, you stay here, darling. I'll get my breakfast and I'll be back when I'm ready. And don't forget I'm watching."

With that, he kissed Golda on the cheek, took the keys from the ignition and got out. He slammed the door behind him and walked away, not bothering to look back.

Golda felt sick and faint. She didn't know what to do. However cruel Alan had been in the past, it had never been like this before. *What was happening?* It felt terrifying, more terrifying than all the shouting and the physical suffering she'd endured in her marriage. What was she supposed to do? If she got out of the car, Alan would be furious and Golda had no idea what punishment that might lead to. He'd been angry enough this morning when she'd done nothing wrong. She didn't dare think about how angry he'd be if she disobeyed him now. Her stomach rumbled and the sudden urge for the ladies' loos became more pressing. But she tried to ignore it.

It was so stupid. Golda felt so stupid, trapped in a situation not of her own making but which was somehow her fault. She didn't know how it had come to this or what she could do to make it better. The main thing – the only thing – she could think of was to do what Alan had instructed. Surely she could do that. She could hang on for the loo until he got back. It didn't matter how hungry she was – she could sleep on the journey and there would be food when they got to the cottage. When Golda had booked it, she'd ordered a welcome pack so there would be something to eat for them. If she did what Alan said and stayed in the car, then when he got back after his breakfast, he would let her go to the ladies' loo. Wouldn't he? This was just a test to see how she would behave. If she passed the test, all would still be well.

Golda took a deep breath, tried to control her tears and simply get through the next segment of time before her husband returned to the car. To distract herself from thoughts of the loo, she gazed out of the car window and concentrated on what was happening there instead.

A little further down the row of cars, a woman was getting out of her vehicle, with a small child in her arms. The child was crying – Golda could hear it even through her own closed window – and the mother was patting its back as she held it against her shoulder and rocking from side to side. Her lips were moving though Golda couldn't hear what she was saying. A man suddenly appeared next to her and Golda gasped, terrified of what he might do and thinking the woman might be in danger.

But the next moment, the man gave them both a quick hug, waved a bag of what must be goodies from the service station shop and then proceeded to make a series of funny faces at the woman and child.

The woman laughed at him and the child stopped crying and stretched out small hands to the man, who surely had to be the father. The woman handed over the child – which Golda could now see was a boy – to the man, took the shopping bag instead and pulled out a chocolate bar. The mother tore it open, had a bite and then offered it to her son. He had a bite too and started to smile. The whole scene was so normal, so everyday and yet so beautiful in ways Golda couldn't begin to understand that she had to look away and think of something else.

When she gathered enough strength to turn to watch the little family again, they and their car had gone. The loss of them felt overwhelming. Golda closed her eyes for a second or two and then looked in the other direction, towards the entrance of the service station shop and café. There was a steady stream of people going in and out, and she felt a stab of jealousy that she wasn't among them.

She risked a glance straight out of the windscreen at the café and saw Alan at the table next to the window, exactly as he'd said he'd be. He was staring at her as he ate his breakfast. A wave of hunger in Golda's stomach and she looked away at once. She could feel the weight of his gaze on her and knew she'd been right to stay in the car. When he got back, she'd beg him to let her use the facilities. Surely he wouldn't punish her for ever? Hadn't he done enough?

The seconds and minutes ticked by and a small and very frightened part of Golda wondered if this was all a horrible dream and also if she would be here forever and time itself had stopped. She was so very thirsty and so desperate for the loo.

Finally, she dared to glance into the café window again and saw the table was empty, and Alan had gone. At once, she looked wildly around, wondering where he was. He had to come back to the car, *he had to*.

But of course he would, she told herself. There was nowhere else to go. This was his car. He wouldn't abandon it. Would he?

A sudden clunk and the driver's door was opened and Alan slid into the seat. He didn't glance at Golda. He started the ignition.

"Alan," she said, her heart skittering wildly. "Alan, please ..."

"What is it?" he said roughly. "What do you want now?"

"Please, Alan," she said desperately, reaching out and grabbing his arm. "I've done what you said. I've stayed in the car. Please, let me go to the loo. I won't eat anything, but please would you just let me use the loo?"

"We don't have time," he replied, shaking off her fingers. "We need to get to the cottage. You'll have to hang on until Norfolk. It's not difficult. Even *you* can do that, can't you?"

Without waiting for an answer, he revved the engine and reversed out of the space. As he drove off, Golda looked frantically back at the service area, but there was no point as they were already on their way again.

She pressed her legs together and tried to think about anything else apart from her own needs. Norfolk and the cottage was at least another three hours' driving. She couldn't last that long. Perhaps, by the time they reached the next service station, Alan would have calmed down and would see sense. She could only hope that would turn out to be the case.

Alan continued to drive in total silence while Golda counted down the miles to the next service station. It seemed to take forever. And all the while, she was aware of the pressure mounting in her bladder and the urgent need for release.

At last, there was about a mile to go and she had to speak to her husband, she had to make him stop.

"Alan …?" she said, finally gathering the courage from her desperation to speak into the silence.

For a moment, there was no response and then he said, "What? What now?"

"Please, Alan," Golda said quietly, not daring to look at him. "Please could we stop at the next service station? It's not far. I promise I won't be long. I promise I won't hold us up."

Golda held her breath for a few seconds, but Alan didn't bother to reply or slow down. He simply kept on driving and didn't even look at the exit road as they passed it. She closed her eyes tight and clenched her fists. The sign after the services exit told her there would be another twenty-five miles until the next one. She wasn't going to make it. The need was too urgent.

She hung on for as long as she could and then Golda finally had to let go. The urine streamed out, more than she'd imagined there would be and the pungent smell filled the car.

"*For fuck's sake*, you bitch!" Alan yelled. "You're disgusting! I don't know why I bothered to marry you in the first place. You're sick, that's what you are. Sick!"

Golda started to cry, putting her hands over her ears to block his words, but it was no good. The seat felt sticky and wet, and her skirt was soaked through.

"I'm sorry, I'm sorry," she moaned. "I couldn't help it, I'm sorry."

Alan kept on shouting and swearing while Golda took some tissues from her handbag and tried to clear up the mess. It was pointless though so, after a while, she gave up the effort and just sat in the car, trying to make herself as small as possible.

Alan turned off at the next service station and parked in the first space he could find in the car park. It was the furthest one away from the services. Golda was shaking, unable to stop, but at least she wasn't crying any more. She didn't think she had any more tears.

"Get out!" he said. "Go and clean yourself up. You disgust me. And be quick about it, will you? You've already wasted enough time as it is."

Still shaking, Golda got out of the car. In the fresh air, some of the smell dissipated, but her skirt and legs were still wet and she felt sick with shame.

She began walking. She tried to keep as far away from people as she could, but a couple of family groups went past, and she could feel their shocked stares on her skin. A little boy laughed and pointed, saying something Golda couldn't hear and didn't want to, but his mother grabbed him and hurried away. Eyes lowered, she stumbled on, her feet feeling wet and sticky in her shoes.

It took forever. Inside the services area, she searched desperately for the loos and followed the signs, aware more than anything of her own stink and the embarrassed looks of those around her.

Golda had never felt so alone and so unhuman.

In the ladies, she headed for the nearest cubicle, locked it firmly, sat down on the loo and sobbed. She'd been wrong about not having any more tears. She didn't know how long Alan would expect her to be or even if he'd be there at all when she came out. For a moment, a fierce joy at the possibility of being abandoned by her husband swept through her. It was like a small window opening in her life and showing her a glimpse of light she had never expected to see.

Still crying and unable to stop, Golda reached round and grabbed as much loo roll as she could find. Then she began making herself as presentable as possible. After a while, there was a gentle knock at the cubicle door.

"Hello?" a soft voice said. "Hello, in there? Are you okay?"

Golda froze, her heart pounding. She couldn't cope with other people. She simply couldn't. She just wanted to be alone, somewhere a long way from here.

But she wasn't.

"Yes, yes," she said, trying to sound normal even though that state seemed so far away. "I'm fine. Sorry."

"Okay," the voice said, and then there was silence, so Golda hoped whoever it was had gone away.

After another five minutes or so, she'd stopped crying and thought she was as dry as she could make herself, though her skirt and tights were still damp and smelly. There was nothing Golda could do about that. Once they got to Norfolk, she could change and wash everything. Perhaps Alan would have calmed down by then. She couldn't afford the time to stay here any longer. He'd told her to be quick, but she hadn't been, had she? Not at all.

Golda couldn't bear the thought of making him any angrier than he already was, so she took a deep breath, unlocked the cubicle door and went to wash her hands.

She found the soap and began to wash. She was still shaking and couldn't bear to think about how she must look. She kept her eyes fixed on the basin, but was aware of a shadow next to her, of someone coming to use the basin next to hers. Before Golda could think how unusual this behaviour was when there were countless other basins to use, the woman spoke.

"I wanted to check you're okay," the stranger said softly. "It was me who knocked on your cubicle door. I saw you with that man in the car. Is he your husband? Things looked difficult."

Golda blinked and turned slowly to look at this woman. She was older than expected from her voice. Perhaps in her sixties or seventies. Her grey hair was pulled up into a bun, and there were creases round her eyes as if she smiled a lot, but she wasn't smiling now. Instead, she looked concerned.

"Are you in trouble?" she asked quietly, though there was nobody else around to hear. "Because if you are, there are people you can go to for help. Your doctor, for instance. Forgive me if I'm being too intrusive, but you don't have to put up with difficult things."

Golda swallowed and somehow found her voice.

"Thank you," she said. "You're very kind, but I can manage. It's not always like this. Not at all. Today is a bad day but most of the time I can cope."

"I'm sure you can, but the truth is you don't have to. I understand things might be hard for a whole variety of reasons, but please understand it's absolutely not your fault. There are places, organisations that can help you."

With that, the woman reached into her skirt pocket, then took hold of Golda's hand, still slick with soap, and pressed something small and rectangular into it. When Golda looked down, she could see it was a business card, but her eyes were too full of tears to work out what it said.

"I'll leave now," the woman said, "but I'll be looking out for you until you go. There are a couple of numbers on the card – the one on the front is for a women's refuge, and the one on the back is mine. Please, keep the card safe and ring either of them any time of night or day. I mean it."

Dumbly, Golda nodded, not taking in any of what she said, but opening her handbag and putting the card deep in an inner pocket. By this time, a few other women were coming into the loos, chattering and laughing together though Golda tried to pay them no heed. When she next looked up, the woman who'd talked to her had gone.

Golda rinsed her hands, dried them, and left. Though she looked around briefly, she couldn't see the woman and wondered if she was watching from somewhere. Even though her trip to the loos hadn't helped her appearance that much and she could still smell the acrid scent of her own urine, something deep inside felt a tiny part lighter. As if somehow she might not be entirely alone.

That feeling stayed with Golda all the way through the service station, out into the car park and across to the car.

All the doors and the boot were wide open, and Alan was busy doing something in the passenger seat. At once, Golda's heart began racing again and for one long moment all she wanted to do was to run. Somewhere far away where she didn't have to watch herself to ensure she did the right thing all the time. But where would she go?

Not that it mattered as Alan looked up, his hand clutching something that looked familiar.

"You took your time," he said. "Where the hell have you been?"

"I'm sorry," Golda said, lowering her gaze. "I was trying to get clean."

She heard him take a breath and wondered if he was going to start shouting again, but she could also hear people not too far from where they stood, and knew he wouldn't do anything where it was so public. Instead, he came up close to her and thrust the object he was holding into her hands.

"Don't push it," he said. "Here, as you're finally seen fit to come back, you can finish up making the car clean. It's your mess, after all."

When Golda looked at what she was now holding, it was one of her favourite summer jumpers, the one she wore for sitting in the garden in the evenings. Now it was damp with urine and she didn't know if she'd ever be able to wear it again. Trying to hold back the tears that threatened to undo her once more, Golda did as he asked, using her jumper to soak up what was left of the mess in the car and then wringing the worst of it out on the verge. He had other clothing – all Golda's – on the car's carpet and passenger seat as well, but she blinked the knowledge away.

Finally, she didn't think she could do any more, so she told him she'd finished.

"Good," he said. "It's about time. Get in the car then."

Golda turned towards the boot, her ruined jumper in her hands.

"What are you doing now?" he snapped.

"Putting the jumper back," she said. "In the case."

"Really?" he said. "I don't think so! I don't want that thing in the car now. Just chuck it somewhere."

"But …" she started to protest, and then stopped at once. Saying anything now would be stupid.

She looked round for a bin, but couldn't see one.

"Oh for God's sake, just chuck it in the grass and we can be on our way. Think yourself lucky I'm letting you get in the car at all – I certainly don't want your disgusting jumper."

Golda did what he asked, placing the jumper on the grass behind the car, and then getting in the passenger seat and closing the door.

Alan went round the car, shutting the rest of the doors and then getting in the driver's seat. He wound his window down.

"Okay," he said, "now you've finished making yourself into a laughing stock, let's get on the road and see if we can have a nice holiday. God knows I need one."

Then they were off. As they drove down the first line of cars, Golda glanced up and thought she saw the woman from the toilets. Afraid to draw any kind of attention to herself, she turned away at once. But even thinking the woman might have been there, watching over her in some fashion Golda couldn't comprehend, made her feel a bit lighter once again, and she pressed her foot against her handbag, knowing the tiny secret card she'd hidden there was still safe. Somehow it made a difference.

She never could remember all that much about the Norfolk holiday itself. Not anything they'd been to visit, nor any sights they might have seen. There were a couple of days when Alan took the car and went out, leaving Golda behind in the cottage. She didn't know where he went or what he saw. She never asked him and he never told her. She was simply glad of a day, even a few hours, when she didn't have to try to work out what mood he might be in and how to best survive it.

The cottage itself was beautiful – she did remember that – it was small and cosy, with a view of the sea and a tiny garden with a table and two chairs for sitting outside. And, of course, the owner was very fond of begonias as there was one in a different colour in every room. After that, the sight of one of these harmless flowers always made Golda feel afraid. When they'd finally arrived on that terrible day of travel, she'd changed out of her soiled clothes and washed them and the ones Alan had used to clean up the mess in the car. She'd then made an early supper, though Alan took most of it for himself. Golda was left with a tiny portion of food which hadn't been enough to ease her hunger. He'd then ordered her to clean the inside of the car properly and she had done so without question.

All this seemed to be enough to calm him down, but Golda spent the whole time away buried deep within herself to avoid any more pain. It was the one sure method of keeping the rising panic at bay.

By the third day of the holiday, her husband had started to allow Golda to eat more normally, and she remembered being pathetically grateful, as she'd been feeling faint with the lack of food. She'd almost cried with relief.

However, as the time of departure came closer, Golda began to worry about the journey back. She wished she could wave some kind of magic wand and suddenly be at home without the need for the long journey, which might well be fraught with danger. She also started drinking less and trying to eat more things which might ease the need to go to the loo. She had no idea if Alan would factor in any comfort break as they travelled this time and she was far too scared to ask. She tried to ignore her growing thirst – she just had to bear it until they arrived home again.

The night before they left, Golda packed everything up and got the cases ready for the morning. Alan said nothing but nodded when he saw how well she'd prepared.

She didn't sleep much that night. Partly this was due to how thirsty she was, but most of it was due to fear. Every now and again, Golda would reach down from the bed and touch her handbag, knowing that lady's card was still there, hidden away where Alan couldn't find it.

The morning of departure went as she'd expected. Alan used the shower while Golda made sure breakfast was how he wanted it. Then, of course, while he shaved and dressed, she had her usual quick bath.

At the breakfast table, he was silent, but Golda took that as a good thing – he couldn't find anything to get angry about, and she prayed that state of affairs would continue. She glanced at him with envy as he enjoyed his cup of coffee, but didn't dare pour herself one. Just in case. She concentrated instead on eating as much toast as she could to soak up any fluids. She simply wanted to get safely home.

It was only when they were getting into the car that Alan spoke.

"I'm hoping you won't be as disgusting on the journey home as you were on the way here," he said, idly, as if he was just chatting about the weather or some other harmless topic. "I don't want to have to deal with that again. We've had a lovely holiday and I don't want you to ruin it."

"No, I won't, I promise," Golda said, heart rate rising at his words and feeling that familiar tension in her shoulders.

"Good," he said heartily. "Let's hope not, eh! You're such a silly woman, Golda. I hope I can trust you."

She nodded. "Yes. Yes, you can, Alan. Thank you."

She didn't know why she should thank him at all, but her words seemed to please him, so that at least was a relief. Throughout the whole drive home, Golda's shoulders ached and her thirst grew, but she was determined to make it back without incident.

They did too. She could hardly believe her husband hadn't found some excuse to find her wanting but they arrived home safely. The first things Golda did after putting her cases and bags in the hallway was to run to the loo – she just made it, thank heavens – and then to drink a large glass of water in the kitchen.

Alan simply laughed but said nothing, and Golda was glad. And so, their normal lives continued – or as normal as their marriage ever was.

Then, just three months after they'd returned from Norfolk, Alan was diagnosed with cancer. And everything changed.

Chapter Eleven

Frankie

What had happened at the garden centre had been shocking in a way Frankie hadn't taken in at the time. When Miranda had fainted, Frankie had switched into a coping mode she hadn't known she possessed. All the way through calling for help, waiting for the ambulance, going to the hospital and then sorting out the plants Miranda had chosen, Frankie had felt unnaturally calm.

It was only when she'd finally said goodbye to Golda and driven home that she'd started to shake. She had to concentrate very hard on not causing an accident and it had been a relief when she'd pulled up in her driveway and turned off the engine.

Gareth had been there, waiting for her. She'd texted him just before she went into the hospital, briefly telling him what had happened and where she was. He didn't say anything. He folded her into his arms when she got out of the car and held her. It was the first time he'd held her like this since she'd told him she wasn't going through with the abortion and it felt like coming home. Even though she knew they still had so much to discuss and decide.

She couldn't seem to stop the shaking but, after a couple of minutes, Gareth guided her into their hallway and then through into the living room.

"Sorry," she started to say but he cut her off.

"Don't be silly, there's no need to be. You sit there. I'll bring tea."

Tea, when Gareth brought it in, came with a packet of chocolate digestives Frankie had forgotten they had. Her husband placed both tea and biscuits on the coffee table and came to sit next to her, putting his arm around her once more and giving her another much-needed hug.

"Are you okay?" he asked her. "What exactly happened?"

Between sips of tea, Frankie told him. He listened in silence, nodding every now and again.

"Did you get to see Miranda?" he asked her when she'd finished.

She shook her head. "No, they wouldn't let us. Her friend Jake saw her and came out to tell us how things are. They think they'll move her to a cancer ward tomorrow, but they need to keep her in overnight, check what's going on. It seems so awful and so unfair that it has to be … you know … terminal. She's just so very young, you know."

And she was right. Because it absolutely *wasn't* fair, was it? It wasn't fair that someone as young as Miranda, with all her life ahead of her, could get a disease like this and in such a way that they couldn't cure her.

"Can you go and see her once she's in a normal ward?" Gareth asked. "That would be better, wouldn't it?"

"Yes," she replied. "Yes, I hope so. I'll ring the hospital tomorrow if we've not heard anything from Jake first. I gave him my mobile number. If he rings with any news, I'll let Golda know too. But, Gareth, what if the news is bad? What then?"

It was stupid, so very stupid, but she hadn't actually thought about this. Not yet. And she didn't want to think about it. Because what if Miranda died tonight? She stared wildly at Gareth, not having a clue what to do or what to think.

Her husband took her face in his hands and she felt the depth of his gaze taking her in, holding her safe.

"I don't know," he said softly. "But whatever news it is – bad or good – you can bear it, Frankie. I know we're having issues at the moment, because of … well, you know. But I'm still here to help you. I promise. Looking at things more positively, the ICU didn't give you or Jake any hints they expected your friend to take a turn for the worse, did they? They didn't ask you to prepare for anything bad. If they'd thought her time was near, they wouldn't have been talking about transferring her out to another ward. They wouldn't have been planning in that way."

Frankie gazed back at her husband and then nodded, feeling distinctly calmer.

"Okay," she replied. "Yes, you're right. Of course you are."

It still took her a long time to get to sleep that night, a fact which was made more difficult by Gareth snoring quietly next to her. It was astonishing how easy he always found sleeping to be. Most nights, his head hit the pillow and he was out for the count. She envied him that. If Frankie was worried about anything, she took ages to get to sleep though once she was asleep she usually stayed that way until a reasonable hour in the morning.

But tonight she was thinking about Miranda and hoping she was okay and would be able to come out of hospital soon. She still couldn't quite believe that her new friend's life was set to be so short. Cancer was a terrible thing. Frankie had never known anyone who was terminally ill and maybe, in that respect, she'd been lucky. The whole thing was unbearable if she dwelt too much upon it. But for Miranda, of course, it was a thousand times worse. Getting upset about it was in fact selfish, wasn't it? It was Miranda who was facing the worst thing of all and somehow coping with it. Not Frankie herself.

No, all Frankie had to worry about was the baby she was still carrying, the decisions she and Gareth would need to make fairly soon, and what any of this might do to her marriage. Which was more than enough to worry about really. On top of the whole situation with Miranda.

She was still thinking about all of it when she must have fallen asleep at last as the next thing she knew it was daylight and Gareth was putting a mug of tea on her bedside table.

"Morning," he said, giving her a swift kiss. "How are you?"

"Okay, I think," she said, stretching and sitting up against the pillows. "I'll give the hospital a ring later if I've not heard from Jake. See how Miranda is."

"Good idea," her husband replied. "But have breakfast first, and let me know if you need me to give you a lift anywhere."

She nodded. "Thank you."

By the time Frankie had started preparing her breakfast, she'd had a text from Jake. Miranda had improved a little overnight and had been transferred to the cancer ward this morning. The visiting hours were the same as for the ICU, he'd added, so that meant afternoons after 2pm.

Frankie felt a wash of relief go through her. The first thing she did, after replying to Jake's text to say thank you, was to ring Golda.

The older woman picked up at once, her voice sounding hesitant, almost afraid.

"Golda, it's me, Frankie," Frankie said before launching into the important facts. "And it's not bad news. Miranda's okay, she's been transferred to the cancer ward so she's not in the ICU anymore."

"Oh, thank goodness," Golda said, her voice sounding stronger even from a moment ago. "That's so good, so positive. Thank you so much for letting me know. Is there any other news?"

Sadly, there wasn't, but Frankie explained about the visiting hours, and the two women made arrangements to visit later on that afternoon. It felt good to have a plan.

The rest of the day went much as Frankie had expected and, on the dot of 4pm, she was round at Golda's to pick up her friend. When Golda answered the door, Frankie thought she looked tired, but was too polite to say so.

"Hello, Frankie," said Golda. "It's good to see you. Do you think you might have a minute before we set off to come through to the garden?"

"Of course," said Frankie and followed Golda through her hallway.

The two women made their way along the side of the house and then into the space designated as Miranda's garden. Frankie couldn't help it. She gasped.

"What is it?" Golda asked, looking at her with a frown. "I've put the plants in the positions Miranda drew in her plan, as best as I could remember it. Do you think it's all right?"

Frankie stared at her friend and then back at the gorgeous garden she'd laid out.

"You are joking, aren't you?" Frankie replied. "This is amazing. It's the most beautiful garden I've seen in ages, maybe even a lifetime."

It was too. It was a wonderful and glorious profusion of white and cream and gold flowers, starting with paler shades and moving through to the darker and more vibrant ones. Even though there were loads of buds still to break out into flower, Frankie could see how beautiful it was now, and also how it was going to be even more beautiful as the summer moved on into autumn.

Golda blushed. "Thank you. As I said, I just tried to follow Miranda's plan."

"Well, it's lovely," Frankie said again. "Absolutely stunning. Miranda's going to love this once she gets out of hospital."

"I hope so," Golda replied. "This was why I brought you through to see what I'd managed to do. Could you take some pictures on your phone? I'm not very good at that sort of thing, so I was hoping you could take them so Miranda can see them. Once she's awake."

Frankie nodded. "Brilliant idea."

She got her phone out and started taking pictures. Golda began to laugh.

"What?" Frankie said. "What is it?"

The other woman waved her hand. "Nothing. It's great. You just look so serious, that's all."

Frankie had to join in the laughter. "Well, photography is a serious business! Besides of which, it's vital to get the best possible shots."

A couple of minutes later and Frankie had finished. She showed Golda on the phone and the older woman nodded.

"That's lovely, thank you. Oh, and on the way through the house, could you take a quick picture of the begonia as well?"

"Of course, no problem," said Frankie.

Once she'd got the picture of the begonia – which Golda had placed in a cream-coloured pot – the two of them were on their way to the hospital.

The cancer ward wasn't as hard to find as the ICU had been, and the whole area seemed to have been newly decorated – it was bright and airy, and packed full of inspirational posters. The windows were larger than in the rest of the hospital, and the ward was designed around a small garden in the middle which today was bathed in late afternoon sunshine.

After signing in at the cancer reception, they were directed to the area where Miranda had been transferred to. At her bedside, a nurse was carrying out some checks from the look of it, so Frankie and Golda waited to one side until she was finished.

When the nurse turned round and saw them, she smiled and beckoned them towards the bed. Frankie saw that she wasn't an actual hospital nurse as she had a Macmillan Cancer Support badge on her lapel. She had kind eyes, and Frankie at once felt more hopeful.

"Hello," the nurse said brightly. "Are you here to see Miranda? I'm just making sure she's settling in okay. My name's Diana."

Frankie and Golda introduced themselves while Diana gave them a quick run-down as to how things were with their friend. They were still doing tests, apparently, but Miranda was now in less immediate danger than she had been the day before and was expected to stay in the hospital for a couple of days or so before being discharged.

"I'll be keeping an eye on her of course," Diana added. "If she'll let me."

"Oh," said Golda. "I see. You're her designated nurse then?"

"Yes, that's right, but of course it's entirely up to Miranda whether she'll see me or not. I'll leave the two of you in peace while you have your visit. She's still asleep but there's no reason for her not to wake up when she's ready. You can hold her hand if you like, and talk to her. She may well hear you even if she doesn't respond."

With that, Diana walked away, and Golda arranged the two chairs allocated to the bed into a more suitable position. She sat down in the one nearest Miranda, and Frankie took the other one.

Miranda looked incredibly small and frail on the bed, wired up as she was to a multitude of instruments, and Frankie's heart went out to her.

Golda took hold of Miranda's hand and began to talk gently. In the occasional gaps in Golda's conversation, Frankie added in whatever she could think of – which wasn't much. Golda had already covered the topics of Pilates and the Little Barn coffee shop, as well as reassuring Miranda – if she could hear any of this – that her plants were safe and well. Frankie could only think about the journey into hospital today and the good weather they were having, which weren't inspiring topics of conversation for anyone, whether or not they were awake.

Finally, Frankie remembered the photos she'd taken.

"Oh," she said. "And we have pictures of the plants you bought for your garden as well. You can look at them when you wake up if you like."

And it was precisely then that – astonishingly and unexpectedly – Miranda stirred a little, groaned and opened her eyes. She looked straight at them.

"My garden?" she said, her voice low and very croaky. "You have pictures? Show me, please?"

For a second, Frankie and Golda stared at each other in amazement and then back at Miranda.

"Yes, of course," Frankie said, her voice not at all indicating the levels of joy and relief she was feeling. "Here they are."

Leaning forward, Frankie took out her phone and scrolled through to the photos.

Miranda looked carefully at the pictures Frankie was showing her, indicating with a slight nod when she was ready for the next one. A slow smile was building up over her pale face.

When she'd seen all that Frankie had to offer, Miranda rested her head back on the pillow.

"Thank you, they're great," she said and then, "I can't remember what happened. Have I been ill?"

As briefly as possible, Frankie and Golda explained why Miranda was here. Frankie thought how confusing it must be for the poor girl and how awful it was that she had no family to look after her. That thought couldn't help but surprise her.

"Shit, so sorry," Miranda said. "What a bloody nightmare. Bloody cancer."

"You've nothing to be sorry for," said Golda, straightening her shoulders and giving Miranda's hand a firm pat. "Don't be silly. And yes, all this is really *bloody*, as you say. But with a bit of luck, you'll soon be out of here and strong enough to start your garden, so you'd best start preparing your *bloody* green fingers for the task."

Frankie snorted with laughter at Golda's determination, not to mention the unexpected swearing, and Miranda stared at her in astonishment.

"Frigging hell, Golda," she said. "You make swearing sound so classy."

This just made Frankie laugh even more, and even Golda smiled.

"I simply wanted to get my point across," she said. "And, besides, *you* were the one who used the word first, Miranda. Not me."

Ten minutes later, Frankie could tell Miranda was flagging so they said their goodbyes and prepared to leave. Just as the two of them were standing up, Diana returned from wherever she'd been and her face lit up when she saw Miranda.

"Miranda!" she said. "So glad you've opened your eyes. You were missing out on a lovely afternoon, and that's a shame. I mean, look at that sky."

As instructed, Frankie, Golda and Miranda all turned in the direction of the window, and Frankie had to admit Diana was right. The sky was streaked with pink, and the light was somehow softening the plants in the ward garden so that everything looked like it was shimmering ever so slightly.

"How beautiful," said Golda.

"That's amazing," agreed Frankie.

"Wow," said Miranda. And promptly closed her eyes and fell asleep.

"Oh," Frankie said. "Is everything okay?"

Diana hurried to check. "Oh yes, everything's fine. Don't worry. Miranda's still very tired. I'm just pleased she woke up to see you both."

"Yes," said Golda. "We were very lucky. We'll try to pop back tomorrow if we can?"

She turned to Frankie who nodded. "Yes, that would be great. I'll text Jake and let him know."

"That's lovely, thank you," said Diana. "I'll drop him a text as well. I think he's coming in later."

That was good news, Frankie thought as the two women made their way back to the car. As she was walking, she texted Jake to tell him what had happened, and that Miranda had been awake, if briefly.

"You young people!" Golda said suddenly.

"I don't think I'm that young," Frankie protested. "But thank you!"

Golda laughed. "You're young enough to be able to send a text whilst walking, and holding a conversation with me at the same time. If I ever have to send a text on my phone, it's quicker for me to get in my car, drive to the person I want to text, deliver my message and then drive home than it is to actually send it."

And Frankie couldn't help laughing at that. The journey home felt far more hopeful than the one she and Golda had shared to the hospital earlier on. It had been great that Miranda had been awake and had seen some pictures of her planned garden. And that lovely sky Diana had pointed out had been magical. Like a gift for the three of them – four if you counted the Macmillan nurse, of course.

After having dropped Golda off, Frankie made her way home. As she parked her car on the driveway next to Gareth's, she could see her husband pottering around the kitchen looking as if he was getting dinner ready. He waved when he saw her, his face breaking into a smile, and a surge of affection for the man she loved to the bone caught her unawares. She was still smiling as she walked into the house. Gareth kissed her and then stepped back.

"You look happy," he said. "Did everything go well? How is Miranda?"

"She's awake," Frankie replied. "Thank goodness. She's in the cancer ward now, but they think – they hope – she might be able to get home in a few days. Maybe early next week."

"That's good news," Gareth replied. "I'm so pleased for you, and for your friend too."

"I'll pop in and see her again tomorrow," she said. "Depending on how things go."

"Good idea," he said.

The rest of their evening was pretty normal and there were no difficult conversations, which Frankie didn't think she could have coped with tonight. They ate together quietly, loaded the dishwasher, watched some television and chatted every now and again. About nothing, or nothing important anyway.

Later, Frankie slept fitfully whilst Gareth, of course, was instantly asleep beside her. Still, she must have drifted off as when she looked at the bedside clock next, it was 3am. Funny, she thought, how that was the time she tended to wake up if she was going to have this kind of night. She was just too hot and her mind was racing, jumping from topic to topic with no resolution and no hope of an answer. And always, always coming back to her pregnancy and the rollercoaster ride of feelings she was having about it.

She spent the next ten minutes or so trying to breathe calmly so she could get back to sleep again, but it wasn't working. She probably needed a drink of water.

Quietly, so she wouldn't wake her husband, Frankie got up. In the darkness of the bedroom, she orientated herself and then padded across to the chair where she'd left her dressing gown. Putting it on, she left the bedroom and made her way downstairs. It was strange in the house at night – it had a different feel to it than it did in the daytime. As if the house itself was resting, waiting for the morning. She smiled at her own fantasy, shook her head to dispel the thought and went to the kitchen to fetch a glass of water instead.

Closing the kitchen door behind her so as not to disturb Gareth, she switched the light on, blinking as everything came into view. She drank her water, leaning back against one of the work surfaces and trying to still her thoughts.

It wasn't working. She was thinking about the pregnancy, what it would do to her marriage, then Miranda, Miranda's illness, the unfairness of it all for her poor friend, and then back to the pregnancy again. All this jumble of thoughts and images whirling round and round her head with seemingly no end to it.

She sighed, refilled her glass of water, switched off the kitchen light and walked to the living room in the darkness. Perhaps sitting down for a while might help.

It didn't. Another fifteen minutes or so passed by, though to Frankie it felt like hours. She did feel a bit calmer by then – maybe the water or the sitting down in the dark had helped. So she retraced her steps to the kitchen, put the glass into the dishwasher and slowly walked back upstairs.

There was a shadow standing at the bedroom door and she gasped before understanding that of course it was Gareth.

"Frankie?" he said, his voice hoarse and uncertain. "Is everything okay?"

She nodded, though she wasn't sure if he could see that and she also wasn't sure if she was okay or not.

"Yes," she whispered. "I needed some water and then I was thinking. Sorry if I woke you."

"It's all right," he replied. "It's just that I turned over and the bed was empty. I waited for a while but then I was worried."

He walked towards her slowly. She stood still until he reached her and then, as if from nowhere, she found the words she needed.

"I'm thinking about us and what to do for the best," she said. "And I don't know. *I just don't know*. And then it all gets mixed up with what's happening to Miranda. And I'm thinking about how her mother gave birth to her and then it all comes to this. All that love, all that worry, *for nothing*."

Gareth took a breath.

"It's a terrible thing," he replied, "and, apart from your friend, I know we've got a lot to talk about, and I don't know what to do either. I don't even know what to think. But I don't see how love, no matter what, can ever be for nothing, can it?"

There were no words Frankie could say in response. No speech that could help right now. So she looked at his shadowy figure, tears pricking at her eyes. Then, quietly and slowly, the two of them returned to bed. Nothing discussed, and nothing decided. Yet.

Over the next few days, she and Golda visited Miranda regularly and each day Frankie thought the younger woman looked stronger. The tests she had to undergo were taking longer than expected, however, so it was estimated Miranda wouldn't be allowed home until the following week. Golda was quick to reassure her that the plants could wait and were perfectly happy in their pots ready for when she was strong enough to plant them.

On a couple of visits, the two women coincided with Jake, and Frankie was happy to catch up with him. She felt that he cared and had a good heart. She was glad Miranda had him as a friend.

Still, all the time, thoughts and feelings were shifting inside Frankie as she went about those days, and she wasn't sure what to do about them. In the end, she knew she and Gareth had to talk again, and the sooner the better.

It ended up being a Monday night. Not ideal, as Monday was always the worst day of the working week, but Frankie had a few busy days ahead, with a couple of her village committees due to meet, so she didn't have any other time. She simply couldn't put it off any longer.

She waited until after she and Gareth had eaten and loaded up the dishwasher though. Then she turned to him.

"We need to talk," she said. "Please?"

He shut his eyes briefly and then nodded. "I know."

They walked together in silence to the living room. There they sat down and it was Frankie who began.

"In an ideal world," she said. "In the world you and I hoped we would have, it would just be the two of us, wouldn't it? Neither of us has ever wanted children and we knew that almost from the start. Perhaps it was what brought us together in some ways? I don't know. I certainly never wanted to get pregnant, and I've never wanted a baby. So when I found out I was expecting, it was a huge shock. I could hardly believe it. I mean, we've been fine all this time, and now ... Now, *this*."

Frankie waved her hand in the direction of her stomach to make her point. Not that she looked remotely pregnant yet, but that didn't stop it from being true. When Gareth remained silent, she carried on.

"At first I agreed with your reaction too," she said. "I wanted rid of it. I didn't want to be pregnant. Abortion was the best option and I honestly thought that would be it. I really did. The baby would be gone once I'd taken the right pills in the right order and that would be that. We could get on with our lives. But, when it came down to it, I just couldn't do it. I couldn't do it. It seemed too cruel and too final. So, here we are. Whatever happens now, I'm going to have this baby, Gareth. That makes me feel scared – more scared than you can ever possibly imagine! – but it also makes me feel something else. Something I'd never expected to feel. Ever. It makes me feel hope."

She reached out and took hold of her husband's hand. His skin felt cold. So cold.

"What do you mean?" he asked quietly. "I don't understand."

Frankie took a breath. The kind of breath that held the whole world within it, but in such a fragile way that it could never be contained.

"Because there are two options for this child," Frankie replied, still gripping Gareth's hand, though he did not respond. "When he or she is born, we can put the baby up for adoption. If we do that, then we can step away. Carry on with the life we have, the life we love now. We never have to think of the child again. But there's another, very different option too. And this is the one that's giving me that sense of hope, though I never imagined it would. We can keep the child, Gareth. *Our* child. We can be parents together, if we want to. We can have a family. In the end, would that be so terribly, unthinkably awful?"

A long silence then. Frankie couldn't say any more. She had nothing more to say. But, even as she'd been speaking, the sea-change in her heart was completed and she knew, without a shadow of a doubt, that she would keep this child. Their child. *Her* child. Not something she'd ever anticipated she'd feel, and with such overwhelming certainty, especially as she'd never wanted a family. But here it was and it wasn't something she could avoid or ignore. She was going to be a mother.

"No," said Gareth suddenly and shockingly into the silence, and withdrawing his hand from hers. "*No!* I can't do that. I can't be a father. It's never something I wanted, and the thought of it fills me with horror. I'm sorry, but that's how it is. I absolutely don't want this baby, Frankie. I was happy for you to get rid of it, as you wanted, and then, when you said you couldn't do that, I assumed you'd have the baby and then give it up for adoption. I didn't like that, but I accepted it. But keeping the child? I don't know. I don't want it. *I don't understand you anymore.* I really don't. I know you have the final say as the mother – of course you do – but I don't know where that leaves me."

"Wh-what do you mean?" she stuttered as he sprang up from his position next to her. "What are you going to do?"

He shook his head furiously. "I don't know. I understand what you're saying and I'm not telling you to change your mind – though if you could, that would be wonderful! – but I need to think. Clear my head."

With that he strode from the living room, and his footsteps resounded in the hallway. Frankie blinked and then leapt up to follow him. In the hall, Gareth was grabbing his jacket from the banisters where he'd left it when he came in.

"What are you doing? Are you going out?"

"Yes. I just need to think. Get some air. Like I said."

"Oh, okay. Shall I come with you?"

"No!" he replied. "No, I want to be by myself. Don't worry about waiting up for me. I've got a key. If I'm late, I'll sleep in the spare room. I won't disturb you. Don't worry."

Then, while Frankie was still catching her breath and desperately wondering what to do to make him stay, Gareth had flung open the front door and was gone.

She was alone, all her hopes and assumptions mocking her, and with not the first idea what she should do now.

Chapter Twelve

Miranda

Hospital was pretty crap, Miranda thought, not for the first time, as she prepared to go home. Then again, life – or what she had left of it – was pretty crap too, wasn't it? She was seriously peed off about how she'd had an episode when choosing her garden. How unlucky was that! Things had seemed to be going so well too – apart from her effing headaches – and she'd hoped that for once they might not mean what they usually did.

No chance. Of bloody course not.

So here she was, sorting her things out to go home and already wondering when she'd next be back here. Jake had been with her for about an hour now – he'd taken today off work to help get her home and she was more than grateful. Her special nurse Diana was also here. She was putting some of Miranda's stuff into bags and sorting out the new medication she'd been given while Jake sat on the side of the bed and held her hand.

A hospital transport minibus, which Diana said was organised by volunteers, had been booked to take her home, which made her feel like a total no-hoper, but there wasn't anything else she could do. She didn't have a car of her own, Jake couldn't borrow one today, and she certainly didn't feel like getting on the back of her friend's motorbike. She could have asked Golda or Frankie for help, but they'd done so much already that she didn't feel comfortable asking for their support again. She was also too tired to argue about her nurse's decision but, by the look of determination on Diana's face, any argument would have been pretty pointless anyway.

"Okay," said Diana, as she zipped up Miranda's bag. "How are you feeling?"

"Fine," lied Miranda, not wanting to admit how she actually felt. Which was exhausted and low, but what good would it do to say it?

Diana nodded, but the look on her face told Miranda the nurse didn't believe her. "I see. Now, when you get home, I'll be there to settle you in if that's what you would like, but as always there's no pressure. I know Jake's going to be there too as he'll be travelling in the bus with you. But, if you let me, what I can do is organise your new drugs, take the old ones away, and leave you the schedule of what you need to take when."

"Yes, please," Miranda said, much to her own surprise as she hadn't intended to agree. But the words had come from somewhere deep inside her and she couldn't help but say them.

Diana blinked. "I'm sorry?"

Miranda took a breath and for the first time that morning looked directly at the woman whose task it was to care for her until she wasn't here any longer. She'd not been making this job easy for Diana, had she?

"Yes, please, Diana," she said. "That's very kind of you and I would like your help. Please."

The smile that came across Diana's face was all sunshine and glitter, and she hunkered down to give Miranda a heartfelt hug, while Jake gripped her hand. She could see he was smiling too. There was obviously a lot of power in being nice, rather than difficult.

"Thank you, Miranda," said Diana. "That means more to me than you can possibly know."

How weird was that. Making people feel good was pretty nice. She'd not thought about this before.

She was still thinking about it when, two hours later, she finally arrived home. Miranda hadn't minded waiting and travelling round with the other three or four people being taken to their homes. It had been quiet, so she'd taken the chance to drift off into a short sleep every now and then. Whenever she woke up, Jake was still there holding her hand and that had been okay too.

It was stupidly exciting to be home. It wasn't much of a flat but it was hers. She wondered if she would die here one day soon. She didn't want to die in hospital, which was full of sick people, and huge and unfamiliar. She supposed she would have to discuss this with Diana, now she was letting the nurse help her properly, but it wasn't something she could face today.

When the minibus stopped, the driver got out and offered Miranda the use of a wheelchair to the front door, but she shook her head. She definitely wasn't at that stage yet! Instead, she leant on Jake as she made her way down the short pathway and got her key out. Just as she was opening the door and the minibus was driving away, she heard a horn tooting and turned to see Diana drawing up at the roadside and waving at her. Miranda waited at the doorway, still leaning on Jake, until Diana got out of her car and trotted down the path. Together the three of them entered the flat. Once inside, Miranda gasped.

"It's so clean!" she said. "And look, there's some bunting. And my bike!"

Jake laughed as he helped her into the tiny living room after she'd given her beloved bike a pat or two. "Yes, once they knew you were going to be coming home, Golda and Frankie insisted on cleaning up for you and returning your bike so they borrowed the key. I hope that was okay? I didn't know about the bunting though – it's a nice touch. Might nick it for my own flat when you're asleep, babe."

"Don't you frigging dare!" Miranda protested in mock fury. "Get your own frigging bunting, you thief!"

She pretended to slap at him in fun, but he easily dodged away. Diana laughed at them both.

"It looks amazing," she said. "Your friends are lovely, aren't they?"

Miranda nodded and was all set to agree wholeheartedly when her attention was caught by a plant in pride of place next to the fern she'd always had – which itself looked a lot happier than when she'd last noticed it.

"Oh!" she said. "It's the begonia I chose at the garden centre."

She picked it up and smiled. Thick green leaves and tiny white flowers – she remembered getting it before everything had gone hazy. There had been something about it that appealed to her, she remembered, and it still appealed to her now, though she wasn't sure why. Maybe it was the ridiculous size difference between the leaves and the flowers? She wasn't sure. She also loved the cream-coloured pot the begonia had been placed in. Whilst she'd been in hospital, Miranda had paid back Golda for the plants she'd bought for her, but she hadn't included any nice pots in the money. That must have been Golda, as she didn't have anything so classy herself. She wasn't sure she had anything classy at all, for fuck's sake. Except Jake, of course.

"Yeah," the man in question said now, confirming exactly what she'd been thinking. "It was the older woman – Golda? – who said it was something you'd chosen at the garden shop. The pot is one of hers, but she was happy for you to have it."

"How kind," Diana said. "It's a great welcome home, isn't it?"

And Miranda could only agree. It was funny to think that these two women she'd met by chance were now her friends. Up until now, she'd assumed friends would be people her own age, not people older than she was. Life was frigging weird, that was the truth.

After Diana had gone, having settled Miranda in and left notes about the new medication, she and Jake sat on the sofa in her living room together. He'd turned on the TV but there was nothing much on. It was just background noise while they drank their mugs of tea, some stupid reality TV programme, which Miranda always hated. She had enough reality of her own. She didn't want any more.

Jake coughed, which was usually a sign he wanted to say something important. So Miranda straightened up and tried to concentrate even though she was so *bloody* tired.

"Babe," he said. "Are you going to take the new medication Diana sorted out for you?"

"Yeah, of course I am," she protested. "Why wouldn't I?"

He snorted with laughter. "Well, because you've not been that good with it before, have you? If we're being honest. And, bloody hell, we should be honest, shouldn't we? I know you say you take it all, but I've found some pills hidden under the edge of the carpet every now and then. I didn't tell Diana. I threw them away because I didn't know what else to do. But I can't go through another hospital episode like you've just had. I really can't. I care about you, Miranda, and I can't bear it if you make things worse than they are. I mean I know things are bloody crap anyway but, please, don't make them any bloodier."

He stopped talking, his voice choking up, and, when she turned to look at him on the sofa, he was crying. He wiped his tears away with the back of his free hand and she squeezed his arm.

"Yes," she said. "I'll take the pills. I'm sorry. I didn't know you knew about the carpet thing, and I'm sorry."

Jake made a noise that was half a sob and half a laugh. "I know you! And when I saw that pulled-up bit of carpet in your bedroom, I knew what I'd find under it. I'm not an idiot."

"No, you're not," she said fiercely. "I know. The pills I was having before were crap. They were crap and they made me feel like crap. And I thought what was the effing point of taking them when I was going to die anyway? I mean, it's just a matter of time, isn't it? What did it matter if I took them or not?"

"It matters to me!" Jake burst out, all but shouting though not at her, not really. "It matters to me and it matters to people who care about you. Seeing you in hospital like you've been this week made me feel afraid, and sick, but mainly afraid. I want you to be here for as long as you can, Miranda, and if it takes all the pills in all the world to give you extra time, then I want you to take them, and I want you to want it too. *Do you understand?*"

Miranda paused. She didn't know if she fully understood. Her head was so crammed with the fact of her own limited time that she didn't know if she had room for what other people, even those closest to her, might feel too. Maybe she'd never fully understand. Maybe that was just how things were but, since being in hospital, something inside had changed. So she nodded.

"Okay," she said. "I mean okay as far as I can anyway. I'm sorry about how the pills thing – and the hospital – made you feel. You know you're the most important thing in the world to me, Jake. I'm sorry I hurt you. I don't know if I can feel any differently about the extra time, and having it or not, but I'll try. I'll honestly try. And I'll take these new pills, as Diana showed me. I promise you that, at least."

"And no more hiding them under the carpet, or anywhere else?"

She could still see tears in his eyes, but there was now a hint of a smile on his lips too. That, more than anything, gave her hope.

"No more hiding the pills," she agreed.

The next day, Jake was back at work, and Miranda spent most of the day asleep, though – as promised – Golda and Frankie did pop in together and visit her late afternoon. She was glad of the company even though she was used to being alone. They didn't stay long – Miranda supposed they could see how tired she was – but their visit made her feel better. Once more, she was surprised how the three of them somehow slotted together as friends even though she supposed they had nothing in common apart from Pilates and a love of cake.

Or maybe that was all you needed to make a friend? It was hard to say. If Miranda had known this truth in school while growing up, maybe life would have been a whole lot easier. Then again, most of the people in her school were horrid, so maybe not. That didn't matter though, as she never had to go to school again and, more than that, she had something to look forward to apart from the unthinkable horror of not being alive, as Golda and Frankie had arranged for her to come over on Saturday to start on her garden.

Miranda wasn't sure she'd be up to cycling across to Golda's, even though it was literally only a few minutes' ride away. But Frankie had said she could pick her up if she needed a lift. They could decide on the day.

During the time before the weekend, Miranda continued to not do very much. She slept a lot. Jake visited, and Diana also visited every day and seemed happy with her progress. By Friday night, Miranda was feeling that all-important bit stronger, but Diana had asked her to go carefully in the garden tomorrow, so she would try to do that.

This thought made her smile – Jake would be amazed if he could see how she was listening to her nurse for the first time! Though, to be honest, Miranda wasn't sure what being careful in the garden meant – she'd never had a garden before so had no idea what to expect, or how to be careful in it. All she wanted was to have those sunshiny colours of cream and yellow and gold around her. It was a chance to start something, when so much – too much – in her life was coming to an end.

When she woke up on Saturday, Miranda wondered briefly if she could after all cycle across to Golda's, but then decided it would be okay to get Frankie to pick her up. By the time Frankie arrived, Miranda had been ready and waiting for about ten minutes.

Whilst they drove, Miranda glanced across at Frankie and thought she looked pale. Was it the pregnancy? She wondered what her friend had decided to do about the baby she was going to have and was about to open her mouth and ask that loaded question when Frankie spoke first.

"I bought some extra garden stuff from home," she said. "I didn't know how much Golda might have and it's better to have too much than too little."

"Garden stuff?" Miranda asked.

"Yes. You know, trowels and garden gloves – we have roses to plant so we'll need to be careful about thorns and anyway gloves are always good. I hate getting my nails dirty."

Miranda nodded her thanks. Did she care about thorns or getting her nails dirty? No, not at all, but she should be grateful for Frankie's organisation skills.

The moment they arrived, Golda was at the door, waiting for them.

"Come in," she said. "I have everything set up outside, along with hats and sun cream. Oh, and the kettle's on as I'm assuming you'd like coffee or tea?"

Yes, coffee would be perfect for Miranda, and tea for Frankie, so Golda poured drinks into mugs, added a plate of biscuits to the tray, and they made their way into the garden.

There, all the plants Miranda could remember choosing were placed in the beds or on the remaining ground in their pots. Just as she'd seen them in the pictures Frankie had shown her in hospital. On the table where Golda put the tray there were also several copies of the garden plan all laid out ready to be used. Frankie had copied them earlier in the week at her office.

Next to this was a work-bench which contained all sorts of items, including trowels, gardening forks, a huge variety of different sorts of gloves, a pile of sun hats, several pairs of sunglasses and more bottles of sun cream than Miranda thought anyone could ever need.

She couldn't help it. She started to laugh.

"What is it?" Golda asked.

Miranda shook her head. "Nothing. It's all fantastic – Frankie was wondering if you'd have enough garden stuff, but *I'm* just wondering how many other people you've asked round today."

"It certainly puts my small offering into perspective," Frankie said, opening the bag of garden items she'd bought so Golda could see. "I don't think these will be needed, that's for sure. Unless there are genuinely at least ten other gardeners coming as well?"

"No, just you," Golda said with a smile. "But you can never be too well-prepared. Besides, it's always good to have choices – nobody wants a fight over which sun hat to wear, do they?"

Miranda supposed that was true, or would have been if a sun hat had ever counted amongst the things on her wish list. Once she'd chosen a hat and a pair of sunglasses she liked the look of, she picked up the plans and smiled.

They started with the roses. For the first one, Miranda shook her head at Golda's offer of a pair of thick gloves but, after she'd battled with the thorns for a few minutes, she changed her mind. In this case, the older woman definitely knew better, Miranda had to admit as she pulled on those all-important gloves and went back to her roses.

It was Golda who showed her how to dig out a hole with her trowel and how to ease the rose from its pot. She absolutely needed those gloves at that point, that was for sure. Who knew gardening could be so dangerous? It always looked like such a gentle thing to do, but there was a lot more to it than she'd imagined.

Before Miranda put her first rose in its new place, Golda started to pick away at the soil around its roots.

"It's a good idea to tease the roots out a bit," she explained. "Before you actually plant it. That way, it stimulates them to grow into the space and settles the plant in better. Plus it helps even more if the plant is pot-bound."

"Pot-bound?" Miranda asked.

"Sorry. That means it's been in its pot for so long that the roots have grown round and round in a really annoying tangle, and it needs to be put somewhere it can have more space."

"Like a garden," Miranda replied. "You really do know a lot about this, don't you?"

Golda smiled. "Gardening has been my salvation. I didn't know anything much when I started, but it was always where I felt happiest, so I learnt as I went along."

Miranda nodded. Everyone had to find something which made them happy, didn't they? She wasn't sure she'd ever found what this was for herself – though cycling came pretty close – and now of course she wouldn't ever get the chance to find out. Though this garden might well help with that, mightn't it? It was what she'd wanted to do this for. A last great push for something positive in her life, before … well … before the end of it all.

Frigging hell, but she sounded overdramatic sometimes. Though it was big, all this, wasn't it? Big and serious too. Too big and serious to think of right now, when the sun was shining and she was at the start of making something beautiful.

Once her first rose was in place, and Golda had showed her how to 'firm it in' by treading gently on the part of the bed just around the rose, Miranda stood back and looked at her handiwork.

"That's the first thing I've ever planted in a garden," she said. "It's lovely, thank you."

To celebrate her success, she treated herself to a biscuit. Then she got back to the business of planting.

At first Miranda wasn't confident she was doing the whole gardening thing right and kept stealing glances at Golda and Frankie to check she was still on track. She'd always thought there was some kind of weird aura about gardening and it was only carried out by very talented or knowledgeable people. But as she quietly got on with digging holes in the bed and planting the roses, she realised maybe it wasn't quite as mystical as she'd thought.

By the time she got to her third plant, the question burning away in her head couldn't be kept inside any longer.

"What happens if one of the plants dies?" she asked.

Golda and Frankie stopped what they were doing and stared at her. She could see they were thinking how best to reply, bearing in mind her own circumstances.

She shook her head. "Honestly, it's just a simple question. It's not related to anything else going on. *Really*."

Golda smiled, though Frankie still looked uncertain.

"That's easy," Golda replied. "If a plant doesn't do well or dies, then we can get another one to replace it."

"Okay," said Miranda. "So why would anything not do well? Is it to do with the plant or is it something else?"

As she asked the question, Miranda wondered if she was in fact thinking about the plants only. Golda, thank fuck, took her question at face value.

"It's hard to say," she pondered, standing up and stretching a little in the sun. "You do get the odd plant that isn't as strong as the others, or there's something in the soil it doesn't take to. A lot of the time, it's impossible to say though there are certain plants which don't like particular types of soil or environment. For instance, a sun-loving plant won't like being put in deep shade, and vice versa. But it's true that some things simply don't thrive, even if you've checked the label and planted it in a spot it's supposed to like."

"So you then replace it?"

"Yes," said Golda.

"But that shouldn't happen in this case, should it?" Frankie chipped in. "All these plants are sun lovers and there's plenty of that here. Hence the need for all the sun cream you've provided for us."

She had a point, Miranda thought, as she turned to her planting mission once more. It was certainly getting hotter by the minute, and she was glad of the hat.

A while later, the three women had filled the first bed with as many roses as they could find room for. Miranda sat back and took in the effect of what they'd achieved so far. The scent was amazing. But far more than the scent was the spectacle of all the roses together in one place.

"Wow!" she said.

Frankie laughed. "I agree. Wow indeed! It does look pretty good so far. Well done to us."

"Yes, it's funny how flowers look even more beautiful when you see them together," Golda said. "I think that's why all the gardening programmes keep on encouraging us to plant at least three, and preferably five, of any one thing so you get the full effect of it."

"Gardening programmes?" Miranda said. "There are programmes to tell you how to do this?"

"Oh yes," said Golda. "There are lots of them. Plus books and articles and all sorts. The world of gardening is big business. But, quite honestly, it's better to get out, have a go and see what works. I've always found that's the best way to learn anything."

Miranda nodded. She could see the sense of what Golda was saying, though she herself would have used TikTok or Snapchat to get the information. Still, in the last half-hour or so, she'd learnt more about this whole garden thing than she'd ever have understood from a book or TV programme, or any social media either.

"There are still another couple of roses we've not planted yet," Golda continued, "but my advice is to put those to one side for the minute and see how we feel later. If we can't find room for them, which I doubt, then we can put them in a pot and use them as back-ups if we need to."

Miranda thought about this for a moment and then shook her head.

"I don't think I want any back-ups," she said, not looking at either Golda or Frankie as she spoke. "I know some things might not survive and it's probably sensible to keep them as spare, but if things die, I don't want to do a second planting. I want to live with that gap if it happens. I want to have it as it is."

When she'd finished speaking, Miranda felt winded but somehow clear inside. As if the words – whatever they might mean for her – had needed to be said and she was glad to have said them.

"All right," said Frankie, her voice low and clear. "I think that's a good idea and we'll do that. Golda?"

Golda blinked for a few seconds and then nodded. "Yes, I understand. No spare pots. We'll plant these two roses once we've got more plants in and we can see where the space is. Is that all right?"

Miranda nodded. "Yes, it is. Thank you."

She turned back to the garden she was making, feeling the eyes of the other two women on her back. She couldn't blame them – she wasn't too sure herself why she'd said what she had, but it seemed important and she would stand by it if she had to.

Luckily, she didn't have to, so instead she pointed at the dahlias before checking with her original plan again. "Shall we plant these ones next?"

And that was exactly what they did. Golda suggested that they put two or three dahlias in the centre of each area and surround them with the geraniums.

At least this time, there weren't any thorns to worry about so Miranda took off her gloves and found this to be so much easier. She could feel the leaves and soil between her fingers as she moved the various pots around until she was happy. Every so often, Golda or

Frankie would make a suggestion, and Miranda would respond, tweaking the would-be arrangements here and there.

By the time they'd got to nearly finishing off the placement in the largest area, Miranda suddenly realised how different she was feeling from usual.

She sat back on the ground and hugged her knees for a moment before looking up.

"Does gardening always make you feel this way?"

Golda smiled. "Very possibly, but what way do you mean exactly?"

Miranda paused for a moment or two, thinking seriously about the question before answering.

"Happier, I suppose," she said. "More relaxed. It's nice to feel the soil. It makes me feel ... I don't know ..."

"Connected?" suggested Frankie, pushing an escaped strand of hair back underneath her sun hat.

"Yes!" Miranda replied. "Connected, that's it! Connected to the earth, I suppose."

Golda nodded. "They say gardening is good for mental health. And you're right about how the soil feels. I prefer gardening without gloves if I can. There's just something about it."

Miranda and Golda smiled at each other. When the three women had placed the final dahlia pots into position, with the geraniums around them, Miranda stood up and stepped back in order to look over what they'd done.

"Amazing," she whispered. "It looks beautiful."

"Yes, it does," Golda agreed. "But let's have a look at it from the other end of your garden as well. We need to consider all angles."

Having done so, Golda suggested a couple of moves for the dahlias and a rethink of the geraniums in one area. That worked better, and Miranda pronounced herself satisfied.

Before getting back to work, Miranda decided now was the time for the question that had been burning inside her all day.

"Have you decided what you're going to do about your baby then, Frankie?" she asked.

Golda drew in a quick, sharp breath and Frankie blinked. Miranda wondered if she should back-track on her words, but her curiosity was overpowering. Besides, surely they couldn't ignore it forever, could they?

"Well," Frankie said, sitting down suddenly at the table. "Well. There's a question. I suppose you could say there've been some developments. Of a sort."

Miranda plonked herself opposite Frankie to listen while Golda poured them all a fresh drink.

"What kind of developments?" Miranda asked.

"I decided against adoption," Frankie replied, clutching her mug in her hands. "I told my husband I was seriously thinking about keeping the baby. It surprised me that I should feel that way now, but there it is. Gareth wasn't happy. Not at all."

"What happened?" Golda said gently.

"He walked out after I'd told him. Said he wanted to think. He didn't come back till very late that night and, when he did, he slept in the spare room. Which is stupid because the bed there is so small. You can't stretch out or anything. And he's been sleeping there since then. Heaven knows what our cleaner thinks as she must realise what's going on. I daren't ask her. Not that I know her that well anyway. I've tried to talk to Gareth a couple of times since then, but he says there's nothing to talk about. Even though there is! So we're just living separate lives at the moment and every day that passes makes it worse. I don't know what to do."

Frankie said all this in a rush, as if the words had been building up inside her for ages and couldn't get out fast enough. Then she started crying. Golda ran and grabbed a box of tissues from the living room while Miranda patted Frankie's arm. Which was the only think she could think of to do right now. What was it with effing men anyway!

"Do you have anyone you can talk to?" Golda asked when Frankie had wiped her tears away. "I mean I know you're talking to us and that's really good, but I mean other people you've known for longer. Or family?"

Frankie shook her head. "That's just it. The people I know – at work or on the village committees – would be so shocked if I told them any of this. I'm just pretending everything in my marriage is fine and nobody's asking any questions of course as they expect everything to be okay. Like it usually is. And I couldn't tell my parents – they live in Spain anyway so that would be no good. We're not that close – they only ever come over once a year at Easter. And

I don't have any brothers or sisters. There's just me. Gareth has always been the only family I've wanted, and now we can't even talk to each other. Honestly, I hate it!"

"I'm so sorry," Golda said. "All I can suggest is that you give it time and keep talking to Gareth. I'm sure he'll come round in the end. From what you say, you have a good marriage and that's something to be treasured. No matter what."

A shadow passed over Golda's face as she spoke, and Miranda wondered what secrets she might be hiding. But she didn't want to ask another question now. Not after the one she'd just asked. So she continued to sit next to Frankie and hold her hand as she drank her tea. What a puzzle the world was. There were so many difficult things out there.

After a while, the three of them got back to work. As they did so, the atmosphere became lighter and even Frankie smiled every now and then. By now, Miranda was almost an expert at getting plants out of pots so the whole process was a lot quicker.

Still, she found she had to have ten minutes' rest after the first bed was done before moving on to the larger section, and she sipped gratefully at the chilled water Golda had fetched for her. It was great to sit in the sun and feel its heat on her skin while she watched the birds come and go from the bird-feeder at the far end of the lawn.

"Do you know what they are?" she asked. "The birds, I mean."

"Blue tits mainly," Golda said as she and Frankie stacked up the empty pots at the side. "Though there is a robin who visits regularly, and I occasionally even see a wren. Nothing special, but I do like watching them."

Miranda laughed. "Honestly, Golda, you know everything, don't you?"

Golda blushed. "I wish I did! I mainly know about the things I like, so that's gardening and any birds that come into the garden. Apart from that, I'm a mine of ignorance. It's you young people who know everything. There's so much information at your fingertips these days whereas, when I was growing up, if we wanted to know something, we either asked our parents or teachers, or went to the library to look it up in a book. We didn't have anything like the internet back then. We didn't even have computers."

Miranda took a moment to take on board the unimagined weirdness of a life without the internet before smiling. "It must have been odd for you when all that computer stuff started then."

316

"Yes, it was," said Golda. "I had to take a course on what to do with computers. It was like a strange new world, I can tell you."

"Handy for keeping in touch with friends or colleagues though," Frankie chipped in, her voice still a little bit wobbly. "I wouldn't be without my WhatsApp work group. A lot easier than having to ring round everyone."

Miranda – unlike most of her generation – didn't much like WhatsApp and had deleted her account ages ago. Jake, as a keen WhatsApp user for bike stuff, had been a bit put out, but she'd been adamant she wasn't going back on it. These days, she was happy to text people – well, Jake, mainly.

She finished her glass of water and went back to work. Though Miranda didn't really think it could be called work, as she was enjoying herself. And she couldn't remember a time lately when that had happened. It made a nice change.

A while later, and the whole of her new and special garden was planted up. Miranda couldn't believe it was done. She'd thought it would take a lot longer than it had – maybe even days – but of course she didn't have any garden experience to compare it with. She also couldn't believe how beautiful it had turned out to be, more beautiful than the plan she'd made and more beautiful than the picture she'd carried in her head.

The roses and dahlias in their various shades of cream and yellow and gold went together brilliantly and the soft greens and whites of the geraniums they'd planted round them created a shimmering base for the whole display. Frigging hell, Miranda thought, she'd gone poetic all of a sudden! It must be the influence of her two friends. They'd even found a space for those spare rose bushes from earlier. The whole thing was effing brilliant.

"I can't thank you enough," Miranda said solemnly. "The garden is so beautiful, and you are both *amazing*."

"That's very kind," said Golda, while Frankie just smiled. "But I think you'll find the plan for this garden is yours and yours alone. We've just been here to help out. So this is entirely your own doing."

"Yes, I agree," Frankie said. "This is yours alone, Miranda, and it's really lovely."

With all that agreed, they celebrated their success with some lunch which Golda had in the fridge and which apparently needed eating up. Miranda soon realised however that Golda's idea of lunch that needed eating up might have been underselling it. Because what came out of the fridge was home-made potato salad with chives, sliced ham, a whole lettuce, some snack-sized pork pies, chopped up tomatoes and cucumber in a lemon and mint dressing (which was pretty yum actually!), all of this accompanied by elderflower cordial and lemonade, and finished off with some tiny cakes which Golda said she'd picked up at the village shop.

Miranda and Frankie looked at each other and smiled, whilst Golda busied herself bringing out crockery and glasses.

"I'm not sure I can eat all this," Frankie whispered while Golda was inside the house.

"Me neither," Miranda whispered back. "But you're eating for two now, and I'm happy to give it a go."

Frankie grimaced and then gave her a smile.

"I suppose I am," she said.

So, the three of them sat at the edge of the brand-new garden and ate their lunch together.

"This must have been what I've been missing all along," Miranda said, as she added more potato salad to her plate.

"What's that?" Frankie asked.

"Making a garden," Miranda explained. "If I'd known gardening was as much fun as this, I would have tried to do some before. It kind of makes you focus just on what you're doing while you're doing it, doesn't it? No matter what other utter crap is going on in your life. If you get what I mean. If you're planting something, you can't think about anything else. You're just thinking about the garden. It's brilliant! Is that why you love it so much, Golda? Did it help you when your husband was ill and after he died? It must have been awful for you when he was gone. You must miss him so much."

Miranda hadn't meant to add those final words – once more, they had just popped out of her mouth and she hadn't been able to stop them. Bloody hell, but she could be a frigging nightmare sometimes!

And when she looked at Golda, she could see her friend's face had turned pale and the fork she'd been lifting was utterly still.

Miranda opened her mouth, this time to say how sorry she was for blurting out something so completely stupid, when Golda spoke first. And what she said was not what Miranda had expected at all.

"I don't miss him in any way," said Golda, slowly. "In fact, I was glad when he was dead."

Chapter Thirteen

Golda

Golda hadn't meant to tell the truth. Not even to these two women who had already been so honest about their lives. That wasn't usually Golda's way as she treasured her privacy with every ounce of her being. But when Miranda had asked the question about Alan's death, something inside her broke open and what she said was the most honest thing she'd ever said in her life.

That didn't stop her wishing she'd not said anything quite so truthful and had kept to the usual sorts of things people said when asked about deaths in the family.

"I'm sorry," she said, feeling her face burn crimson, as both Miranda and Frankie stared at her, eyes wide. "I didn't mean to say that. I shouldn't have said it. It was ridiculous."

Frankie was the first to recover. "Don't be sorry, Golda. You can say anything to us, of course you can. You don't have to be sorry for telling us what you really think. God knows you've listened to enough of my problems in the last weeks. If you didn't like your husband, then you didn't like him. And if you're glad he's dead, then I'm glad too, for your sake."

With that, Frankie poured her a glass of water. Golda took a few swallows and felt instantly calmer.

"Why didn't you like him?" Miranda asked, and her direct approach made Golda smile.

Golda closed her eyes for a moment or two before responding.

"Alan was a cruel man," she said at last, slowly. "In the end. Though when we met, I fell in love with him so very quickly and a part of me always loved him, no matter what. I didn't realise his cruelty when we met and not for a while after we were married."

And then Golda told them how her married life had been and how she'd slowly come to fear her own husband. They listened without interrupting to what she said, and she was grateful as she didn't think she could deal with any questions. Golda still had enough questions of her own, as to why she'd put up with it for so long and why she'd stayed. Questions she could never now answer.

She kept her story brief, but when she came to that terrible holiday in Norfolk, Miranda gasped and gripped her arm as Golda told them what had happened on the journey.

"The bastard!" she whispered. "The utter *bastard*. I'm glad he's dead, and I hope he died horribly. Please tell me he did, Golda. What a *fucking* bastard."

Her passion made Golda smile, even in the midst of telling her friends about the disaster that had been her marriage. But she couldn't help but wonder how they would both feel about what had come next, after Alan's diagnosis.

Back then – and how it seemed like a lifetime ago – the cancer had hit her husband hard. Treatments weren't as effective as they would become, and the attempts to cure him, or at least slow the cancer down, were bloody. Alan had a nurse, the same kind as Miranda had today, but of course he was furious he had to accept this kind of help. The nurse did what she could, but he was never an easy patient.

Golda liked this nurse very much. She liked her even though she had to hide so much of what she was doing from the woman's watchful eye. Because Golda wasn't providing the kind of support for her dying husband the nurse should have expected. Something changed inside her the moment she knew how ill he was and that he would die from this disease. Before Alan's cancer, she'd thought of herself as a decent woman – a terrified one, yes, but a decent and kind-hearted one. After his diagnosis, none of that was true.

Where Golda should have been supporting Alan, looking after him and making sure he was as comfortable as he could be as he slowly and agonisingly set about the business of dying, she was instead doing the exact opposite – or as much as she thought she could get away with without the nurse or any of the doctors noticing anything.

After his treatments, she would pinch his arm at the place where the drip had been set up as he lay exhausted so that he groaned in pain. She would 'accidentally' let the scissors slip when she was cutting his nails every now and again so that she drew blood. She didn't make any of his favourite foods – not that he could eat much anyway – but instead provided the things he'd always hated: spinach, carrots and lamb. She would leave him for two or three hours at a time and go out walking or shopping when she knew the nurse wouldn't be there and, if he'd messed the bed when she returned, Golda would take her good time cleaning him up and changing his clothes. Once when he'd wet himself after the nurse had left for the evening, Golda didn't change him until the hour before the nurse was due to return in the morning and she remembered how happy she'd felt at his fury and how ineffective that fury was. Alan couldn't hurt her, not now, not in the state he was in. Instead, it was Golda's turn to hurt him, and how good that had felt.

Yet, even when she was doing all these terrible and inhumane things to a dying man, Golda understood how petty it was, and how mean. But she also knew how good it felt to be giving Alan a taste of the terrible and inhumane treatment he'd given to her for so long. More than anything, Golda didn't want him to die in peace, not after he'd caused her so much misery. She wanted him to stay alive for as long as possible so he could understand in some way how it had been for her all these years.

She also wanted him to die.

And so, even though she knew in her inmost being exactly how cruel she was being, she kept on doing it. Every time Golda caused her husband pain, she counted it off against the balance sheet of all the times he'd mistreated or abused her, though even then the scales would never be equal, would they? There was little Alan could do about it. A couple of times he complained to the nurse and told

Golda he'd done it too, but the nurse must have thought he was hallucinating as she never said anything about it. Golda simply smiled at him and said nothing. After that, his eyes followed her around the room, and his expression was halfway between confused and afraid. As if he couldn't understand why she would be like this, and it was this lack of understanding that made her carry on her secret cruelty.

When his drug needs became more pressing, in that last month before he died, Golda even started giving him fewer of the painkillers than the nurse had recommended and then, sometimes, none at all. By then, she was worried she might be found out so she simply flushed those she didn't use down the toilet. She knew he suffered more because of what she did, but she was glad of it. And then shocked at herself for feeling that way.

The end for Alan came sooner than the doctors thought it would, though – as the nurse told Golda as she held her hand – there were no guarantees with cancer. All bets, as she said back then, were off. That last week, there were duty nurses in the house all the time, so there wasn't much she could do to hurt Alan. He wasn't eating and all he could do was lie in bed waiting for death to come.

The main nurse had suggested he would be better off in a hospice, but Golda shook her head at that idea. Not because she was the kind of loving wife who wanted her husband to die at home, in familiar surroundings. Not at all. No, it was because she absolutely didn't want him to be comfortable during his final days. She wanted him to die in the kind of pain and torment he'd made her live in.

Yes, Golda knew how much of a monster that made her, but it was the driving force of all she did and felt on her road to becoming a widow at last.

In the end, Alan died in his sleep. The duty nurse woke her at 3.04am – Golda would always remember the time – and gently said it was probably best she should say her goodbyes now. Golda struggled to keep the joy and relief from her face and instead to appear shocked and serious, as normal wives would do.

The night was cold – it was winter – but the main bedroom where Alan laying dying was warm as a portable heater had been left on. Her husband's breathing was harsh and loud as if he couldn't find enough air.

"I don't think he has long," the nurse whispered. "I'm so sorry. I'll leave you with him for a few minutes."

And then Golda was on her own with him. She supposed she should sit on the bed next to this man she had once loved, but had learnt to hate and fear, or even hold his hand until he died, but she did neither of those things. Instead, she crouched down next to him and spoke quietly but with intent the words she held inside.

"You have been the worst and cruellest husband to me," Golda said, not knowing if he could hear her but hoping he could. "Not at the start. I loved you so much then, Alan, but you killed that love and now I wish with all my heart I'd never met you. I wish we had never been married. I hope you die in pain soon and, when you are dead, I will walk away from the life you made me live and never think of you again. Or, if I do, it will be with pleasure that you're no longer alive, I promise you."

There was nothing more she wanted to say. For a few minutes, the only sound apart from the hum of the heater was her husband's stuttering breath. Then, as she was looking at him, his eyes opened and stared up at her for a moment. They were clouded and full of fear. The kind of fear she'd learnt to live with. Golda turned away from the bed, and it was then that his breathing stopped.

She waited for a few minutes to be sure he was gone. Then she smiled before composing her face to what others expected it to be and went to find the nurse.

The funeral was as small and quiet as she could make it. People kept offering their condolences until Golda thought she might scream the truth out at them, but she never did. They would never understand. The only thing that got her through the lies and deceit she had to pretend to during those weeks was the utter wash of relief that she was finally free. She felt as if she'd been living inside a cage where she couldn't open the door, let alone find the key, and then suddenly the cage disappeared, and she could breathe again.

Golda wrote to the woman who had once helped her. The woman she'd met in the service station on the way to Norfolk, the one who had been so astonishingly kind. She used the address of the refuge on the card she'd given her which she still had, and hoped they would know who the woman was and pass it on. Golda simply reminded her of how they'd met and said that her husband was dead now and she was free, and she wrote to say thank you as well, because it had been waiting for a long time. She didn't say anything about how Alan had died or how she'd treated him while he was dying. This was for her to know, and her alone. It was a private matter, or so Golda believed. She didn't give an address so she knew the woman could never write back, if she ever received it. And she made sure to post it from a town an hour's drive away and not to put her name.

Of the many good things arising from the death of Golda's husband, his unexpected wealth was one of them. She hadn't known he'd saved so much money during his life – he'd always kept his finances secret and she had never dared ask. She'd never even thought of it. But it meant she didn't have to worry about money, and she would never have to. It was a blessing she hadn't expected, but she knew deep down how much she deserved it after the years of pain.

Eventually, Golda sold the house and moved several times before settling into the village she lived in today. When she moved the first time, she took nothing to remind her of Alan. Some of his things she burnt, and others she threw away. She didn't have the heart to give anything he'd owned to charity – she didn't want other people to have in their possession anything touched or worn by a cruel man. So she got rid of it all.

And when that was done, Golda walked away from the life she'd known and started again. She never looked back.

When, at last, Golda finished her story, there in the quiet peace of her garden, she felt as if a dark place buried inside her had somehow been made brighter. She wondered what her two friends would think and for a moment felt the kind of gripping fear she'd not felt for so very long, not since Alan had been alive.

She hadn't needed to worry. When she opened her eyes, Golda could see Frankie was crying. Her friend got up, hunkered down next to Golda and wrapped her arms around her.

"You poor, poor thing," Frankie whispered, her voice thick with tears. "I'm so very sorry you've been through those awful things. What a truly horrible man. I'm so glad he's dead, and you're quite right to feel as you do about him dying. You poor thing."

"Too bloody true!" Miranda chipped in. "What a total bastard! You're lucky to be rid of a shit loser like that, Golda. And I'm glad you paid him back before he died – though if it had been me, I would have been far nastier. You should have taken his fucking drip out and shoved it so far up his arse that it came out of his mouth. That would have finished him off good and proper! What a *wanker*."

Golda turned in amazement to Miranda, who looked furious on her behalf. As if the younger woman would jump up and kill Alan herself if he suddenly appeared in front of them.

"Miranda!" said Frankie. "That's … that's …!"

"… the right thing to say?" Miranda cut in. "And isn't it good you never had his children! Who wants those kind of genes in the world?"

Frankie opened her mouth again, but nothing came out. And suddenly and unexpectedly, Golda started to laugh.

"Yes, you're right," she said. "Alan's genes definitely wouldn't have been welcome. I used to think he might have been kinder if we'd had a family, but it never happened for us, and now I think that's a good thing. After all, it wouldn't have been a very happy environment for any child to grow up in, would it?"

For a moment, Golda worried she might have said too much, especially bearing Frankie's situation in mind. There was a brief silence and then Frankie sat back and started to smile, though with a touch of wryness. Miranda simply shrugged.

"Now, Miranda," Golda continued. "Just think, if only you'd been there, I might have escaped from my marriage a lot earlier than I did."

When her two friends left, they both gave Golda a gentle hug. Miranda, however, added a wink as she let go.

"Definitely should have been meaner to the nasty fucker," she whispered so Frankie couldn't hear.

Which only made Golda laugh again. And that, surely, was something good.

Indeed, it was amazing how much lighter she felt. She'd told the deepest, darkest truth about herself and hadn't been judged. Certainly not as much as she'd judged herself over the years, in spite of her promise to walk away and never look back. And that, surely, was a gift Golda had never expected to be granted.

Chapter Fourteen

Frankie

When Frankie got home, after the big day of garden creation and after Golda's startling confession, the first thing she did was go straight to the living room and sit down. Gareth was out at the shops but would be back soon, according to his text message. He hadn't added any kisses as he usually di, but at least she knew where he was. That was progress of a sort, wasn't it?

It had certainly been a day to remember, but for sad reasons as well as good ones. Though the good reasons were always going to be sad as well, weren't they? Because of Miranda and because of the whole purpose of making this garden. Frankie had expected she would be both happy and sad. The main thing was it achieved what Miranda wanted to do and she thought it had definitely done that.

What Frankie hadn't expected was for Golda to open up about her past and how her marriage had been. She'd felt like crying when the older woman had been telling her story and she felt like crying now. What a truly horrible man Golda's husband had been. She couldn't imagine being with someone like that for so long. How lucky she was in Gareth, she thought. No matter what problems they were having now, she was so very lucky in ways she'd never truly considered. She, like Miranda, was glad Golda's husband was dead and she understood completely why Golda had been less than supportive while her husband was dying.

Frankie thought about everything for a while longer, and then she made a cup of tea, added a teaspoon of sugar as she felt she needed it, and sat down to do more thinking.

She pondered how Golda had been stuck in an abusive marriage and hadn't been able to free herself from it. Not until her husband was dead. She didn't know why Golda's husband had been a cruel man and she certainly wasn't going to ask her new friend for more details she might not want to give. Friendship wasn't just about sharing things, was it? It was equally important to accept and live with the silences. The same for marriage too, she supposed. Though the current silence in her own marriage wasn't a good one, was it?

Still, it seemed such a waste for Golda. All that time married and then only truly being free when her husband was dead. If she was Golda, Frankie would have been bitter. She was sure of it. But Golda didn't appear to be bitter. From the short time Frankie had known her, Golda seemed to be perfectly happy in her life. She'd had no idea about her new friend's past. Until today, Frankie had assumed Golda's life had been a good one, with the only real sorrow in it being the death of her husband. But the truth was utterly opposite. The good thing had in fact been Alan's death, and the life Golda had created for herself afterwards.

She'd also assumed Miranda's life was normal though, hadn't she? Whereas in fact it was anything but that. She was glad Golda – and Miranda as well – had felt able to trust her with some of their secrets, as she had trusted them with hers.

Funny how with some people – no matter how unlikely in terms of age or life experiences – you just clicked. It was a gift, Frankie supposed. A real gift.

And another gift she'd not thought of until today was Golda's ability to move on and recreate her own happiness, in spite of what she'd had to go through and the feelings of guilt she'd carried with her. Golda hadn't allowed trauma or personal difficulties to dictate her life now, but could she, Frankie, say the same?

Not that the circumstances were remotely similar: Golda had survived years of domestic abuse and was now living the life she wanted to live; whereas Frankie herself was merely pregnant and going through some challenging marital issues because of that fact. Surely these issues were temporary. Oh God, she hoped so! She couldn't bear it if Gareth actually decided to leave her because of the baby. Would he do such a thing? No! Because it would be insane, wouldn't it? She and Gareth loved each other – Frankie knew this truth as if it had been written on her heart even before she'd been born – and she would fight for the two of them, and for her marriage, no matter what. The *three* of them now.

The three of them.

Frankie looked down where she sat on the sofa and, for the first time ever, she laid a careful hand on her stomach. There was a baby in there. Somewhere. An actual baby. Made from Gareth and from herself in a blend of blood and flesh and bone she couldn't even begin to imagine. A fierce surge of love swept through her that she'd never expected to feel and the power of it made her gasp.

They were going to be a family. She and Gareth. They were going to be parents. And it was the scariest and most beautiful thing in the whole world. In the whole *effing* world, as Miranda would say. It was the scariest and most beautiful thing and she, Frankie, was going to fight for it. With every single breath she had. And for as long as it took.

Ridiculously, she started to laugh and then almost at once started to cry. And it was in that position of laughing and crying that Gareth found her when he came home ten minutes later.

"Frankie, what is it?" he rushed to give her a hug where she sat, which was exactly what she needed. And as if all the recent terrible tension between them had never been there at all. "Are you all right? I'm so sorry I've made you cry. And I'm so very sorry for being an utterly stupid idiot in how I've treated you over all this. It's not your fault, I see that now. I'm sorry I've been so distant. I've needed time to think things through but that doesn't excuse my behaviour to you. I love you, Frankie. Please, can you forgive me?"

This was surely more than Gareth had said to her for ages and it made her cry even more as she hugged him back.

"Yes! Yes of course," Frankie replied when she could talk again. "I know you needed time to think. That's okay. And you know I love you too. So very much. You have no idea how much! But, Gareth, I need to tell you something. And it's important. Very important."

Gareth took hold of her hand. "Okay. Go ahead."

"It's always just been the two of us, I know," Frankie told him. "But now, no matter what happens, it's more than that. There are three of us. We're a family and, whether you stay with me or whether you don't, this is still your child, and always will be. I want you to know that."

It might have been the hardest thing she'd ever said, but she knew she had to say it. He blinked and gazed at her, a look of concern in his eyes.

"Frankie, I'm not going to leave you," he said quietly. "Not because of this and not ever."

"But I know you don't want to be a father," she replied. "You've never wanted to have children. And even though I was the same and never wanted them either, I've changed my mind. But just because I have, it doesn't mean you have to as well. I do see that."

"Yes," he said, running his free hand through his hair, which left it sticking up in strands Frankie longed to smooth down. "That's what I thought too. But, as I said, I've been doing some thinking and talking, and things seem a bit clearer now."

"Talking?" Frankie asked, with half a smile even in this difficult conversation.

Gareth half-smiled back. "Yes. Talking. In a way. I thought I needed a sounding-board and didn't know who that could be if it wasn't you. And I didn't want to talk to my sister or my parents when everything was so up in the air for you and me. I just couldn't do that. So I signed up for some online counselling, even though I hate that kind of thing, and actually it's been helpful."

"What?" Frankie couldn't help her reaction. "You? Counselling? *Really?"*

"Yes, I know! Your strong, silent husband talking to a counsellor. Who'd have thought it? See! You're not the only one around here who can make big changes in their life, are you?"

For a long moment, there was utter silence in the living-room. And then, in the manner of all basically strong marriages everywhere, the two of them began to laugh. Holding hands on the sofa, Frankie and Gareth laughed and then looked at each other and laughed again. Until all the pain and confusion they'd been experiencing had melted away in the warmth of what each of them meant to the other.

"So, what did you discover when you were having counselling?" Frankie asked. "Oh! Am I allowed to know? You don't have to tell me if you don't want to. I know these things are private."

"That's fine," Gareth replied. "I do want to tell you. The counsellor – he's called Peter, by the way – did a lot of listening and helped me to see things in a different light. He basically reminded me that being a father isn't unusual, whether it's been planned for or not, and that lots of men are worried about it. I wasn't alone. That made me feel better for a start. And then we talked about you and our marriage, and Peter pointed out that you and I seemed to be a pretty good team."

"Which we are!" Frankie agreed.

"Yes, indeed. And then Peter moved on to asking me if there were any good points I could see about being a father. And I realised that there were. But there was one major good point that really changed my mind about it all."

"Oh? What was that?"

Gareth smiled. "The child will have half of your genes in it, Frankie, and that, as far as I'm concerned, is the best start in life anyone could ever have."

There was nothing she could say to that. Nothing that wouldn't make Frankie cry all over again. In a good way. So instead, she reached across and kissed him.

When the kiss had finished, Gareth hugged her once more and then said, "There's something I bought for you this week. Well, for us both. It arrived at work yesterday and it's still in the car. Would you like to see it?"

"I'd love to," she said.

Her husband hurried outside and Frankie followed him into the hallway. She heard the slamming of the car boot and then Gareth was at the front door, struggling with an enormous box.

"What on earth is that? What have you bought?" she asked.

"Open it and see," he said, carrying the present into the kitchen. "If you don't like it, I can send it back and get something else. But I saw it and thought it might be perfect. See what you think."

Frankie opened the box and took a breath when she saw what it contained.

It was a cot.

Gareth gently took it out of the box and placed it on the kitchen table for Frankie to see. It was a thing of beauty and so simple in design. The headboard had teddy bear carvings on it which were repeated around the rest of the frame, and the wood was smooth and light in colour. Alongside the cot was a matching set of yellow bedding decorated with darker yellow teddy bears. For their baby. For their family.

Frankie turned towards Gareth and took hold of his hands, feeling their warmth within her own.

"It's the most beautiful thing I've ever seen," she said.

Chapter Fifteen

Miranda

It happened in her kitchen. It was weird as she'd known for about a week that things in her head hadn't been right. More frigging not right than usual. On the second day of these weird sensations – which she'd not told anyone about, not her nurse, and not even Jake – Miranda stood in her bathroom and stared at her reflection in the mirror.

She looked pale. So very pale. Her blue eyes stood out more than usual, somehow making her look like a ghost. Her head hurt a lot too, though she was used to her head hurting. Too used to it.

Her reflection blinked and looked as if it were about to say something incredibly important. Miranda wondered what it might say, her image in the mirror. She saw her lips move and words come out. They weren't what she had imagined.

"Is this it?" she heard her reflection say. "Is this going to be it now? I don't know if I'm ready."

She waited for a while, but her reflection gave her no answer. So she got on with her week – which was basically resting, taking a stupid number of drugs, listening to her doctors and being with her nurse and of course with Jake. She also went to see her garden and spent some time with her two friends. She'd done a tiny amount of watering but then had to sit down because she was so tired, and let Golda and Frankie finish off the task. They did the weeding too, while she sat and sipped her glass of water, and breathed in the scent of the roses.

It was lovely being in her garden. Miranda tried to hang on to every moment she spent there, but it was hard to do as time didn't stop just because that was what she wanted. Looking at the flowers made her happy, and it made her happy too when she could enjoy a small bunch of them at home. Their scent in her flat covered the smell of vomit from when she was sick – and she was increasingly being sick now, especially in the afternoons – and it covered the smell of her fear too. Which she definitely didn't like to think about. She was, in all honesty, trying to live in the moment but only when the moment was good – and that too was harder than she'd ever thought possible.

Still, she kept on trying. She'd thought about taking photos of her day, but she wouldn't get time to look at them, would she? And if she did spend time looking at the pictures she'd taken, it would mean she wasn't paying attention to the moment as it actually happened. So Miranda tried to fix each small part of the day in her mind as a special treasure. It did seem to help her a bit, and at the very least it meant she wasn't then thinking about the time to come when she wouldn't be able to see or think anything.

Oh no, she definitely wasn't thinking about that. Was she? Well, maybe she was, but she was trying not to. Because there wasn't an effing thing she could do about it, was there? Bloody cancer. Her *bloody* luck. She was doing the best she could do and that was all there was to it.

It happened in the kitchen. She and Jake had been chatting in her living room. He'd been moaning about work and then talking about some new colleague who'd just arrived. He'd told Miranda her name but she couldn't remember it right now. The information had gone straight into her head and out again, even though she'd been concentrating on what Jake had been saying. Weird, that.

Miranda had gone into the kitchen to switch on the kettle. A simple task. Nothing difficult about it. Then she was standing near the sink though she couldn't recall getting there. Had she been in the living room just now? She was at home, wasn't she? Who was here with her? Jake? She couldn't remember.

Kettle. The kettle. She needed a coffee. That would be good – she could almost taste it already. And then there was an explosion of colour in her head – how did that happen? And after the explosion, a strange silence and then the walls around her were dancing. And all the stuff in the kitchen was dancing too: the taps, the cups, the kettle. For a long moment, it was the most beautiful thing Miranda had ever seen and then it vanished away, and there was only darkness.

She didn't know how long the darkness lasted, or how long she lay in it. Whatever was going on, it was weirdly peaceful. She could sense movement every now and again, and also the occasional hum of voices from a long way away. The voices didn't interfere with the darkness though or with the soft beat-beat-beat of her heart. She could hear that all right. It gave her comfort. She would be quite happy to stay here.

Then there was nothing for a while, so she must have slept. And when she woke up, the darkness had gone, and she couldn't hear her heart as much as she could before. But it must be doing its job though as she was definitely breathing.

When she opened her eyes, the inrush of light – so different from the darkness she'd loved so much – made her gasp and moan, and she felt the touch of someone holding her hand.

"Hello there," a voice whispered. "You're awake then."

It took Miranda a moment or two to recognise the voice. It was Diana, her special nurse. She blinked and tried to smile, but her face felt funny. When she tried to speak and ask what had happened and where she was now, she couldn't form the words and instead what came out of her mouth was nothing more than a series of grunts and moans. She felt Diana grip her hand even more tightly.

"Don't worry," said Diana, leaning over the bed so Miranda could see her whole face. "Try not to talk. You've had a major episode in terms of your health, and you fainted in your kitchen. That was a couple of days ago but luckily Jake was there with you. He heard you fall and called the ambulance. And then he called me. You went to hospital and they did a series of tests. And then, this morning, you were brought here."

Miranda moaned again, trying to make her groan into a question she desperately needed to be answered. By some miracle, Diana understood her and nodded.

"Yes," she said. "You're in the hospice, as we discussed, and we're making you as comfortable as we can. It's a lovely room, and Jake has brought in some things from your flat to make it more familiar. And your two gardening friends have brought you some flowers too."

Miranda took a breath and screwed up her eyes. She could smell roses. She'd thought that was yet another trick her brain was playing on her, but they were real. She opened her eyes again and turned ever so slightly towards the scent. The movement caused a flash of pain to jump through her head, but she tried not to think about that. She could see the vase now, filled to the brim with large cream and gold roses, the shape of them so utterly perfect that it all but made her cry. She turned slowly back to Diana and smiled. At least she could still do that. She felt far too tired to even think of trying to form words.

She remembered discussing hospice care with Diana, of course she did. It was just it had seemed very distant when they'd been talking about it. Somehow, Miranda had assumed she would die at home, quickly, without any frigging fuss. It was what she'd hoped for. It was what she'd thought she'd wanted. But she was glad of the flowers and the chance to see them once again. She was glad too of the items Jake had provided which she could see on the table: the cushion from her bed; her favourite mug; and a photo of her on her bike which had been taken a couple of years ago. She'd always loved that picture.

She wondered if she'd ever be able to go out on her bike again and then at once decided not to think about it because she was being stupid, wasn't she? If she was here, in the hospice, then this was finally, absolutely, the end.

Diana was holding her hand, and she was still speaking.

"Jake's here, Miranda, if you would like to see him? Your two garden friends are here too but I think you should only see one at a time as you've only just woken up. I'm assuming Jake first and then see how you go?"

Miranda nodded. Her head was a strange place – half in pain and half singing with words she couldn't make out – so nodding was all she could do.

Diana let go of her hand and Miranda closed her eyes. She could have sworn it was just for a moment but when she opened them again, Jake was sitting next to her on a chair near her bed. She'd not

heard him come in. How long had she been asleep?

She tried to smile at him, but she wasn't sure how that was

working out as her mouth didn't feel right.

"Hello, Miranda," Jake said, not sounding like himself. "Babe,

don't worry about talking. Diana said you might have difficulty with

that, but don't worry. You gave me a bloody scare in the kitchen,

you know! Please try not to do that again. At least not on my bloody

watch, eh? Mind you, you look a lot better than you did then, so

good to know the doctors are doing their job. That's one thing to be

thankful for, isn't it?"

Then he burst into tears, and Miranda felt her heart crack. She

felt as if she were flying and drowning at the same time. Not a

feeling she liked. She reached towards his arm where it rested on the

sheet and touched his skin. It felt warm and somehow it grounded

her. She snorted, trying to offer him both comfort and strength

without the use of words, and he half-laughed, half-cried again. Then

he wiped away his tears and took hold of her hand.

"Yeah, I know," he said and this time he sounded more like the

Jake she knew and loved. "I need to man up a bit, don't I? Thank

God you're here to sort me out, babe. Try and hang on a bit, won't you? I don't know if that's what I'm supposed to say or not. Fuck knows. But I love you so much, Miranda. Always have and always will. I want you to know that."

But she did know it already. She always had. And she felt the same about him, this special friend she felt she'd always known. She wanted to say exactly the same to him but could only smile her weird smile again and squeeze his hand.

She didn't know how long he stayed but she must have drifted off to sleep again – shit, what was she like! – as when she next woke, Jake was gone and Diana was in the room. The nurse was studying her wall chart which Miranda couldn't see as it was behind the bed but it must have been interesting as Diana's face was a picture of concentration. Miranda stirred slightly, and Diana at once hunkered down and gazed kindly at her.

"Jake's gone now," the nurse whispered. "But he's here in the waiting room if you would like to see him again. Golda and Frankie are here as well. You can see them if you would like? As you've stabilised a bit more, I can send them both in."

Miranda nodded and again must have dozed off as when she woke up, her two friends were sitting next to her. She hoped they'd not been sitting there too long. Golda was holding her hand, but the two women were having a quiet conversation together so hadn't yet realised she was awake.

She made a groaning sound to let them know, and they stopped speaking to each other at once and turned their attention to her. Miranda wanted to thank them for the roses, for everything they'd done, but instead she settled for a smile and turned her face towards those wonderful flowers, breathing in the scent once more as she did so.

She hoped they got the message. They spoke for a while then, both of them, but she couldn't understand what they were saying. Not that it mattered. Because the important thing was they were there and she took comfort from them. She thought she might have tried to say Jake's name and maybe one of them had understood as she was sure Jake arrived too, with Diana, and they were all there, surrounding her.

This felt so good. It was funny how the important people in her life were here with her now, and it was all that really mattered.

Maybe there were people from her past who should have mattered too – her foster families and the people she'd known when she was growing up, for instance, or maybe even effing *boyfriends* – but Miranda couldn't bring herself to care enough about her own past to think about them. It was the present moment and the people she knew now that counted, wasn't it?

And then there was just Diana and it was so annoying how she couldn't speak to her nurse, not properly, as there was something she wanted to do – two somethings actually – and she had to work out a way of letting Diana know. And then she must have made her meaning clear because Diana brought the things she wanted and sat beside her and helped her as she used them. The task was simple but it seemed to take ages, or maybe that was because working out how much time had passed or not passed was beyond her. And when finally Miranda had finished, and Diana had tidied everything away and promised her she would do what needed to be done, time seemed to be coloured like a rainbow and perfect in every possible way, in all the ways Miranda had ever imagined or hoped for, but had never dreamed could be possible.

And she closed her eyes and felt the amazing colours fill her up inside until she had no more room for anymore and until she felt utterly and absolutely free.

Chapter Sixteen

Frankie

It was stupid. Frankie knew it but she couldn't help it. It wasn't as if she hadn't been to funerals in the past. Of course she had. Her grandmother's, to name only one. But she was sobbing like a child and she couldn't stop herself. She was here in the smallest room in the local crematorium, gripping Gareth's hand as if she'd never let it go, and feeling Golda's arm around her shoulders from the other side.

Jake was standing at the front, saying a few words about his lovely and very special friend. He'd started out shakily but had gained courage as he continued to speak. She didn't know where he found the strength from. She couldn't concentrate on what he was saying. All she could think about was Miranda's face when her garden had been completed, and then how small and tired she'd looked in the hospice bed. She didn't know if Miranda had heard what Golda and she had said when they were there. Not that they'd said much. Golda had talked about the garden and how beautiful it was and how happy Miranda should be that she'd thought of it and created it. Golda's words were what Frankie had wished she'd said, but in fact her sole contribution at Miranda's bedside was to take hold of the dying girl's hand and tell her how much they would miss her, even though they'd not known her for very long.

She didn't know if it was the right thing to say, but it was all she had to offer. It seemed so unfair that Miranda was dead and they were here in this crematorium, remembering her. When instead, Miranda should be alive, riding her bike, weeding her garden, taking flowers home to enjoy in her tiny flat. If there was any justice, that's what she should be doing. She had been too young to be dead, and Frankie was emptied out inside with the injustice of it.

There weren't that many people present, which was why they were in the Crematorium's smallest room. Diana the Macmillan nurse was in attendance, sitting across the aisle. And behind her there was a scattering of what must be other nurses and doctors, as Diana had been chatting with that group when they arrived. Frankie didn't recognise them.

Behind them was a small group of younger men and women and it was in this group where Jake had been sitting. Frankie imagined they might be Miranda's old work friends or perhaps people from school or who had known her when she was growing up. She wasn't sure. So there were no more than twenty people here to say goodbye. It wasn't enough, not for a life. Not really.

The funeral seemed to last forever, and then suddenly it was over. The coffin – which was so very small! – had gone and she, Gareth and Golda were out in sunlight, and she was still blinking away tears. It was the end of August and the sun felt cruel.

Then Jake was in front of them. His face was stained with tears, which he didn't wipe away.

"Thank you for coming today," he said, hesitantly, though of course they had come. Why would they not? "Miranda would have loved you being here."

"Thank you for thinking of us," Golda said, and thank goodness she did because Frankie couldn't think of any words at all. Not now. "We appreciate it, Jake, as I know we weren't friends with Miranda for very long. I very much wish we had been."

Frankie nodded at this, and Gareth pulled her close.

Jake smiled briefly and then said, "I didn't get the chance to let you know but we're having a small get-together at the pub down the road. Nothing formal as Miranda would have hated that. Please, you're all more than welcome to come."

Golda glanced briefly at Frankie and must have picked up on her thoughts as she thanked Jake but said she didn't think they were quite up to it. A sentiment with which Frankie could only agree. She wanted nothing more than to be at home with Gareth, somewhere familiar where she could be herself, and start to think things through at her own pace.

Jake understood and left them. As Frankie watched him disappearing back into the group of friends he'd come with, she wondered if she or Golda would see him again. Miranda had been the connection with Jake, and now Miranda had gone. Then Golda was hugging her goodbye and walking away to get into her car to drive home.

And it was just Frankie and Gareth, getting into their car also. Preparing to drive home and get on with the rest of their lives, and all the time moving away from Frankie's unlikely friendship with Miranda. Because Frankie had enjoyed Miranda's company, even though the younger woman had been so very spiky and direct, and she was sorrier than she could say that she would not see her friend again. She had Miranda's printed-out text in her handbag – the last thing she had ever done, according to Diana. It had been sent to Golda and to herself, and Frankie had read it over and over since receiving it. There'd been a separate message for Jake too, but of course she would never know what that had said. It was private. When Frankie first read her note, she'd laughed and she'd cried, at the same time, and it had given her a great deal to ponder on.

It seemed hard to turn from all this, and think about the future, but she knew she had to do so. She and Gareth had made their choice and, one day soon, their baby would be here and they would be a family. How everything had changed since she, Miranda and Golda had become friends. Odd friends, yes, as they were all so very different from each other, but they'd somehow muddled through and they'd even made a beautiful garden, for Miranda. That was something positive, wasn't it? Something to hang on to. Maybe it was true that good things could come from terrible circumstances. That had been true of their friendship, and it was proving true at a more personal level for Frankie and Gareth, as they prepared for parenthood together.

"Are you ready?" Gareth asked her gently.

"Yes," she nodded. "I think so. Let's go home."

Chapter Seventeen

Golda

Golda thought the funeral was what Miranda would have wanted it to be. Yes, there hadn't been many people there, but Miranda wasn't the type of woman to have huge numbers of friends, so it didn't much matter. She hadn't been able to cry – not then – although this was probably a good thing as poor Frankie had been unable to hold in her grief. Golda had tried to comfort her, but hadn't been sure anything she said or did would be helpful. Sometimes grief was what people had to go through. It was the price they all paid for being alive.

Jake had given a very moving speech, and Golda wondered if in fact he'd been in love with Miranda all along. It wasn't something she'd thought about before, but perhaps there'd been more between them than she'd imagined. She hoped so, for Miranda's sake. No matter how long or short life was, it was important to have love in it in some way or other.

Here, back home, the day after the funeral, Golda wondered if love had ever been a positive force in her own life. In her marriage, it hadn't lasted, had it? In fact, in the end, love had turned to hatred. But love took many forms, didn't it? Love could be kindness, it could be the simple duty of looking out for other people and offering help where it was needed, whether or not that help was taken up. Oh yes, it could be that too.

And it could be friendship. Miranda had been her friend, for a short time, yes, but Golda would miss her. On a whim, she went outside, took a chair and sat in the space Miranda had made her own for a while. It was early evening, and Golda could hear the call of a song thrush nearby and the faint hum of the occasional car on the road outside. The smell of the roses Miranda had planted filled the air and it was this, more than anything, that brought the tears to her eyes at last. Miranda would never smell this glorious scent again and never feel the rich warmth of soil between her fingers.

After a while longer, Golda wiped away her tears. She took out the message Miranda had sent them at the very end of her life, and which Frankie had printed out for her. Thank goodness she had, as Golda would never have worked out how to do it. She was of the generation that preferred to read things from paper rather than on a screen, and so she'd been grateful for Frankie's concern and her organisational skills. When she thought about it, Golda was sure Frankie was going to make an excellent mother indeed.

She unfolded Miranda's note and read it again. The words made her smile. Closing her eyes, Golda remembered the secrets of her marriage she'd shared with Miranda and Frankie, here in this beautiful garden.

She'd told them everything, and they'd not judged her for it. Her hatred for Alan and how she'd wanted him to die in pain for what he'd done to her. They'd listened to it all. That was a precious and perfect gift.

So Golda sat and thought for a while. About life and how cruel it could be, but also how unexpected and how wonderful. She folded Miranda's note up and put it carefully back in her pocket. For another half-hour, she sat there quietly, listening to the birdsong and gazing at the flowers. There and then, she decided what to do with Miranda's garden. She gathered her thoughts and went inside.

Chapter Eighteen

Miranda's Text

For Golda and Frankie, my 2 fav pilates frends. Just want to say thank you to you both. Ive sent a txt to Jake too, but you have a special one just like he dos. Yay! Thank you for all youve done for me. Im sorry Im dying, as I would have liked to no you for longer, but glad I didnt die when I fell off the bike the first time I met you. I wanted to die then but glad I didnt as I woudnt of got to no you. We all have such secrets dont we but thats ok. Thnx for telling me some of yours. Know nobody can tell peple everything bout their life but thats cool, youre both still my frends WHATEVER. Thnx also for the garden – its been the best thing. You are both special and perfect – like a gift I didnt expect but really loved. Really hope everything works out for you both just as you want it to. Enjoy your baby, Frankie -hope it loves pilates one day. So glad you decided 2 keep it, yay! And you are the best, Golda – your garden is beatiful and so R U! Ill be watching from wherever I am – tho not in a scary way LOL!! Promise not to haunt you!! – and cheering you both on. Will save you some cake in the nxt life – honest!! All my love M.

Epilogue

One Year Later

It wasn't too hot for an August afternoon, and there was a pleasant breeze drifting through the new garden at the hospice. The space was filled with roses and dahlias and geraniums in gorgeous shades of cream and yellow, gold and white. The hospice had been thrilled to accept Golda's offer of Miranda's garden and the area they'd allocated to it was, in Golda's view, just about perfect. It wasn't big but that didn't matter. What mattered to Golda was it was near enough to the room where Miranda had died so that – if she'd still been alive today – she could have looked out and seen them. And how lovely that would have been if it had been possible.

Nonetheless, Golda was sure Miranda was present, somehow. She was certainly there in their memories. Their gathering was a small and private one, but utterly special and perfect in every way. Golda smiled to see Jake in a rather smart suit. She hadn't even known he'd possessed one, though she and Frankie didn't know him that well. These days, they caught up with him every now and again, but she wondered how long it would be before he moved on from contacting them. Not long, she suspected, and of course it was to be expected, really. He was here with what he called a 'new friend' whom he'd introduced to them all as Amy. She was dressed entirely in black with a shock of bright orange hair being the only contrast in what Golda thought might be called a 'goth look.' Amy and Jake were colleagues and they'd been working together for about a year, but Golda had seen the way the two young people looked at each other and how they held hands when they thought nobody was looking, and it had made her very happy indeed.

However, what was making her the happiest of all was taking in the almost palpable joy of her friend Frankie as she hugged her baby Grace close to her heart, and the way her husband Gareth gazed at them both. As if he couldn't believe his extraordinary luck.

A few nurses from the hospice, including Diana, who had been with Miranda until the very end, made up the rest of the party.

Golda smiled across at Frankie, who smiled back. Then she cleared her throat and prepared to speak.

"It's lovely to be here today," Golda said. "Thank you all for coming and a special thank you to the hospice for allowing us to plant this very beautiful garden here. I won't say much but I will say that Miranda was a very special person, and both Frankie and I – and all of us – are very proud to have known her. Very proud indeed. Her friendship was a gift we never expected to have and it helped us in ways we'd never anticipated. So thank you, Miranda, and I hope our friendship was a gift to you too. As we meet together in her new garden for the first time, I'm sure Miranda is very much with us in spirit as well. So, without more ado, I am very happy to declare *Miranda's Garden* well and truly open."

Then, just as Golda finished speaking, a sparkle of sunshine lit up the plants and flowers, and the celebration could truly begin.

The End

Cover design by Danna Mathias Steele

First edition
May 2024

Acknowledgements

With thanks to The Literary Consultancy for their amazing editing skills, as ever, and I am also grateful to Danna Mathias Steele for a wonderful cover. Special thanks must also go to the village of Elstead in Surrey, where I have made my home, to my wonderful Pilates class and, last but not least, to The Little Barn Café for their truly excellent cakes.

About Anne Brooke

Anne has been writing contemporary fiction and fantasy for over twenty years. She is the author of women's fiction novels *The Old Bags' Sex Club* and *Thorn in the Flesh,* both available at Amazon. Her website can be found at www.annebrooke.com.

More Books from Anne Brooke

Anne's Amazon page: Author.to/AnneBrooke

Any questions or comments, please email: annebrooke1993@gmail.com

One Last Thing ...

Reviews, however short, are a lifeline for independent authors such as myself, and so if you've enjoyed *Three Perfect Gifts,* I would be very grateful if you could take a few seconds to let other readers know by leaving a brief review at Amazon. Thank you!
All the best
Anne Brooke

Printed in Great Britain
by Amazon

54739949R00205